TURN DOWN MAN

TURN DOWN MAN

RON McLARTY

Epigraph Books
Rhinebeck, New York

Turn Down Man © 2023 by Kate Skinner McLarty

Paperback ISBN 978-1-960090-03-4
eBook ISBN 978-1-960090-04-1

Library of Congress Control Number 2023902496

Book design by Colin Rolfe

Epigraph Books
22 East Market Street, Suite 304
Rhinebeck, NY 12572
(845) 876-4861
epigraphps.com

I DEDICATE THIS BOOK TO ALL
THE FANS OF RON'S WRITING

WE MISS YOU,
MY BELOVED HUSBAND

ACKNOWLEDGMENTS

Many thanks to Doug and Linda McLarty,
Peter Maloney, Mark Hampton and Colin Rolfe.

Since Harlan had died, he had not gone to the window. There was no point in it. The routine of longing seemed as senseless as the scratching at low ceilings or the figure eights his long nails made in the cold red clay of the cellar floor. So he would squat, perched upon imaginary cushions braced by dream hands, with elegant fingertips caressing his neck. When the narrow shoot of light dusted onto his toes from window he would think highways or bridges, the expanse of escape, the possibility of, somewhere, flight. When window vanished into a cold darkness and the creatures of that darkness scurried over his legs, he would think of arrows filling the air, everywhere arrows, and water. He never slept.

If a year could be determined by the flow of the moon and a season by temperature, then a day in its place by window light, door latch, meal, the ceremony of food. Harlan had darted to the door at the first sound, and pounced madly on hard rolled dough and water. He had not moved. He would not turn his head. Finally it was no longer thrown in but brought and placed and presented. Hard, round balls of brown dough. Laid upon a flat stone, garnished with a finger of water, filthy with the country's dust. If Lumpapa was at door he would demand the food be eaten. In great roars of bluff Lumpapa would wash his hands of his death, cleanse himself of responsibility. Koro would enter quietly, squat with him. When Lumpapa left, Koro would lower his elegant black fingertips into the water, anointing his lips and eyes, until at last, he reached, as a dreamer for the dough. Koro smiled, uttering a low hymn, a hallelujah of the dry land.

★ ★ ★ ★

Charles Marshall was tiny in death. From the shining mahogany soles of his Italian loafers, to the blood red bow of his tux, the number one box office mega star of the entire universe couldn't have stood (or laid) more than five-six.

Flowers tumbled to the granite floor. Roses, lilies, carnations, more roses. Charles Marshall held a rose. Wreathes encircled the entire church. Thousands sniffled at the green stems.

". . . and not simply a great artist, oh no," Smiling Jack Runyon addressed the invited mourners.

"Oh no, no. This was a man of power and wealth and fame who would always be willing to give of his time and his fortune . . ."

Outside a line of mourners jostled for position from the large oak doors of the Crucified Christ down the marble steps to Santa Monica Blvd. for a glimpse of the tiny Charles Marshall, dead of a fabulous combination of excesses at thirty-three.

Smiling Jack paused for effect, wiped an imaginary tear and turned.

"Well Charlie," he trembled, "I . . . I guess this is goodbye."

The Governor of the State of California stepped from the front pew and announced the placing of a wreath from the President of the United States. In slow-step an honor guard of Marines glistened up the aisle with a horseshoe of snow white carnations. They wheeled left in pivot and gently lay the mob-like display in front of Charlie. It read, 'You were great.'

The Rector stepped forward and shook the Governor's hand. He reached for 'The Smiler' who flashed his teeth and gave the Hollywood squeeze.

"Ladies and gentlemen, the service has ended."

The Rector at first was stunned as the audience rose and applauded but immediately relaxed into a happy wave. 'The Smiler' worked the crowd. Some got a kiss, some got a shake, some got the squeeze, the hand limply extended, a split second tightening of the finger muscles, an incredibly quick release and pullaway. It meant you were, if not absolutely nothing, then not much of anything. Andy Nef pushed up the aisle with Smiling Jack's coat and hat. Wives, boyfriends, and lawyers surrounded the corpse. Outsiders began to bang at the oak doors. People sobbed, unable to restrain themselves. Some wept on others' shoulders, many proffered film scripts they had inadvertently brought with them. Andy slid the overcoat over Smiling Jack's arms and placed the hat, cocked at the angle he liked, a slight angle, an angle that said 'I've got the money and the power to really hurt you.'

"Mr. Runyon is not accepting manuscripts at this time," Andy announced pushing a path to the vestry room and escape.

"But this is different, this is perfect, this one is about life, this one is about death, this one is about children and hornets and cowboys and women with huge breasts," they screamed.

"Sorry, Mr. Runyon is not accepting ...."

Andy closed the door of the vestry. There were forty minutes to get to Peakskill Films for the story conference, he spoke as he moved, and lunch with Mrs. Runyon might have to be moved ahead also.

"Fuck her, I'm depressed enough."

"Yes sir, a great loss," said Andy, opening the door and leading Smiling Jack onto the sidewalk.

"Marshall? Fuck that drugged up, boozing no talent fuck brain. I piss on him. How long I gotta shelve my picture? Answer that Mr. Big Deal college boy bastard. I piss on you too."

"Peakskill," Andy told Smiling Jack's driver, Wills, as he climbed into the back of the Rolls Royce.

"So Wills," Smiling Jack dribbled to the driver who never, never spoke. "Nobody knows. Right? Nobody. I got me seven and a half million in pre-production. I got Prussian uniforms, I got gold shit for the Czars, I got fifty-two hundred black horses on hold, I got half the fucking bastards in this town on hold and nobody knows when I can make my movie cause some fuck brain asshole booze shit breath bastard drops dead. How long I gotta wait? Fuck you. I piss on you too. Aim the air conditioner on me. I'm dying back here."

Andy adjusted the back-seat vents and pressed the Rolls computer air setting to arctic. Smiling Jack settled back and closed his eyes. Outside, the town passed in silence. Some Chicanos in a gleaming Oldsmobile with extra grill and white walls painted crimson, smiled and flipped him the finger. A girl on an English racer passed as the traffic creapt across Wilshire.

"Go through Westwood," Andy commanded, watching the girl's haunches move piston like, out of sight.

He lit a cigarette and cracked his window a touch. As they turned onto Veteran Avenue for Sunset he considered his life from the gardens of apartments on the right and in the huge Veteran Cemetery across the street. Acres of dead. It had to mean something. Such contrasting symbols of life and death had to have great significance, even if he wasn't sure what it could be.

Sunset Blvd. always disturbed him. And now as the Rolls floated east, as Smiling Jack snored and the hard lithe creatures of self fulfillment puffed their long distance muscles up the Westwood slopes, he felt loss. Another feeling he couldn't finger, yet must have profound meaning.

"Piss," Smiling Jack snored.

Sure, he thought. Why not piss? It might mean piss. It would be a lot easier if it meant piss.

A young blonde man jogged easily toward the car. He studied the gait, the swing of arms. Jackie had run like that. Serenely. Andy opened his wallet and flipped to the picture of his golden brother. Always tall and beautiful. Always amazing to see. Next to him stood Andy, two years older, a generation behind. Suited more to potato farming. Balding even then, and somehow tired, tired, tired. Mother had taken the picture. Dad's hairy arms draped over the boys' shoulders. Andy was like a ballplayer whose good luck depends upon wearing the same filthy socks or touching his nose before each pitch, his fear was in not holding that picture at least once a day lest he forget those bucolic features or balk at the mention of joy in the dream of Jackie Nef, ten years disappeared into the memory. Andy hit the photograph against his thigh softly fulfilling his daily duty.

The offices of Peakskill Films were housed in an art deco, yellow brick building originally slated to be a nursing home. In 1933, less than one week before construction was completed, a minor credit snafu allowed Peakskill's founding father, Julian 'The Elder' Franklin, to pre-pay a small bank loan, thus, by a statute in State law as creative as any scam used by street hustlers, it gave 'The Elder' the entire western corner of Havenhurst and a brand new building to boot.

"Build one in the valley," he chuckled to the previous owners, "or go piss on yourselves."

Smiling Jack's eyes popped open as though he could smell the big deals being cut, upfront or behind backs, foreign money or U.S. greenbacks, knives in the back or face-on disembowelments, and savored the waking breath of life. He was out of the car in a blur, Andy ran to keep up. Smiling Jack's energy at sixty-seven was amazing. He could hold five conversations at once, balance multiple phone calls, close deals so complicated his phalanx of lawyers couldn't understand them, find time for tennis every afternoon, engage in a variety of sexual misconducts and understand. And herein was the key to Smiling Jack Runyon. He understood. Power, money, people. He did not sweat the small stuff. The art of his business was the manner of wielding his fantastic wealth and power in a subtle yet creative way. No, Smiling Jack understood the marrow of things. People were to be pissed on, money was to cajole, to display, to lure. And Power was to make it all, all of it, hurt. He understood.

Smiling Jack usually worked out of his Rolls or in his Jacuzzi surrounded by phones. This was his Connection Time. Afterwards he would move his operation, his two fulltime attorneys, his office manager, several secretarial squeezes, some legit secretaries, and Andy Nef, his right hand man, into whatever studio the connection was made with. Smiling Jack was an independent and no shit brain was ever going to deny him his right to sell high and free.

His Peakskill office in the recreation room of the old nursing home was on the first floor of the Ambulatory wing. Over the security desk at the entrance to the building, suspended by invisible wire, two crutches dangled, crossed in the air. Smiling Jack loved the touch. 'The Elder' was some pisser. Through the swinging doors, down the hall and into the office, the mourner roared, followed by Andy, jogging alongside.

Gene Moniz leapt up and slipped into his jacket as the tornado chugged by him.

"Eddie, Stan, Rebecca," Gene said, in his monotone. Instantly the team materialized behind Gene, dropping pens and conversations to the ground and marched into the back of the office suites.

Smiling Jack stood silently looking out the window at the slow roll of apartment houses sloping down to Santa Monica Blvd. The team stood silently at the edge of Smiling Jack's lucky Persian rug, an incredibly beautiful work of art of great intricacy and mystery, laying at the corner of his oval desk and nearly covering the shuffle board floor. Over the desk, a banner announced the title, The Last Prussian. The desk was immaculate, no papers, no pens. Smiling Jack remembered everything. Andy took his place at the edge of the rug next to Rebecca.

Gene spoke.

"Dobs Kane is available."

"He ought to be," sneered Eddie Burke, Hollywood lawyer and Gucci enthusiast.

"Joel Wakeman is too," chimed in Stan Echols. Silence was deadly and Stan the man knew the rules. Who needs a production manager with no ideas and three outstanding paternity suits? Bad enough his wife was mad at him, he wasn't about to compound it by being quietly thoughtful around Smiling Jack.

". . . and Wakeman's a helluva actor. He was great in that last thing."

"He didn't talk in the last thing," sneered Eddie.

"Yes he did," answered Stan, "I think he did."

"No, no he just killed the bad guys and fucked what's her name."

"Cynthia Colby?" asked Stan.

"Yea, yea."

"Really?"

"Yea. No. In the film for chrisake," Eddie answered irritably pulling at the gold chain laying between his neck and the lizard collar of his orange shirt. "She goes for girls."

"Oh," replied Stan thoughtfully.

Gene again.

"That's Kane and Wakeman. That it?"

"Billy Briar is finished with the Paramount deal," sang Rebecca Haycroft.

"He's black for chrisake," moaned Eddie.

"He's funny," Rebecca smiled sweetly, "and brilliant."

"But this is a picture about a blonde, blue eyed, one hundred percent Prussian. We need an All American for this."

"What was Charlie Marshall doing in it then," smiled Rebecca.

"I piss on him," uttered 'The Smiler'.

Andy lit a cigarette and watched the sweat explode through the back of Stan's blue shirt.

"The thing is," Andy announced, "if we we're going to retain the continuity of the situation, if we want to keep the project rolling and not close down, which is death, we have to make the connection. So let's make it with all of them and let's make it with whoever else might ..."

As he spoke he stepped away from himself and viewed his countenance with a sigh. What a dreamer can do if he tries hard enough, how far he can fall up the hill. The continuity of the situation my ass. Who cares? The world should stop because Charlie Marshall self destructs and Smiling Jack can't find a star for his eighty one million dollar movie about a Napoleonic German with a perpetual hard on? My god, he thought, that's me. That's my hair combed over my bald head. That's my belly hanging over my Giorgio di St. Angelos. That's my mouth flailing and my tongue licking the air. That's me. He wanted to whip out his wallet and show them the photo. The guy on the right is Jackie, the guy in the middle is my dad. Jesus. And that's me.

". . . if at all possible and, of course, everything is possible. Also we should not overlook other venues, script change, etc., to accommodate."

A silence filled the room. Smiling Jack had sucked the very sound off the face of the earth, the air conditioner whine was the only vestige of hope in a world gone quiet. Finally, softly, Smiling Jack spoke without moving his eyes from the window.

"Rebecca, come here."

Dutifully Rebecca crossed the room, studiously avoiding the lucky rug.

"Yes, Mr. Runyon?"

"That blue building with the red sign."

"The Havenhurst Lanai," she read slowly.

"Yes, second window from the left, middle floor, see it?"

"Yes sir."

"Is that two people fucking?"

"Why yes sir, I believe it is."

★ ★ ★ ★

The first explosion drove the waterbugs into the center of the room. A living floor he thought. A rolling, shifting, breathing floor. He rose solemnly like a willow, and floated through the mass of bug and smoke, to the doorway.

The settlement of seven white huts was empty. The children gone. The women gone, the hunters gone. He watched a goat stop in flight, turn to him and disappear in a puff that also sucked the well into itself sending muddy water over the dry earth. He turned his gaze to a small rise over the rusty tin of the school roof. On the slope thirty-five people scampered almost comically, wildly up to nowhere. It was morning. Some were naked. No skin could be blacker. No skin drier. Children cried and women hushed them. Mada turned and looked over the roof to him. He stepped out of the doorway onto the dusty ground. The large ebony woman raised her fists into the air and like some giant death bird screeched into heaven. And instantly he was in shadow.

Slowly, effortlessly in a glide of a slow motion dancer, the whirlblades moved above him over the school toward the villagers. Mada continued to scream, the fists now flailing in the air. The willow moved further into the light. He opened his mouth. And in a fraction, a pause of a moment, a child's hold of a breath, they were finished.

He fell back. The helicopters turned softly in the air and gently touched the earth by the schoolhouse. Soldiers, black, tall and full in neatly pressed fatigues, camouflaged in brown and gold, eased from the war machines and stood for a moment. Talking. A cigarette was lit. A laugh, a sweet-good casual laugh was shared. He rose trapped in himself. They moved toward him shouting greetings. He reached for the carcass of the goat and held it over his head. Red black blood dripped onto his filth.

★ ★ ★ ★

Andy pulled his socks into alignment and thought of rumpled men and his Dad, the King of the Rumples. He thought of the rumpled card games, and rumpled bowling and the rumpled times Jackie and he would sit in their rumpled PJs watching the Gillette fights on the old black and white, surrounded by Mom's popcorn and great big . . .

"Jesus Christ," gasped Bobby Tucker, senior vice president of Peconic films, putting his Bloody Mary on the table, "that asshole is beating him."

Andy stood and looked out onto the court. Oh Jesus he thought, I'm daydreaming and that moron is actually trying to beat him.

If you drive over the hills into Burbank, past the oversize Quonset huts of Warner Bros., through the middle class neighborhoods sitting like dying dinosaurs, a monument of a time when everyone could own a home and be warm and regarded, you will come to a hedge encircled like a wagon train connected by an eighteen foot mason wall with selected broken glass pieces inlaid on the top, pointing upward toward heaven. Within its boundaries is the Green Glen Golf and Tennis Club.

Anyone is eligible to join the Green Glen. After an initial application, those invited to join pay a ninety-five thousand dollar good faith new member fee which is refundable after ten years at no interest rate. A yearly fee of eighty-five hundred dollars, and clubhouse dues of two thousand dollars a month entitles you to become an associate member. At the end of ten years, the full members vote on the elevation of Associates to full Membership. Smiling Jack had bought a membership for Andy. The kids'll like it he had said, only don't let them run all over the fucking place, talking and yelling and stuff. Andy had never taken the family, even though Susan dutifully wrote an obscene check out every month. He did not like tennis, or golf. He could not relax with the snap of a deal in the air, although courtside was a deal restricted area as was the clubroom, and locker room. Business could be discussed on the course, in the dining room, and in the Red Lounge only. He had seen a rather high profile attorney physically removed from the clubroom for breaking the code. It was a serious rule. Check all scripts at the door like Dodge City six shooters.

It was also, however, important to maintain the connection even in restricted areas. Over the years the practice of court stroking had reached an art form. Some could lose more stylishly than they could win and some stories of past champion strokers were the stuff of Green Glen legend, like Brian Mose, a nineteen thirty-one amateur tennis champion who at the age of twenty-six, not only lost straight sets to a ninety year old studio head to whom he was trying to peddle his script <u>St. Theresa: Unauthorized</u> but in his zeal to congratulate the ancient tennis master hugged him to death, cracking him like an ice sculpture. The movie was not made.

It seemed no one had explained this to Bobby's executive assistant, for there, before Andy's horrified eyes, he was running poor old Smiling Jack all over the court, not allowing him one point in the first three sets.

"He's beating him," Andy uttered.

"Oh Jesus!"

"You didn't tell him?"

"You saw him. He's . . . limp. I figured 'The Smiler' would kill him."

On the court Smiling Jack crunched his teeth together. Across from him, Bobby's assistant smiled.

"Going for the shutout old timer," he called at Smiling Jack.

"Oh God," sobbed Bobby, "the shutout, he's going for the shutout."

Andy turned and strode to the bar.

"There's a page, Mr. Runyon."

Smiling Jack pointed to the young man.

"Don't go anywhere you little bastard. I'll be right back."

As he stormed to the bar phone Bobby leapt from his seat and grabbed the startled assistant by the front of his shirt.

"You goddamn little shit," he nearly screamed, "you're beating him."

"I . . ."

"You beat him and you'll never work in this town again. That's Smiling Jack Runyon for christsake. He owns twenty-percent of Peconic."

Andy sidled up to Smiling Jack who slammed down the receiver.

"Nobody there."

"No there isn't. I paged you Mr. Runyon. I used the phone as a ruse. Your arm sir. You're not locking it at the elbow. You're giving away your power."

"My arm?" Smiling Jack asked.

"Lock the elbow and you'll ..." Andy chose his words carefully, "... annihilate him."

"Heh, heh," wheezed Smiling Jack, wiping his chin on his terrycloth cap and running back to the court.

"I'm ready, you little bastard, let's go."

Andy's observation was pinpoint. With arm locked firmly at the elbow, Smiling Jack Runyon began a tennis comeback of epic proportions. His overhead drives so unnerved his opponent that he simply could not return any of them. His athletic grace boggled the young man so, at one point he served six straight net balls. Finally, it was over. He had, once again, come back from the abyss. Returned from the brink. Snatched victory from defeat. Won.

Andy waited while 'The Smiler' showered and dressed, then they walked to the Red Lounge for drinks with Lloyd Kennedy, the Kennedy Hardware King, and a possible connection. Kennedy was a kindred spirit, a down and dirty Mick who could root in the mud with the best of them. And he was rich, and Smiling Jack liked that. And he was straightforward, and Smiling Jack liked that. And he could hurt you and Smiling Jack appreciated that.

"My kind of guy," he said happily as they got into the Rolls. "His old man and my old man both got out of Belfast. 'Course he's Protestant but what the fuck."

"The Guesthouse," Andy instructed Wills, who nodded silently.

"Wills," 'The Smiler' said, leaning forward and speaking to the glass partition, "you got the sound on?"

Wills nodded.

"I'm playing this limp dick asshole right. He's got me down, almost for the count, right? Only he says, you were there Nef, he says, 'I'm going for the shutout Old Timer.' Can you believe that?"

"Mr. Runyon destroyed him."

"Fucking annihilated him. And I'm not gonna forget that tip you gave me. I forgot I got to keep the elbow straight. Great game. I feel great. Shut the fucking sound off Wills."

The Rolls rolled past small two bedroom stucco homes,

planned in early Fifty's confection, to look and taste the same. Andy was raised in such a home, clapboard perhaps, New England maple maybe, but the content of the tired man arriving, and the kids happily whizzing, were the same. Through Burbank they crept up to Mulholland Drive for the day's last event, a six o'clock cocktail and buffet at the home of Claire Guest, party giver to the stars, widow of Toby Guest and granddaughter of Knewl Henry Porter, builder of an early twentieth century athletic support empire whose protected millions multiplied in pre-income tax America into a private fortune as obscene as the marble testicles on the Greek Olympic statues flanking the driveway to Claire's estate.

"Such sad news about Charles Marshall," Claire said sympathetically offering Smiling Jack her cheek. "Where's Althea?"

"She's home. She's sick. Yes it is sad news," he answered licking her skin. "You remember Nef, my executive assistant?"

Claire nodded in Andy's direction.

"Alan Hunter is here and word is he's having trouble with Paramount," she reported squeezing Smiling Jack's arm.

"That's very interesting, Claire. Thank you."

"He's taller than Marshall was," she chuckled.

"Heh, heh, heh," added Smiling Jack.

What a gal. At fifty, Claire Guest was the flower of Hollywood's social stratosphere. A progressive link between the old and the new, who without breaking stride could display a banquet of rare California wines for old friends as easily as she could offer a feast of the finest cocaine, presented with engraved baby spoons, for new ones.

This particular buffet was to celebrate her acquisition of Daybridge Winery in Napa Valley. A small operation bottling some three thousand litres a year. Claire announced none would be sold, only given as gifts with the remainder stocking her extensive cellars. The name of this dry yet disturbing table wine would also be changed to 'Howard's Best' after the young man who shared Claire's exciting hostess life.

"Now I'm not a pushy woman, darling, you know that."

"Yes Claire, I know."

"But you did offer my Howard a screen test a year ago."

"Has it been a year? Tell him to call me on Monday."

"I love you Jack," she swooned.

"I love you too," he lied.

"My Howard would be better in that part than Charlie Marshall could ever hope to be."

"Monday, Monday," he smiled.

Andy walked to the edge of the ballroom with Smiling Jack.

"Fucking house smells like a museum."

"Yes sir."

"I piss on houses that smell like this. Is Alan Hunter a good idea?"

"He's very good."

"So what? What's good got to do with any fucking thing?"

"Well," Andy began, "He's prone to thoughtful, intelligent choices of roles. His last film ..."

"You see it?" interrupted Smiling Jack.

"No sir."

"He was a guy dying of black lung. Had a big family all fucking talking. He talks too fucking much."

"Yes sir."

"Anyway feel him out. I'm going to the pisser." Smiling Jack started up the stairs then came back down. He looked at Andy thoughtfully.

"Can we show pretend fucking and still get a family rating?"

"I don't know sir."

"Something to think about."

Alan Hunter sat oddly alone on the terrace watching the gardener trim a dwarf grapefruit tree.

"Mr. Hunter. Andy Nef, Mr. Runyon's executive assistant. Looks like you've got the quietest spot around."

"I guess I do," smiled Alan. "Where is the monster?"

"In the bathroom."

"This about Charlie?"

"What?"

"You coming over here. You talking to me. Sure, I'd like to read a script."

"Well . . . great."

"Poor Charlie. Nobody cared about him. Nobody. And it wasn't just because he was a preening star, which we know he was. He was the shallowest person I've ever met. He couldn't take joy in anything," Alan said quietly, watching the gardener's nimble fingers.

Andy left the terrace, walking through the garden to the swimming pool. He stood a moment by the diving board, then sat and lit a cigarette. Susan would be putting Elliott to bed, then Tom. Jackie Jr. was ten now. He could put himself to bed. Almost ten, and named for the vanished. Ten years. When he'd first disappeared, Dad refused to bend to the sorrow that engulfed his Mother. He'd flown there twice, twice to harass the officials, pay private police, once even rented a jeep and headed into the burned land himself always coming home empty. He never wept for Jackie and that's what killed him, at least Mother thought so. She died less than six months after Dad.

Andy tossed his cigarette into the pool and walked around to the front of the house. He sighed. The heavy air, the lush rush of rose and fruit tree was suffocating. He sighed again. Most of the drivers stood by the stairs chatting. Wills sat alone in the Rolls. He'd been with Smiling Jack for nearly seven years and Andy had never heard Wills utter a sound.

The beast appeared at the front door.

"What the hell? What's going?" Smiling Jack shouted. Andy bounded up the steps.

"Just taking a smoke sir. I spoke with Hunter. I'll be sending him a script in the morning."

"Saturday?"

"I mean Monday."

"Good. Let's get out of here."

"Should we say goodnight to Mrs. Guest?"

"Fuck her."

Wills cut down the spiral road towards Beverly Hills. It was nearly ten by the time 'The Smiler' finished his weekend instructions and strode toward his light pink and brown palace. Wills steered back onto Sunset and headed toward Laurel Canyon. The neighborhoods descended. Taj Mahals slowly shrank to the crisply efficient boxes and towers.

Andy thanked Wills who nodded and drove off. Elliot's tricycle blocked the long stair to his three tiered, redwood and glass house, he moved it under the carport. He drooped to the stairs, then stopped and shuddered. He turned toward the Merrill's home across the narrow street, then fled up the stairs from where it squatted against a black Mercedes, watching him, in the almost shape of a dog.

★ ★ ★ ★

Monton was no longer a provisional town. Roads and water make the incidentals. Road to water. Water to the roads. A genius of a town, Monton. Brigadier Hec Lanee, head of police, cut an orange, sucked deeply, and adjusted the braid on his light blue uniform.

"They come," the policeman shouted, banging open the door of the head office.

Lanee waved him off disdainfully. Could he not hear the blades spinning over the dead trees? Must my policemen babble in tribal grunts? We are in Monton. Fat cows and potatoes grow in Monton.

He grabbed another slurp of fruit and briskly walked down the stairs to the edge of the heliport. Don Lawton, regional Peace Corps commissioner, jogged over from an animated discussion with several men. They shouted after him.

"Got a minute Mr. Lanee?" he breathed importantly.

"Brigadier Lanee," he corrected, watching the choppers rise over the distant burnt ridge.

"Brigadier," Don said impatiently, "those men were telling me the robbers are still coming and going with impunity."

"Coming and going?"

"The robbers. The gang."

"Ah yes, I know about that and I am taking the measures. We will always take the measures. We killed one last week. Big fellow. Had a wheelbarrow and some flour."

"You killed him?"

"Cut his head off. Put it on a stake," Lanee lied, laughing to himself. The missionaries are full of advice. No one needs to tell the Brigadier his duty. He will take measures against those who steal, only in the dry land it is not so easy to find them.

"Cut off his head?"

"Fed his genitals to the dogs."

Don turned his gaze toward the choppers. The first two landed on a patch of packed dirt about a hundred yards from the heliport. The third suspended above them for a moment then perfectly set down in the middle of a concrete slab. Two soldiers emerged from the side panel, reached in as another soldier handed the cargo, draped in a khaki blanket, to them. They moved from under the blades towards Don and Hec Lanee. The soldiers stood before the head of police holding their blanket between them. Suddenly the cloth slipped to the ground. Lanee, wide eyed, stepped back.

"My good Jesus Christ," uttered Don.

★ ★ ★ ★

Andy fumbled with his keys, then banged the door open. He locked it quickly, jogged between Susan and the television and stopped in the shadow of the living room window. He moved the curtain slightly aside.

"Damn."

"What?"

"Something by Merrill's car. Can't make it out. Kids alright?"

"They're sleeping."

"Check on them will you?"

"What's . . ."

"Please, check the kids."

Andy got their neighbor, Al Merrill, on the phone.

". . . so I moved the bike you know, but I felt something watching me, I turned and there it was against the Mercedes. How should I know? I'm gonna call the police. Alright. Give me a minute."

"What are you going to do?" Susan asked.

"I'm gonna call 911 then I guess I'm gonna meet Merrill outside."

"Outside?"

"I'm supposed to defend my home."

"From what?"

"The thing out there, come on, where's Jackie's baseball bat?"

"In the carport."

"Oh, that's great. The carport. What can I take down? Merrill will have that shotgun. I'm getting one you know. No more arguments. First thing tomorrow, double barrel, lots of bullets. A knife. I'll take a knife."

He chose an eight inch master meat slicer with an off-white plastic handle.

Andy inhaled deeply, stepped out of the house and onto the landing. Susan closed the door behind him. Two houses down, Bill Cramer smoked marijuana and listened to Bob Dylan rasp out 'It's all over now, Baby Blue'. Down the stairs crept the defender of the cave.

"Fucking Puretz," Al Merrill said stepping out from behind the stairs.

"Jesus," Andy gasped losing his footing and falling off the bottom step.

"It's just me."

"Don't creep, don't ever creep up on me again," Andy quietly screamed.

"Where's my knife?"

"You don't need a knife for Christ's sake. I've got this." Al confidently presented his 12 shot automatic, gas locked shotgun, capable of destroying all life in most small towns.

"I had a knife," insisted Andy.

"I'll be a son of a bitch."

"What?"

"What kind of knife?"

"White handle."

"It's sticking in your goddamn leg."

Andy looked at his leg and indeed, on the side of his right

thigh, the slicer had penetrated about two and a half inches. He suddenly faltered and lurched toward the ground.

"I'm stabbed. I'm stabbed."

"You stabbed yourself."

"Fuck you."

"Shhh," whispered Al. "Hear that?"

He pumped the shotgun once and walked slowly to the middle of the street. Andy viewed him from the ground, the angle lending height and importance to this upwardly mobile portrait of manhood who had taken his Ph.D. in Child Psychology from Pepperdine.

"Over in the bushes. Hear?"

Andy stood precariously and listened. The knife bobbed back and forth.

"By the hedge."

The rustle of the hedge stopped. Nothing moved. Now, Dylan's 'Subterranean Homesick Blues' banged out into the night. The shape of the dog was nowhere. Suddenly the sound of running, leaves, and wind rang from behind. Al whirled and fired, the pellets slicing their way through a mimosa, severing it in half. Al pumped a new shell in the chamber and fired again, this time killing a large black and brown cat. Al pumped his weapon again and even Andy, who had in effect, attacked himself, realized he had to be stopped.

"Al, Al, you killed a cat," Andy screamed, pointing to the Pollinis' neat white stucco home, now decorated with cat face and tail.

"A dead cat," screamed Al, into the darkness. "I know you're out there. Well, you came to the wrong neighborhood." And with that Al Merrill pumped the remaining shells into every spot that could conceivably conceal an intruder.

As the last explosion ricocheted down the hill and smoke rose from the avenger's staff, Susan crawled from the cave.

"Andy!"

"Oh shit," he cried, as her embrace drove the slicer in another inch or so.

"You've been stabbed."

"Stabbed himself," Al corrected.

Sirens were thirty seconds away when the neighbors began to emerge. Al waved his shotgun happily at the Pollinis and their children.

"It's all under control folks. Nothing to get alarmed about."

Police arrived and ordered Al to drop the gun. He gently laid it down. An ambulance was called for Andy. They were both read their rights.

Bill Cramer ran toward the patrol cars carrying what appeared to be the tattered remains of his neighborhood entertainment unit.

"Officers, they destroyed my goddamn stereo, my goddamn window, my goddamn record collection. Merrill, you're a son of a bitch."

One of the policemen sympathetically walked over to him, removed the joint he'd neglected to take out of his mouth and put him in the cruiser's back seat with Al.

Fifteen minutes later, Susan stood in the street and watched the ambulance and patrol cars pull away. One by one the neighborhood retreated into their homes vowing revenge for slain animals, murdered shrubbery and destroyed automobiles. Squatting under Merrill's carport, leaning against the Mercedes, it rose in the shadows. She stepped back.

"Please."

It stepped out of the dark, into the street.

"I'm very tired. I can't walk very well."

Afloat in a sea of brown suit, mad yellow hair, sky blue eyes drifting in a shell of the head, long thin arms and legs, feet too large and hands holding itself, stood a picture of The End.

Susan turned to run up the stairs.

"Susan." It called, "Susan."

She stopped mid-flight and turned. It moved to the bottom of the steps on seadog legs. It raised its head painfully, tilting its head to one side.

"Susan Nef?" it said.

"Yes."

"Susan Nef?" it repeated.

"Yes."

It turned away and walked a circle in the street. Then returned to the bottom of the stairs looking up. A smile danced across its face. A smile she had seen before but could not remember. It did not go with the face, the hair. The eyes too. She had seen the eyes.

"Who are you?"

It turned away and walked another street circle, the smile leaping and twirling then it stopped by the bottom stair again. Its eyes flashed up to her and it drew a deep breath.

"I'm Jackie," it said, "I'm Jackie Nef."

★ ★ ★ ★

Don Lawton had planned to take his laundry into Francistown thirty-five miles to the north. He signaled the driver on, passing up the once a week trip, and crossed the square from his small room to Hec Lanee's two story headquarters.

Brigadier Lanee was straightening his latest selection of uniform in front of a full length mirror. For today he chose a lime green military cut suit with marine green corduroy buttons and a sash of crimson.

"Mr. Lanee?" Don said, knocking on the open door.

"Brigadier," Hec Lanee corrected. "Help me here."

Don refastened the sash to the side of the Brigadier's brown military belt.

"How's your guest?" Don asked.

"Still sleeping. Sleeping on the floor. He hasn't spoken at all. We tucked him into bed. He moved to the floor. I thought you were going to Francistown with the mail truck?"

"I thought if he spoke English I could be of help."

"Ahh yes," smiled Hec Lanee. "This here big black man cannot speak English at all. Thank the almighty God in heaven for the great white missionaries He has seen fit to bless us with. Where would we be without them? They can speak English. They can read textbooks. They can build schools. Great God for our good fortune. You would be surprised to learn, that here before you, is one big black man that can speak … English, and … German and … French. There before you is a big black multi-lingual fellow of great intent and thank you very much!!"

Hec Lanee walked smartly to a small window by his desk, clasped his hands behind his back and watched two policemen sleeping under a tin awning on the other side of the square.

"Actually," he continued, "we are not certain what language he speaks. He has not spoken. We bathed him and cut his hair. Doctor Ano put some salve on the sores. His neck is tender. But he has not spoken."

"Any idea who he could be?"

"No. We called Gaberones. Nothing. Many disappear. The world is a difficult place."

"He looks kind of American to me, what does he look like to you?"

"All white people look the same to me," smiled the Brigadier.

Hec Lanee took a deep breath and looked back out of the window. The two policemen had not moved a muscle. He knew duty dictated him to kick those pathetic Bakwenas awake and whip them across the square to their duty posts but the heat and the sweat and the discomfort of responsibility would more than likely put an unpleasant edge to his newly uniformed day. He drew the blinds closed. "He's in the barracks."

Monton's prosperity, its very existence, owed as much to the contingent of troops from the Bakwena tribe and their Bamangwato officers as it did to the European Engineers who cut the two hundred forty mile duct from the Letiahau River, past the Shukudu hills, to the southern tip of the Kalahari desert. They did not have a settlement in mind. In nineteen seventy-one an Afrikaner prospector crossed over into the desert and promptly showed up in Gaberonos waving a six pound rock so infused with highly pure gold it seemed to flame. Examined by government officials he agreed to take them to the area of this amazing discovery. Ecstasy moved over this poverty ridden capitol. Streets were paved. Whitewash was applied. Europeans were consulted. First a canal or pipeline of sorts would have to be designed and built, for the tons of gold must be sifted and washed and of course, workers had to drink. Tracks could be laid later for the unearthly riches that would have to be trained out for smelting, pouring into molds and coins and stacking in Government bins to be used to purchase everything the world offers.

Moving at lightning speed the small waterway was completed in only six months at the bargain price of two hundred six million dollars which would of course, be one small train load of washed gold ore.

The end of the canal was named Monton. Neat rows of barracks for workers and soldiers sprung up overnight. A two story white stucco police headquarters and ore evaluation building was set center, bordered by instant shops and framed by an asphalt parade square. Trees were planted. Banners were draped. A ceremony was performed and the heavy trucks and back hoes and gasoline tractors and diesel earthmovers roared over a small rise to the exact spot indicated by the Afrikaner, who had received the incredible sum of eight hundred thousand South African Rands, before he left for parts unknown.

For several months the workers drove deep into the earth, a spiral hole two hundred yards across. Kyanite ore was discovered and noted for possible future pursuit after the years and years, possibly decades of high grade gold ore which they soon would absolutely hit, had dissipated. They did not hit the gold. One afternoon the Minister of Mines, reclining in a chaise, steeped in a new importance and authority, a confident man who had casually settled into the routine of signing a three million dollar daily Monton ore voucher received a curious phone call from his counterpart in Windhoek, Nambia. Missing from Nambia's National Museum of Ore repository was a glorious six pound pure gold infused rock. He had just discovered the loss only recently and as it was an extremely old treasure taken from the earth nearly eighty years ago, he would greatly appreciate, if the Minister hears of anyone so bold as to try to actually sell the rock, for the Minister to please contact the Nambia Office of Mines and we, of course, would cooperate in kind with Botswana, and thank you and goodbye.

The earthmovers and diesels burned in the sun. The fuel evaporated. Workers moved back into the business of goats and hills. The Europeans snickered onto chartered flights. The Minister of Mines tried to land on his head after he hurled himself from his four story office building but the wind turned him and he landed flat on his back. A Renault Dauphine motored over his extended legs, the panicked driver in his hysteria threw the car in reverse and backed over them. Still he would live to try again. Most of the police were removed. Only Hec Lanee, thirty policemen, and four old but true helicopters remained. The shops kept cattle. The water kept people. The road for the heavy equipment lived on in its outline.

Don entered the sweltering barracks and asked some dice throwing police where the white man was. They ignored him so he asked in Bantu. They still ignored him so he walked on alone. "Fuck you guys," he uttered.

"Fuck you too," as they all laughed. The Peace Corps was a bitch. He continued past the rows of bunk beds toward several private rooms. He tried a door, then another. As he swung the door open into the third room, a porcelain figure, reclining stiffly on an Army cot, rolled his head toward him.

"Hi," Don said awkwardly, "everything okay?"

He said nothing, only rolled his head back on the pivot of the pillow and looked into the ceiling.

"Getting used to the bed. That's a good idea."

Don watched him a moment. Nothing moved. He lay extended as though he were a cadaver on an embalming table. His long fingers open and motionless lay across his stomach. He wore only the short brown pants of a policeman and his grotesque feet, colorless and the left toeless, dangled over the edge. Even his chest did not rise and fall. Don quietly turned to leave.

"Creature comforts," he said.

"What?"

"Creature comforts. Creature comforts."

"You speak English. American?"

"They cut my hair."

"Gave you a bath."

"I'm clean now. I can feel that. But I have no hair."

"It'll grow back."

"Maybe."

"My name is Don Lawton. I'm in the Peace Corps here, almost eighteen months now."

"Harlan is dead. It's clear now he would die."

"Harlan?"

"Harlan and the electric boat," he said, swinging his legs over the side of the bed and sitting up. "Harlan has died."

"Would you tell me about Harlan?" Don asked sitting on the bed.

"He's gone."

Across the square Hec Lanee sat at his desk with belt loosened reading Agatha Christie and loving Miss Marple. He considered her powers of deduction fantastic and hoped the study of her might be useful one day against some unsuspecting goat rustler.

The door burst open and corporal Demi ran in gesturing with both hands and babbling his regional Bantu incomprehensibly.

"Slowly, slowly," Hec Lanee said, looking up from Miss Marple.

"They are dead. They are dead."

"Who is dead?"

"Two policemen on the other side of the square. You can see them there." He pointed to the window. "Somebody cut their throats."

★ ★ ★ ★

Eddie Burke strolled down the white and blue hospital aisle toward Emergency. His crotch hugging jeans snapped with each step, keeping time with the clink of his metal tipped Italian loafers. Andy was sitting on a stainless steel examining table, while a young female physician applied the sixth and last stitch.

"Hey sweet cakes," Eddie announced.

"What?" the doctor said.

"I was talking to him."

"Oh."

"In a manly way," he added fuller voiced.

She resumed her minor operation. Andy grimaced and Eddie grinned as the needle moved the flesh tight.

"Hurt?"

"Did you talk to the police?" Andy asked.

"Yeah. They told me you're a first class fuckhead."

"Jesus Christ."

"They said the guy you were with went crazy. Shot the hell out of everything. They're not pressing anything against you. Your partner's in trouble though."

"Fuck him."

"Police took his gun, charged him with reckless endangerment and released him on his own recognizance."

"That's lawyer talk baby. Eddie Burke Attorney at Law."

The doctor half smiled at him. "Your wound," she said to Andy, "must be bathed twice daily. It will get black and blue but nothing has been severed and you should be fine in two or three weeks. Your attorney is not as lucky. He'll be an asshole for the rest of his life." She left the room.

"Feisty chick," Eddie said pensively.

"I can go then?"

"I just told you."

"You see my wife out there?"

"The delicious Susan?" Eddie sneered. "No."

"I'll get a cab."

"I could drop you."

"Great."

"But I got a piece of you-know-what in the car. Oh yeah, that other guy is in deep shit."

"Who?"

"The guy with the drugs."

"Cramer?"

"Yeah. He's fucked. They set bail at ten thousand. See ya."

He had the cab let him out at the bottom of the street and slowly hobbled up the steep slope. Near his home he paused by a converted van and lit a cigarette. The match illuminated the blown away front. Pellet holes everywhere. He smoked it down then climbed his stairs.

Susan ran in from the kitchen and hugged him hard. Harder still.

"It's okay," he said.

"Andy."

"I'm fine."

"In the kitchen."

"I couldn't eat a thing. Anyway here it is. Leg's fine. No charges. Merrill's home. Cramer is in jail. I'm going to bed."

She grabbed his wrist.

"What? The kids?"

She turned and pulled him slowly into the kitchen. Andy saw the back of a head sitting at the counter. He looked at Susan. Tears washed down her face. He moved around the counter studying the rounded wild blond hair, the slant of chin, the large ears. Eyes were closed. He had fallen asleep in a stiff upright position. Andy continued on until he was exactly in front of him. Only the slightest wisp of air seemed to travel in and out of his nostrils. Andy pushed back and looked at Susan. Then he walked around the counter, down the hall, pushed open the bathroom door and closed it behind him.

Jackie Nef, Jr. sat straight up in bed and called for his mother, as his father's sobs shook the foundation of the world.

★ ★ ★ ★

Harlan met Mada on a sidewalk in Port Alfred. He wore a clean white shirt with the Electric Boat emblem on the pocket and a metal helmet, also white, save for the emblem. It was the golden boy he was walking with that caught her eye.

"Hey sweet thing."

"Hello," she whispered shyly.

"I am Mr. Harlan A. Baker, executive."

"I am Mada."

"I'm Jackie Nef," the angel smiled, his perfect teeth catching the low sun.

Harlan and Jackie had only recently met. Both had been heavily recruited by Electric Boat. Harlan was chosen for his excellent educational credentials in Virginia State's School of Business and the color of his skin. Harlan understood this and fully intended to use whatever advantage he could to rise to the top level of the huge corporation.

Jackie was an inch taller at six foot two. He also wore a white shirt. However he had tailored his to highlight the slope of shoulder, the bulge of bicep, the slant of torso onto the thin waist. His shirt said he loved his body and it was so.

"You are beautiful," said Mada.

"He's white," laughed Harlan.

"Still beautiful."

She smiled at the blue eyes and turned away. Her tight hair danced in a sudden hot breeze. Tall for a Bangwaketse, a hunter, her flowing robe covered the long lank of malnutrition, the stamp of the dry land.

"I think you're very beautiful too," Jackie said. Harlan started to speak but was interrupted by a policeman. "Would you please step off the sidewalk onto the curbing?" They looked at one another, and complied. Mada instinctively pulled out her identification. He looked at it, then at her.

"Bangwaketse?"

"Yes."

"From?"

"Botswana."

"Papers?"

"I am not working here."

"Stand by the pole," he ordered moving in front of Harlan.

"Colored?"

"Black," Harlan answered testily.

"From?"

"Louisville."

"He with you?" Jackie nodded. The policeman continued. "Think you were issued Identification Tags for no reason? Blacks like her, Coloreds like you must display them. Come on then," he yelled at Mada, who obediently fell in line behind him as he crossed the street.

"Where are you taking her?" Jackie asked.

"She knows," answered the policeman.

Jackie and Harlan watched as Mada disappeared into a police truck.

"A white man's dream, South Africa," Harlan muttered.

"Unbelievable," said Jackie.

They walked toward the generator throb of the propeller factory. Jackie and Harlan had been given this two week 'inspection' tour before beginning work at the Connecticut headquarters.

"Companies like this all over the world," the foreman said happily to Jackie, ignoring Harlan. "Bitch of a Corp. hey?"

"Real bitch," smiled Harlan.

"Been to Groton yet?" the foreman asked Jackie. "I been. Company paid all expenses. Connecticut. That's the place. Headquarters. Electric Boat is some bitch of a Corp. hey?"

The bitch operates itself. There is a Board, of course, a Chairman, a president, divisional presidents and operating officers but essentially like a snowball down a hill, growing on its own momentum, occasionally losing a section but embracing gravity as its course, so rolls Electric Boat.

Begun in nineteen twenty by William Kite in Groton, Connecticut, as a company mass producing row boat oars, it added oar locks in twenty-three, row boats in twenty-five and small gasoline motors in twenty-eight. Kite did not want the motors but his partner Louis Prisco insisted. They argued. Kite killed Prisco with an oar and was sent to the State penitentiary. Mrs. Shirley Kite held a meeting with Nolan Powers, another of her husband's associates. If Mr. Powers would see to it that Shirley got fifteen thousand a year then he could continue to run the company unfettered by herself. Her husband protested but he was a murderer. Powers soon added another shipyard in Brooklyn, two in Rhode Island, one in Boston, New Bedford, Portland, Virginia Beach. Each facility was larger, the latter ones not only turning out pleasure craft but capable of designing and building naval hulls and shafts. By nineteen forty, when Mr. Kite was released from jail, what had begun as a small, family run garage size business was now a giant. Nolan Powers was scheduled to cut a ribbon in San Diego opening the largest Electric Boat venture yet, the Electric

Boat Frozen Food Center, when Mr. Kite came up behind him and killed him with an oar as he had done to Shirley earlier in the day. The company, however, by now could feed itself. The bitch was loose to grow and prosper and screw in the bed of free trade.

Harlan caught Jackie's eye as the foreman recounted the function of the Propeller, the Driveshaft and the Waterpump, and put a finger to his nostril. Jackie bit his lip.

"That's the place then," the foreman finished.

"Well thanks for sharing it with us, bossman," said Harlan.

The foreman turned to him for the first time and smiled.

"I'm not the bossman. Bossman's office is on the north wing. Day Foreman, that's my job. Any questions?"

Outside the facility Harlan checked his watch.

"Ten thirty-two."

"Was that it?" laughed Jackie.

"That, my friend was our inspection tour of Electric Boats Propeller factory in South Africa. Now what the fuck we gonna do for twelve more days?"

"Get a tan by the pool."

"Fuck you."

"Fuck you. Anyway I got my own pool. What the fuck they send me here for?"

"Hello again," said Mada, suddenly in front of them.

"Hey mama, we thought we seen the last of you," said Harlan.

"They only make things difficult. You are members of Electric Boat?"

"It ain't no club."

"We work for Electric Boat," answered Jackie. "We just started."

Mada stared hard at him for a moment, then at Harlan.

"My friends enjoy Americans. We knew some in Botswana. A dance company."

"We ain't dancers."

"They were very free. Some could stay in the air for a long time. They . . . would descend like a flower."

"Hangtime," said Harlan.

"You speak English very well," said the Golden Man.

"Thank you. Would you like to meet my friends?"

"Where are they?"

"Botswana."

"What was your name again?"

"Mada."

"Well Mada," said Jackie, "see Botswana is quite a ways off."

"That's right. We're here on official business," said Harlan. "We got no time for . . . where."

"Botswana."

"Yea, no time, dig?"

"I am very sad then. You would like my village. My village is like paradise."

"Africa," said Harlan.

"Real and true," said Mada.

Harlan looked at Jackie. "They don't eat white people do they?"

"No," Mada answered seriously.

"Can we rent a car?" asked Jackie.

"Shit, I don't believe this. Africa. What the fuck?"

"Can't stay long," said Jackie.

"What the fuck," said Harlan.

"What the fuck," smiled Mada.

★ ★ ★ ★

The guestroom door was closed. He pushed it open. Jackie wasn't there. He checked the kitchen, the living room. Through the family room window he saw him. On the redwood deck. Standing. Looking at the sun. Naked. Andy moved slowly to the window. His brother, back from the dead, looked dead. He had shrunk several inches and couldn't have weighed more than a hundred pounds. Andy grabbed a bathrobe and walked onto the deck. Jackie turned to him in his painful nakedness.

"Got to . . . got to put some meat on you," said Andy softly.

"The sun feels good."

Andy put the robe on his shoulders and hugged him gently, careful not to crush his alabaster brother. The rare, the rare, rare brother.

"I had a baseball dream," Andy said, stupidly wiping a tear. "Everybody was in it."

"Everybody?"

"Thatcher was pitching, 'The Cat' was behind the plate. Ever dream about the guys?"

"No."

"I do all the time."

"I dream about root beer. I dream about A&W root beer."

"In Riverside, by the pond, the A&W stand?"

"Just root beer."

Andy made breakfast while Jackie watched the sun and they ate on the deck. He watched his faded brother pick through pancakes, putting tiny bites into his mouth and chewing a slow circle of teeth.

"Nobody called us. Told us."

"I know."

"I wish they had."

"I asked them not to."

The children in Saturday morning cartoon pajamas pressed at a corner of the sliding glass door watching.

"Mom and Dad ..."

"Yes."

"They're dead."

"I know. But I see you are alive. I see three children watching. I smell good smells of life in this house. Your house."

"Eat some bacon," said Andy.

Jackie picked the longest strip and raised it slowly. He did not bite it as much as nip the end. Andy began to cry.

"Papa's crying," whispered Tom.

"Shut up asshole," whispered Jackie, Jr.

"Who's crying?" asked Elliot.

"Jesus Christ. What happened? What did they do to you?"

"Harlan is dead. Mada. Koro. I am here."

"They should have protected you. The people who sent you. Jesus. Jesus."

"They gave me money."

"Bastards."

"What else could they do?"

"How can money make up for whatever . . . happened to you?"

"Five hundred seventy thousand dollars."

Andy's tear ducts dried. A desert loomed.

"Five hundred . . . What?"

"Five hundred seventy thousand dollars. Also they want me to go back."

"Five . . . Where?"

"My pants . . . I think."

Andy went to the guest room and went through the pant pockets. Empty. The suit jacket the same. He saw it on the floor by the dresser. It was not five hundred seventy thousand. It was six hundred seventy thousand. And the attached note of Electric Boat's appreciation indicated taxes on the amount had already been paid. He walked back to the deck. The children were with Jackie. Elliot was holding his hand.

"Kids. This is Jackie. My brother."

"The dead brother?" asked Elliot.

"Am I dead Elliot?"

"No."

"Good."

"You don't look good," said Tom, the middle heathen.

"Tom, Jesus."

"He doesn't. You don't. You're skinny."

"Well, I am going to eat my good food and gain weight."

"And exercise," said Jackie, Jr.

"And sleep," said Elliot. "I go to bed early."

"Because you're an asshole."

Elliot grabbed a handful of syrupy pancake off Jackie's plate and chased Tom into the kitchen.

"They're assholes," Jackie, Jr. explained.

Andy thumbed Jackie, Jr. off the deck.

"Jackie. It's six hundred seventy thousand not five."

"Oh."

"That's a lot of money."

"Yes."

"What do you want to do with it?"

"I don't know. I have to use the toilet."

Andy watched his brother walk across the boards to the sliding glass door.

"Your toes. Your toes are gone."

Jackie looked down at his foot then back to his brother and smiled.

"A toeless man."

Andy stared.

"A toeless man with six hundred seventy thousand dollars."

★ ★ ★ ★

"*I got a feeling* I come from around here," said Harlan as the Wagoneer rolled past the final border gate and into Botswana. "What you think girl?"

"I am sorry. I did not hear you."

"I say, I got a feeling my people came from this part of Africa."

"Oh, well, maybe."

"You dig, we were all slaves."

"Oh. Yes."

"I got the feeling though. My people were warriors. We know that much. We were bad motherfuckers."

When the European confab of churchmen and physicians first arrived in Botswana or Buhuanaland in the early nineteenth century, they found it hard to establish their faith in a land so torn with tribal warfare. The Bakwena, goatmen, were fighting the Batawana, goat killers, and both were trying to ward off the Bangwaketse, the people killers. They warred over food, slaves, water, soil, rocks, salt. This madness continued unabated until approximately 1885 when the Boer War led to a British protectorate. As had happened in many other British protectorates, tribal fighting waned because British soldiers killed most of the tribal warriors. Eighty years later the British gave the country back and the dry state of Botswana, the subtropical frame of the Kalahari desert, was formed.

"Dry," said Harlan.

"Africa baby. Africa is dry below the equator," said Jackie.

"I might come from here. My people might."

"I don't think so."

"Fuck you, man."

At Gaborone they found in-tourist accommodations at a surprisingly pleasant government run hotel. Mada would not enter the hotel, told her companions she would meet them in the morning and disappeared into a busy street.

The next day they stayed on asphalt through Molpolole, Mosomane, Dibete and Parris Holt, turning onto packed dust just outside the mud village of Palapye.

"It gets very dry now," said Mada.

"That wasn't dry back there?" asked Harlan.

"No."

They drove past the abandoned hole of Monton, the heavy equipment laying dead. Fifty more miles and the dryness tore at the layers of moisture on the roof of their mouths.

"The village of Dete," Mada pointed to the distance. Seven white buildings of bleached mud and rusty tin roofs gleaming under the sun.

Jackie parked the jeep by the well in the center of the village and looked at Harlan who grinned and rolled his eyes.

"My village," said Mada.

Mada got out and the Americans followed prying the dust from their clothes. Several children ran to Mada who lifted them and said greetings in Bantu. A short man in a grey uniform with a tiny camouflage cap walked from a building toward them followed by three other men similarly dressed. When they were next to them the short man looked at Mada who pointed to Harlan and Jackie.

"Electric Boat," she said and walked briskly away with the children.

The men drew revolvers.

"Got you," said the short man. "Got you, you big sons of a bitch."

★ ★ ★ ★

The crisis was averted. The world was spared. Smiling Jack Runyon passed the mantle from Charles Marshall to Alan Hunter. He had agreed that this thoughtful, well respected actors' actor could play the lead in The Last Prussian at least in principle. A telephone directory size contract stipulating everything from salary to the size of the toilet in the star's private trailer was in negotiation. Prepoduction continued towards the April shoot, four months away.

Jackie swam with the boys, walked through Ralph's Grocery with Susan and gained weight. At the Westwood Medical Center a plan of nine small meals daily was devised plus vitamin shots and liquid supplements. His hair grew. His last seven teeth were pulled and he was fitted with false ones. He was fitted with special shoes and his toeless limp became a rolling gate. One morning Andy saw him with the gardener. The tiny Asian held one of Jackie's hands and gestured with the other. Andy could not tell what he was saying but Jackie raised one finger and the man stopped talking, then he touched the side of his head and the man closed his eyes. Jackie walked away.

"You see that?" Andy asked Susan.

"What?"

"Jackie and what's his name, the gardener."

"What?"

"I don't know. Nothing I guess. Listen we have to get a sitter for Friday. 'The Smiler's' having a birthday party for Althea."

"Who?"

"His wife. Think Jackie would like to go? Get him out?"

"I guess. How does he seem to you?"

"Gaining weight."

"Does he seem odd?"

"He was locked up somewhere for ten years."

"Something is off."

"Jesus Christ," snapped Andy.

"I don't mean 'off' bad. I mean, I don't know . . . different."

Friday evening Jackie and Susan waited on the top of the stairs as Andy reviewed the two page instructional document with the sitter. Phone numbers, neighbors to call, location of thermometers, etc. Thirty minutes later the trio walked the meticulous Beverly Hills sidewalk to the Runyon Estate.

"The filthy rich," laughed Andy. Jackie nodded. Inside the antechamber of marble they were met by Rebecca Haycroft.

"Mr. Runyon wants us all to stick close. Seen Gene? Hi Susan."

"Hello Rebecca."

Jackie walked between them and glided into the room.

"Creepy," smiled Rebecca.

Susan followed Jackie.

"Andy has to stick with that group. They work for Jack Runyon."

"You do not like that."

"They fawn a little too much."

"I see."

"But then, he pays them to fawn."

When the five retainers linked up, they moved, almost in step, from the antechamber into a supportive position behind Smiling Jack, who stood stationary, glad-handing and waving to the large crowd. Althea stood next to him trying to be correct. Her hair, done in the afternoon by Les Chicks on Rodeo Drive was wilting under tension, the sweat under her arms burst through her roll on protection and stained the designer's dress.

"Don't sweat so much," dribbled Smiling Jack out of the side of his mouth. "I hate it when you sweat so much."

"I can't help it," whined Althea, "I feel like everybody is staring at me."

"Nutcase," hissed Smiling Jack.

Althea began to cry softly. Her hair tilted ever downward, sweat cascaded.

"Rebecca. Take my wife upstairs and dry her off."

"Althea? Want to come with me?" Like a small child she walked tentatively to the stairs with Rebecca.

"Gene?"

"Yes sir."

"Monie here?"

"Yes sir. She's in the library."

"She don't sweat," leered Smiling Jack. "Wait here."

"You know what I can't figure out Eddie?" said Gene pleasantly. "How can you stand upright with all that cheap jewelry around your neck?"

"Twenty-four carat," Eddie snapped.

"C'mon guys, shhh," Andy said as he turned away and reviewed the gathering. Most of Smiling Jack's pals from the Green Glen were there. Competing Centaurs. With these guys 'The Smiler' knew he could see the bullets coming. Carlos Martinez, the Hispanic Producer who specialized in bringing second rate

American films south of the border, dubbing, and billing them as gigantic Gringo hits, snaked his way to Andy.

"So?"

"Good evening Mr. Martinez," said Andy.

"Where's the fucker?"

"I think Mr. Runyon has gone to the bathroom."

"Yes, yea," laughed Carlos. "So?"

"What?"

"What's the fucker got into his sleeve? Who's doing the Russian thing?"

"You mean the Prussian thing. Still up in the air."

"I heard Alan Hunter."

"Still up in the air."

Martinez spit into his hanky and walked away.

"Creep," said Eddie.

"Shhh," whispered Stan.

Andy crossed into the dining room. A flamenco band bounced its music off marble walls and red porcelain tiles. Susan was at the buffet table.

"Crab," she said holding out a piece for Andy.

"Where's Jackie?"

"He's just here and then, he's not here."

Smiling Jack patted Monie Tooles' bare butt and watched her disappear into the bathroom. He pulled his trousers on and moved to the window adjusting his tie in the reflection. Outside a couple strolled, talking animatedly, a young girl dove into the pool. Alan Hunter walked slowly into view along with a strange, slightly bent man of indeterminate age. Hunter talked passionately. His hands pounding the air. The strange man reached over and took one of Hunter's hands out of the air and held it. He raised a finger and Hunter stopped talking. Then he reached over, in the delicacy of glass-like fingers, and touched the side of his head. Hunter closed his eyes.

"What the fuck?" blurted Smiling Jack.

The library door opened and Althea peeked in.

"I'm all dried off."

"What?"

"I'm all dry."

"Oh, well good."

"What are you doing?"

"Fucking Monie what's her name."

"I meant at the window."

Smiling Jack looked at her, then out the window, then back again. "I just saw the strangest fucking thing."

★ ★ ★ ★

Mada divided the water and dough into nine even portions. She handed them to the children. Nema, the oldest at eleven, whined for more. Mada glared him into silence. She left the seven in the cool of the school hut shade and carried the remaining two portions across the village center to the cellar house, a small hut with a hole under it which the villagers had dubbed Lumpapa's cave. When he had labored alone in its construction, he was aware of the laughter, of the children mocking him. But a revolution without a prison? A Peoples Front without secret holding areas? He labored on, comforted by his vision, even before he formulated a coup de grace, a kidnapping and ransoming of the Electric Boat personnel. Money. Rands for revolution.

Lumpapa ran across the center, his baggy grey uniform flapping in the breeze.

"Woman," he screamed. "Woman."

Mada stopped and turned. Her eyes burned him a little as he looked up into her face.

"Oh no," he growled. "No, no, no."

"Dough and water," she growled back.

Lumpapa looked hard and cocked his head to one side, then the other. He knew Koro watched from the Peoples Revolutionary

Hut. He knew the children watched. He knew whatever happened at this moment between himself and this huge taloned bird would be discussed for weeks. She had criticized him at revolutionary meetings. She had emasculated him with a word or a sigh and always had pulled herself up to that great erect height diminishing his authority. No more. He held up one finger.

"One. Prisoners should be treated like prisoners. Two. I am the leader. Three. You are a huge woman."

Satisfied with his amazing logic, he gave his head a small confident wiggle. He placed his hands on his hips and spread his legs into a modified but confident, parade rest. This made him shorter and sensing this, Mada drew herself to new heights.

"Dough and water, little man."

"No, no, no," he repeated nervously.

After a moment Mada, sensing his fear, the impossibility of a Revolutionary leader's position, turned abruptly and walked back to the school.

"You see now I am totally correct," he shouted suddenly arrogant, after her. She wheeled facing him, eyes narrowed to a laser.

"I see a tiny thing," she hissed and walked away, her bare feet kicking explosions of dust.

Harlan and Jackie watched from the space between the hut, a natural window slit. They bent quietly as Lumpapa strutted back and forth raging in Bantu. Raging at his political prisoners from Electric Boat. Beating his breast in an orgasm of righteousness. Koro called to him and he took his Mussolini walk back across the village center to the Revolutionary Hut.

Harlan turned back into the darkness. Something moved on the other side of the hole.

"You hear that?"

"Probably a rat," said Jackie.

"Too small for a rat," Harlan hoped. "A mouse. That mother-fucker was a mouse."

"Yes, a mouse. That was a mouse."

★ ★ ★ ★

Smiling Jack sat at his glass desk, tilted back in his chair, looking out the window. Most of the staff at Peakskill Features had left for the day and Andy, anxious to catch the last half of Tom's bantam soccer match, eased himself into the office.

"The Hunter percentage clause is pretty well completed Mr. Runyon. I should have it on your desk by the end of the week. I'm taking off now."

"C'mere."

Andy walked in and closed the door.

"I'm down," 'The Smiler' continued, "I'm blue."

"I'm . . . sorry sir, if . . ."

"Althea. She had a heart attack. Got a call on my private line about ten minutes ago."

"I . . ."

"When you're young, when you're a kid, like you for fuck sake, you don't think heart attack. You just don't."

"Mr. Runyon I'm ..."

"You don't that's all. The whole fucking world should spin off its prick bastard axis. Young people don't give a fuck. It's hard is what I'm saying. It's all hard."

"Yes sir."

"I come here, this fucking town, it's like I'm a toilet, I'm a ...

what are those things," Smiling Jack asked shaking an imaginary penis in Andy's direction.

"A urinal?"

"I'm a urinal. I'm a piss catcher. I'm a dumb Mick toilet and they reach for the old cocks and start pissing. It's hard, I'm saying. But I was young. I was a young toilet. I had porcelain that wouldn't turn yellow no matter how much they pissed."

Andy nodded.

"I'm pissing now. I'm the pisser now. You know 'The Elder'? Stole the nursing home? I was an office boy for him. Old bastard. He fires me. Fires me. He gets old, he goes senile, family puts him in the Chester Nursing Home, which by now I own, so I tell them to get the fucking bum out. They move him to the Alexandria Nursing Home in West Hollywood. I buy that, he's out. They move him, I buy the place, he's out. Fucker died in an ambulance enroute to a home in Palm Springs that I pulled out of negotiation to buy when he cashed out. Fuck him."

"Yes, sir."

"He shouldn't have fired me."

"Oh yes sir."

"It's a game of youth until you're old, then it's a game of money."

"Yes sir."

"Rebecca tells me Sid Morris offered your brother a walk-on in his film at Althea's birthday party."

"What?"

"I don't even know you have a brother and I come to find out not only do you have a brother but he's working for Sid 'and I hope he dies soon' Morris. What am I paying you?"

"Mr. Runyon I had no . . ."

"How much?"

"Two hundred thousand."

"Is that good? I don't know if that's good."

"I think it's good."

"Good."

"Sir, I had no idea Jackie had been offered any sort of job."

"No big deal. Just fuck Sid Morris. Sid Morris is a scumbag. And I know scumbags."

"Yes sir."

"You tell your brother ... who?"

"Jackie."

"You tell Jackie, Morris is a scumbag. You tell him if he wants to act he can play a part for 'The Smiler'. He don't have to do no fucking low piss nothing walk on. I'll give him words."

Smiling Jack tossed across a sheet of typing paper. In the middle were the words. 'I will stable it.'

"Rebecca typed that," 'The Smiler' said lethargically. "It's one of the stable boys. Lots of horses in this fucking movie. See he can speak in my movie. Give it to him."

Andy took the sheet in his hand.

"I will, yes sir. And please give my best to your wife. I hope she's feeling better."

"She's dead," Jack Runyon said. "She's fucking gone. Dead, dead, dead."

Andy drove to the sports field at Immaculate Conception Grammar School and watched the game. Tom hated soccer. The seven year old preferred the one-on-one delicacies of big time wrestling to team sports. The opposing coach roared onto the field and confronted a twelve year old referee over an offside penalty. The hulking coach threatened the boy's life. The boy, unintimidated, threw a red flag and the coach was history. Tom had squatted in the center of the field and fashioned a dirt mound during the commotion. Tom could really give a shit. He looked over to the parking lot where his father leaned against his car.

"Up Nef, c'mon, play soccer," his coach screamed. Tom rose from his mound of dirt, gave it a stamp and fled in the direction of the ball.

Driving home Tom slouched against the door.

"Tired buddy?" Tom nodded.

"Me too."

"Joey Hebolt says they found this guy frozen and they melted him and he's okay. Is that true?"

"I never heard that."

"Could it be true?"

"I don't think so."

"Joey Hebolt's a liar."

"Maybe he saw it on T.V. Some people think what they see on T.V. is real."

"I don't like Joey Hebolt. I'm supposed to believe him and he don't believe me."

"Doesn't."

"He doesn't. I told him how Jackie walked across the swimming pool. He called me a liar."

Andy laughed.

"I'm not lying."

"Your brother can't walk across the swimming pool."

"Not my brother. Your brother."

Andy stopped laughing and looked at Tom quickly then moved his eyes back to the ferocious Los Angeles Freeway.

"You know Tom, it's okay to make up stories as long as you know they're stories."

"Jackie walked across the pool. I saw him do it. He didn't get wet."

The car pulled into the carport and Tom bounded out, crushed a cabin made of Lincoln Logs that five year old Elliot had spent untold hours assembling and headed for the stairs.

"Asshole," cried Elliot, throwing a plastic fireplace after the heathen.

"Elliot watch your mouth," yelled Andy, "and Tom you go to your room, and don't you dare turn on cartoons."

Elliot grabbed Andy's leg and buried his face in it. He blew his nose. The pant leg shined.

"Jesus Christ."

"Watch your mouth," sobbed Elliot.

Andy helped rebuild the cabin, then climbed the stairs.

"Tom go to his room?" he asked Susan.

"I don't know."

"Didn't you hear me screaming at him to go to his room?"

Suddenly Woody Woodpecker's laugh erupted from the family room.

"Little bastard," muttered Andy, charging into the room.

"I said to go to your room."

"I didn't hear you. Don't shut if off. It's Woody."

"I'm counting to three."

"One."

"I didn't hear you."

"Two."

"I didn't hear you."

Andy took a deep breath. He had never reached three. Had the heathen figured out nothing would happen? Was the final line of defense about to come crashing down? Had three lost its meaning?

"You didn't hear me?"

"No, honest."

"I don't like it when you bully Elliot. You're not a bully."

"I'm sorry."

"Okay then. Okay you can watch Woody."

Andy walked back into the kitchen. He took a beer from the refrigerator and popped it.

"Where's Jackie?"

"Which one?"

"C'mon."

"Jackie your son's over Josh Cain's house. Jackie your brother is out."

"Out where?"

"Out. I don't know where. He's alright."

Andy sipped his beer. Susan sliced a cucumber.

"Althea died."

"Who?"

"'The Smiler's' wife."

"Oh no."

"I'd better call Gene. Listen sweetie, after he told me about his wife, he said something about Jackie being offered a part in a movie."

"That was funny."

"You knew about it."

"About them. I think there were two of them."

"Two offers."

"Well they weren't really parts. He'd just be in them or something."

"Why didn't you tell me?"

"It wasn't a big deal. I left him for a few minutes and went to the girls' room. When I got back he was standing with the band members and about six or seven guests, telling some kind of story. They laughed and laughed and then just walked away smiling like all get out. A couple of guys told him they wanted him in their movies. Turned them down. No big deal."

"Jackie had them laughing?"

"It's odd alright."

"Not odd, Susan. Jesus Christ. Give the guy a break. He was always quick. A funny guy. He's not odd."

"He's odd good. If you can't deal with odd-good, then don't. But he is odd-good. I love him. You know that."

Andy drank the rest of his beer.

"I'm sorry. You've been great. Just great."

"I know."

"I worry about him."

"Me too."

"Tom told me in the car he saw Jackie walk on water."

"That's funny. I saw him heal a cripple in the farmer's market."

"What?" said Andy, rising.

"I'm kidding for God's sake."

★ ★ ★ ★

Jackie drew squares upon the hard earth.

"Okay, each square represents a hut."

"Okay," answered Harlan softly.

"Right here is where all the uniform guys go."

"I can't see. You're standing in front of the light." Jackie stepped aside and the slim shaft of window light flashed onto the floor.

"Here. See?"

"I see."

"Now the Wagoneer is parked behind that place. I saw them put it there. Tonight we're gonna get that car and get the fuck out of here."

"Well great. That's great. That's some plan. We're gonna go. We're splitting. We're history. You're some smart motherfucker you know? I never thought of that plan and I've been thinking and thinking. We're just gonna go over there, get the keys, get a little gas and we're gone."

"Shhh."

"Don't shhh me, motherfucker. I don't need no shhh. I need to get home. I need to get on with it. I'm sick man. I'm sick of this shit."

"That's why we're getting the fuck out."

"How long man?"

"Tonight."

"No man. How the fuck long they keep us here?"

"About ten days."

"Oh shit. I'm dying. We got to cover the shit with dirt."

"We are."

"I cover the shit but it smells man. It smells so bad. You got to cover it."

"I do."

"You got to. It smells so bad."

Jackie looked across the village center.

"Tonight," he whispered harshly. "Tonight."

They fell asleep in the dry bone ache of a calcium free country. Koro sighed, slumped on a stool, and hovered over the twelve disconnected pieces of M-16. Lumpapa had instructed him to break and clean the weapon. It stripped down easily but two days later he had managed to connect only two pieces. He rose after a moment and walked to the hut door. Across the yard men bent in a cellar. Lumpapa had created his ransom demand of weapons and food and cash. Mada had traveled two hundred miles to a desert station to mail the document from a distant province and Koro had attached a tiny spring to what appeared to be a trigger mechanism or something. Lumpapa had promised the children and the parents chemicals for fresh water. Just add some drops he had said. He promised soy cakes and cans of Spaghetti-O's he had tasted once in Garbone and never forgot, milk and more milk and handfuls of flour. Yet the cellar men made Koro uneasy. Lumpapa marched by.

"Ho, Koro," he laughed.

"Ho," saluted Koro.

"How is your weapon?"

"I . . . fine."

"Fine."

Lumpapa stood in the sun, his amazing blackness absorbing the light. He carried his notebook and pen clutched in his tiny hands. An on-going record of revolutionary activity, sayings, proverbs and general thoughts of this miniature authoritarian. He smiled proudly at Koro and opened his notebook.

"I read from Lumpapa's people's revolutionary notebook." He cleared his throat. "Although the land is dry and the hot wind heavy, men draw strength from the air."

"Ho," said Koro after a moment.

"Do you see my friend?"

"Oh, ho, ho," answered Koro.

Lumpapa closed his notebook happily, performed a smart left face, and marched off toward the school for the day's revolutionary children's council. A council of starving children. The eyes, the soft eyes wide in the heat. Koro turned back into the room and sighed onto the stool. The pieces of M-16 laughed into his fat face.

"What do we know of the people?" barked Lumpapa, striding into the school hut. The seven children stood on spindle sticks.

"We know the people are good."

Lumpapa swaggered confidently back and forth in the front of the class. Mada had delivered the letter. She would not be snickering against the wall today. At least not today.

"Yes, oh yes. The people. The people are good. Sweet and fine under the sun. Together the people are true. We know this. Together they do not break."

"Why do people not break?" asked the nine year old Kuana punching a fly from her eye.

"Together. I said together. People do not break together," smiled Lumpapa patiently.

"My father and my mother and Toomos' brother were together and they broke."

"Sand broke them," concurred Toomos.

"You must believe in people not being broken. Let me read from Lumpapa's people's revolutionary notebook. Ahh. Here. 'Let me not be like a weed trampled by goats but many weeds grazed upon at noon.' Do you see my children?"

"I do not see," answered Kuana, picking her nose.

"Do not pick your nose while the children's revolutionary council is in order."

"Sorry."

"Okay."

Heat lingers. Even the evening stayed stale under the stars. From an afternoon temperature of one hundred fourteen the thermometer fell to one hundred five. This cool front activated the mighty rodents of Lumpapa's cave. Jackie woke violently as one large grey rat pounced onto his foot and scrambled up to his hair and out the window slit, leaving tiny scratches for him to ponder in the impossible filth of his imagination.

"What man?"

"Jesus. Nothing. It's night baby."

"The rats. I hear the fucking rats."

"Fuck the rats."

Jackie raised himself to the window.

"It's quiet."

Harlan joined him. Jackie reached up and pulled some loose dirt into the cellar. His fingernails dug at the wall. The window slit grew. Harlan tugged at some jutty rock.

"We're getting out of here."

"I hear you."

Lumpapa smoked a cigarette by the well hoping of armies and

command. Koro loved his wife, then sat quietly with her outside of their place in the warm breeze. The children slept. Wild dogs scampered over the rise above the schoolhouse and somewhere a lioness yawned horribly.

Jackie watched Lumpapa toss his cigarette into the well and walk to the revolutionary hut. The family sleeping in the hut above them rolled in their sleep. He eased his square shoulders through the opening and pushed out. He lay for a moment stretching under the stars. Harlan followed. They ran to the well and dropped the scoop stick in. Lumpapa's cigarette danced in the brown water. They drank deep. They anointed their lips and eyes. Jackie pointed to the back of the jeep. Instantly they were inside. The key was still in the ignition. The engine turned over. Jackie roared around the hut whizzing past the astonished Koro. Lumpapa ran from the revolutionary hut and Harlan showed him an American finger. The engine pumped past the schoolhouse.

"Fuck you assholes," screamed Jackie.

"Motherfuckers," screamed Harlan.

They slapped palms. They shook with the absoluteness of escape. The children looked out sleepily from hungry eyes. Koro wept, holding pieces of his M-16 helplessly. Lumpapa struggled to remove his pistol from its holster, cursing the world. The wild dogs looked up together. The lioness ceased her occasional sigh. The sleeping birds fluttered. The engine stopped.

"What man?" asked Harlan.

"C'mon baby, c'mon," said Jackie, turning the empty engine.

Lumpapa had the pistol out, he fired twice at the Wagoneer.

"We're gonna die. Oh Jesus. We're gonna die," cried Harlan.

"Got to run man," said Jackie.

"I can't run. I'm too afraid to run. I don't want to die."

Jackie watched a split second as the sobs wracked Harlan's

body. Feet were running across the village center. He fled alone toward the rise. Lumpapa fired again into the night.

Amazing. So amazing, thought Jackie, to be a fleeing man and not afraid. He knew, of course, fear is all regard. He had not had time to regard an empty jeep. Nor regard bullets. He decided he would regard only escape and the sensible gait of a runner. He slowed himself to a comfortable stride and cleared his head, allowing the constriction in his chest to stop. He breathed deep. The town. The town then. Where? How far? Twenty. Yes maybe twenty miles. A single tree shimmered under the hot moon. He would run to the tree and once there would branch left. Relax, he breathed out loud.

Harlan was dragged out of the Wagoneer and struck hard across the back of his head by Lumpapa. He fell to his knees and wept. Lumpapa leapt into the jeep and turned the ignition. In the silence he pummeled his face with little fists.

Jackie neared the tree then veered off easily to his left. He unbuttoned his shirt, took it off and ran with it in his hand. His pace was good. He thought of the body. He filled his brain with distraction.

"Dogleg left, blue over, on two."

Jackie nodded in the reality of memory. Hope High School had East Providence on the ropes 12-7 less than a minute to play. The crimson spread in a tight wing formation against the waiting blue and white Bulldogs from Hope.

"Hut, hut."

The ball, snapped, turned dangerously on the quarterback's fingers. The pitchout was not smooth, end over end, but on belly target and Jackie nestled the pigskin perfectly against his bicep and wrist. The play had surprised the Bulldogs. He hurled himself fifteen yards from scrimmage, stopped on a dime and crossed the field toward the open spaces. Nothing touched him. Run Jackie. Set it out. Feel the stadium roll with your wonderful legs. Run. Near where the Bulldog band assembled, the crimson warrior turned upfield. He could not be stopped. The goal line. A memory of score.

Jackie smiled at the abeyance of Bulldogs and ran on dropping his shirt. He turned his head left and smiled as the Bulldogs of memory faded then turned his head right. More Bulldogs dropped back. Hungry men, ten days caved, see Bulldogs clear. Is that a Bulldog, Jackie? No, not a Bulldog. Run Jackie. Pick up your pace. But what school is the Lions? Cranston? No, no Rhode Island Lions. Yet what is that? Looks like a lion. Run, Jackie, run.

It hit him on the hip, two huge front paws stripping him to his knees in midstride. He rose instinctively, a passive expression washed through his white cellar face. He moved away but the cat reached slowly out and ripped into his buttocks, pulling him down to his knees. He rose again. The cat watched him stagger away and fall and try to rise again. The cat sat and stretched, licking the blood off his paw then delicately walked over to Jackie, took the toes of his left foot in his mouth, and bit them off.

★ ★ ★ ★

Leonie had gotten the the lead in the senior class play at Hoover High. It was an accident. Most everyone agreed that Candy Fecabrini, who was so fabulous as Mother Superior in last year's <u>Sound of Music</u>, should have gotten it but Randy Corsentino drove her home one night after a basketball game and set Candy on the road to motherhood. Mr. Pennington, the music director, drafted Leonie out of the chorus and into the role of Nellie Forbush in <u>South Pacific</u>. At assembly a few weeks later, dressed in her Navy uniform and sporting a 1943-do, Leonie dazzled her classmates. She would never forget the applause or Mr. Pennington looking up from the orchestra pit and smiling or the rose sent onstage from the principal or Candy Fecabrini squeezed into her seat wiping her eyes. The flush of victory reddened her light skin. Even now when she thought of that glorious afternoon it was always one high point after another. The memory firmly locked against Jimmy McKay, who dragged his overweight Emil Debeque out from stage left, drunk on a six pack of Coors, belching a tuneless version of 'Some Enchanted Evening', then falling into the orchestra pit. Leonie refused to remember that the standing ovation was reserved for a swine. The bug bites deep.

Leonie locked onto the dream. After two years at Fresno State it was New York and Hell's Kitchen and the Neighborhood

Playhouse to hone the skills, sharpen the focus, define the dream. By thirty, her ingénue departing, she realized the limitations of the stage: money. Hollywood beckoned. The gold coast, a few films, some guest shots on T.V. Maybe even a series if the right vehicle could be found, then back to New York and the legit life. You got to have a plan. You got to have a dream. You got to be out of your mind.

Leonie took an apartment with a girlfriend. It was above a Mexican vegetable market on the Barrio border. It was a temporary stop in the valley of hope. She bought a used Volkswagen, had new pictures made up, stapled her long resume of off and off-off Broadway roles to the back and set out joyfully to market herself.

"So lie," Dennis said. "Put down some characters in films and if they call you on it tell them you got cut out."

"I don't lie very well," answered Leonie putting the beer down gently.

"I lie. You got to lie."

"Want me to tab this?"

"Yeah. Anyway I lie. I lie a lot. How do you think I got that cab driver in Hill Street? See it? I saw a crime, you know, but was afraid to come forward. I lied to get that, told them I just played a cabbie on a new Alan Hunter film."

"He's great."

"He's lucky. Not great. What time are you finished?"

Leonie tallied up the bar slips, changed her mini-skirt and waved goodnight to Oogles and Sandy and the rest of the girls on the 10-2 shift. They could have it. A few extra bucks is just not worth the extra hands. Creeps. Beats sales at May & Co. though. Oogles was the best job she'd had in nine years. And so what's wrong with being a waitress? Okay, barmaid. A person has to live. A good and true thirty-nine year old dreamer has to survive.

Dennis followed her out the door and walked with her to the Volkswagen.

"I'm starting to think you don't like me."

"I like you fine."

"Well how come you won't go out with me? Wasn't I a good guy the last time?"

"I had fun."

"So what's the story?"

"Actors always burn me."

"All actors aren't the same."

"I'm really tired Dennis."

"Hey, that's cool, just asking."

Leonie watched Dennis turn and walk back into Oogles. Sometimes you have to be a little hard. She didn't like that about life, but sometimes . . .

Leonie snuck through the back streets of West Hollywood, turned south onto La Cienega and headed for her nine year temporary digs above the Cuchara Vegetable Market. She slipped a tape from the musical <u>A Chorus Line</u> into her cassette player and sang happily with it.

Leonie pulled around the back of the market, stopping by the dumpster. She grabbed her tights from the back seat, thrown in after dance class, and walked across the lot fumbling with her keys. At the bottom of the stairs to her second floor apartment she stopped cold. Seven members of L'hombre, a neighborhood street gang sat halfway up the steps. Leonie would not like to be near these cold blooded Mexican teenagers with their dead eyes even on a sunny day surrounded by police. The amazing despair of children. Hopelessness you could feel. Sitting now above her, studded pants catching the street light, red and black bandanas worn around their right legs, shirtless, cut down vests, names inked into their taut biceps, flat black broad brimmed hats arrogantly slanted and faces empty of expression, individualized only by the varying degree of scars and bruises and of course dead eyes.

". . . and then I get enough and then I go back and I'm a big deal. You know?" said Chaca.

"Ahhh," answered a man in the middle, lost in a raincoat.

"Just a dream man, no big deal."

"No big deal but it's all he ever talks about," laughed Pedro.

"They got fields there asshole."

"Got a brother in Bakersfield moved next to a field," a little boy named Mookie said, "woke up one morning they filled his field with junk."

"It's just a dream," said Chaca.

The man in the raincoat held out his hands, palm down and brought them together. He spoke slowly, softly. The boys leaned in close. Leonie could not hear what he said. He reached over and held each boy's hand and touched the side of their heads. Quietly each one rose, walked down the steps.

She waited a moment for the raincoat to follow the boys but it just sat there looking at its hands, so Leonie walked up the stairs, passed the man, to her apartment. She opened the door, triple locked it behind her and looked out her kitchen window. Still there. She drew the curtain tight, made a cup of tea, checked the trades. A melodrama in Arizona (but it rehearsed in L.A.) a definite possibility. New films were circled in red and pinned to a bulletin board. Her service called with a message to call Dennis. He already caught up with me thank you very much. She looked out the window. Still there. Still bent over his hands as though frozen in the light of the street. Leonie picked up the phone and dialed 911. Immediately she put it down, walked back to the window and looked at him, adrift in a sea of raincoat. He rose stiffly, standing for a moment as though balanced on a pin. Unsteady. He stepped down, holding the rails tight for balance. Stepped again, then fell to one knee, keeled over his right shoulder and rolled to the bottom of the stairs. Leonie rushed out of her apartment and helped him to his feet.

"Are you alright?"

"Overdid it."

"Can I call someone?"

"Walked too far. Overdid it."

Leonie held his arm. He sat on the bottom step. "I'll get some water."

She watched him hold the glass in two hands and sip a tiny amount. He wet his fingers and rubbed them into his eyes. He looked at her and smiled.

"It doesn't take a whole lot for me to overdo it."

His eyes danced, his sloppy hair stood out hedgehog fashion. Leonie surprised herself.

"Why don't you come upstairs and rest awhile."

"And eat something, I have to eat."

"I'll make some soup."

She held his arm and they rose to the top of the stairs. He stopped for a moment, caught his breath, then looked at his hands again.

"What?"

"My hands."

"What about them?"

"Something about these hands."

★ ★ ★ ★

He slept four days dreaming of cats. Harlan unwrapped the bandage on his foot, smelling for gangrene. Harlan had never seen gangrene but his Grampa always said don't look for it with your eyes. Look for it with your nose. Boy, he would say, if you can put your face near a wound, breath in through your nose and not wince and turn from the stench then he ain't got gangrene. Jackie's foot smelled dirty. Looked awful but only smelled dirty. Ain't gangrene.

Lumpapa had followed him with Koro and Suni, a tall fifteen year old, bringing him back on a litter.

"Dumb bastard man," Lumpapa screamed at Harlan. "This is a dumb bastard man. Lion eat him."

Lumpapa shook with rage and pointed his revolver at Jackie's head, making a loud whiney cry. Then stormed off to the revolutionary hut, cursing at the early sun. A cool night wasted on the chase. Big dumb white bastard man.

Koro and Suni moved the two families living above Lumpapa's hole, which could not hold prisoners again until some stones sealed up the escape hole, and pushed Harlan into the hut. They lay down Jackie, dazed with pain.

"If this man drool foam. If this man's leg rot right off. You yell for Koro."

Jackie looked over to him glassy eyed, then sunk into a four day sleep. Harlan wept.

Lumpapa cursed himself. He removed his shirt, belt and shoes, stretched to heaven and kneeled on his straw mat. He closed his eyes and saw children warm and full. Saw them teethy with milk, clear eyed, vegetables chasing away the cataracts. Saw their bow legs straighten. Lumpapa pulled his knees to his chest, smiled, and held himself into a dawning sleep.

★ ★ ★ ★

Smiling Jack looked down on Althea and shook his head. He looked up at the ceiling of the Thomas Reilly funeral parlor and noted pink pastel. There appeared to be three or four shades. Cheap bastards. Smiling Jack was one son of a bitch but not cheap. Hell no. Not by a longshot. He motioned to Reilly who moved solemnly over to him, keeping his hands folded into one another as though holding the weight of death itself.

"What the fuck," asked Smiling Jack Runyon, pointing up to the ceiling.

"Sir?"

"The fucking ceiling. You got three, four shades of pink. So?"

"I'll have it re-done this evening," groveled Reilly.

"Never-fucking-mind. I don't fucking care. You got to get more air in here though. Look at her fucking hair. People are going to be coming here in droves. I'm a fucking big deal guy."

"Oh yes sir I know that."

"So fix her hair, more fucking air. Hey that rhymes."

"Yes sir it does."

"Something funny?"

"Oh no sir."

Smiling Jack looked down solemnly again on the puffy face of the former Althea McCann Runyon. People die, he thought.

People can actually croak. Interesting. He hardly gave it a thought before. Most of the people he buried to date, Charlie Marshall included, somehow deserved the departure, but Althea? The nice girl from Bensonhurst who worked at Bergdorf-Goodman on break from Hunter College and who fell for Jack's dick humor? Senseless. People die who shouldn't die. Guys like Sid Morris go on living. Go figure. 'The Smiler' looked up at the ceiling, the three shades of pink like stripes of a rainbow, and sighed. He looked over at Reilly.

"Fuck God."

"Oh yes sir," said Reilly solemnly.

"What time do people start coming?"

"In about a half hour."

"So put on the fucking air," said 'The Smiler' as Reilly bounded from the room, hands still clenched in front of him, like a huge ballerina leaping from the stage.

Andy Nef put eye drops into each eye and closed them for a moment. They burned a bit, then a sensation of cool. He leaned back and stretched out slowly on the bed so as not to wrinkle the dark blue suit.

"Jesus."

Susan adjusted her pearls.

"Don't get all wrinkled."

"Where could he be? I didn't sleep at all last night."

"I'm sure he's fine."

"How can you be so sure?"

"Look, we called the police. We can't do any more than that. He's fine. How's Mr. Runyon holding up?"

"He could at least call."

"Runyon?"

"Jackie. Out all night. Jesus Christ."

"C'mon sweetie."

Norma Merrill, daughter of the shotgun avenger, met them in the kitchen already complaining about her three charges.

"Tommy urinated in the potted palm, Mr. Nef. He won't listen to me."

"Tommy! Listen to Norma."

"Thanks for sitting honey, I left all the numbers on the kitchen table," said Susan.

"Daddy's trial for disturbing the peace and assault is next Tuesday. Can you make it? We're all excited."

"We'll see."

"I hate funerals," Andy sighed as they walked into the carport. He moved the hot wheels, the ten speed Ross, Elliot's cozy coupe, Tom's shoebox of bones and 'dead things' and backed out of the drive. He jammed on his brakes.

A low rider, blood red nineteen sixty-nine Chevrolet Impala, gleaming in acrylic splendor, blinding in high gloss chrome, screeched to a halt not one inch from Andy's BMW.

"Lock your door," he said out of the corner of his mouth.

He watched his side mirror as a lean young Chicano eased his hobnail boots to the street and arrogantly, dangerously walked over to him. Andy lowered the window and tried a casual laugh but nothing except air escaped his mouth.

"Hey man, almost got me that time. I'm looking for Andy Nef."

"He's Andy Nef," said Susan.

"C'mere man."

Andy looked at Susan, took a deep breath and unlocked his door. The Chicano was already at the low rider. Andy walked over as the back door was opened. The boys and Norma watched the scene from above, summoned by the screech.

"Hey daddy," Tom screamed. "Punch the asshole out."

"Shut up idiot," screamed Jackie, Jr.

Leonie stepped out of the car, half pulling the lost Nef to his feet. He leaned against her. Andy looked at the brother and reached for him.

"I'll take him. He's mine."

"He's everybody's man," said Chaca.

"I'm Leonie Polk. Jackie stayed the night with me. At my house. I made soup."

"Vegetable man, good soup," added Chaca.

"Then Jackie just fell asleep. I figured he needed the rest."

"Yes," said Andy. "He's . . . he's been through a lot."

He watched them both.

"Well, I've got him okay now."

Leonie nodded and got back into the low rider. Chaca said something in Spanish to Jackie and then got into the car. The low rider roared fifteen feet, stopped fast, rose up on hydraulic springs, descended all the way to the ground, up again to normal and powered down the street, complete with the horrified Leonie Polk.

"Let's get you upstairs."

"I'm fine. I feel okay. You're going somewhere. Go."

"I can't leave you like . . ."

"I'm fine. I'll tell you. You go, I'll sit in the back of the car. Get something to eat."

Andy knew there was a better solution but he wanted someone else to come up with it.

"Okay. We'll get you something to eat on the way over."

Andy held his shoulders and walked him to the car.

"Is he gonna die?" screamed the heathen Tom.

"Shut up asshole," screamed Jackie, Jr.

"Bye daddy. Bye mommy," screamed Elliot happily.

Andy and Susan left Jackie with a hamburger, fries and chocolate shake sitting in the back of the BMW in the funeral home's parking lot.

Rebecca met them at the entrance and pinned a large carnation on Andy's lapel.

"Gene wanted us to wear armbands. You believe that?"

"Hi Susan."

"Hello Rebecca."

"How's 'The Smiler'?" asked Andy.

"Better now that they've got her hair curled again. They did a shitty job on her."

"Hey doll," snarled Eddie Burke. "How do I look?"

Like a Forty Second Street Peep Show Operator.

"You look great," lied Susan.

"Fucking white carnation is for shit."

Althea lay out in an ornate cherry wood coffin adorned with flowers and wreaths. Smiling Jack sat next to her head sipping a coffee. Gene Moniz and Stan Echols stood attendant behind him, Stan's hysterical eyes darting constantly about the room. Andy and Susan knelt by the coffin. Eddie thought 'The Smiler' looked at him for a split second and vigorously crossed himself. Susan shook Smiling Jack's hand. Andy took the beast's paw. Smiling Jack pointed up. Andy looked at the ceiling.

"Three, four shades pink."

"Yes sir."

The room filled. The power brokers barely regarded poor Althea, wilting center stage. They slid up to 'The Smiler', dripped studied sincerity and left. Alan Hunter came alone, stood quietly by Althea and closed his eyes.

"Embarrassing, huh?" murmured Eddie. Stan shook with the possibility of someone overhearing.

"Fucking movie star pretending to pray."

"Shhh," pleaded Stan.

"So terribly sorry Jack. She was a lovely woman."

Smiling Jack nodded and Alan moved off to retrieve his coat.

"Something about that guy I don't like. Keep an eye on him."

Smiling Jack put his coffee down and stretched. He walked over to Althea and stood quietly for a moment. He reached out and tucked a piece of wayward hair under a curl. He looked again at the ceiling.

"It's pretty, isn't it?"

Jackie had come into the parlor and was standing next to Smiling Jack and all his unusual grief. Smiling Jack turned and looked at the ridiculous Jackie Nef smiling at the ceiling.

"It's a sense of line going on. A ceiling that moves in color."

Jackie walked to the head of Althea, his smile holding him upright.

"She's in the light now," passing his hands over her face. "She surely is in the light."

Smiling Jack moved close to him and regarded Althea. They stood together in silence, then, without moving his eyes from her, Smiling Jack reached out a few inches and took hold of Jackie's hand.

Eddie, Rebecca and Gene stared open mouthed. Susan rose from her seat. Andy somehow gained control enough to move over to Jackie. He put his hands onto his shoulders.

"My brother, Mr. Runyon. He's tired. He hasn't been well. Come on Jackie."

Jackie smiled at 'The Smiler' and turned with his brother. They were nearly out of the parlor door when Jack spoke.

"Forget that stable part. There's a part of Milo, the Irish expatriate. It's a good part. I'm sending the script home with your brother tomorrow. I'm paying top dollar, top."

Jackie turned slowly and smiled. The room of film people flashed their eyes on him.

"Milo?"

"Irish soldier in the Russian Army."

"I know soldiers. I'm really not interested in Milo or movies."

Jackie turned and walked into the hall leaving Andy staring across the room into Susan's astonished eyes. Smiling Jack watched as Jackie disappeared, turned back to Althea, then looked at the ceiling and laughed.

★ ★ ★ ★

He opened his eyes slowly breaking the seal of four days sleep. The room was dark. The night was cool. He pulled himself into a sitting position and edged backward until he pressed against the wall of the hut. It hurt to breathe. He could not see his feet. Harlan snored, occasionally whimpering as sleeping pups do. A lioness roared once in the stillness.

His ass ached. His torn buttocks, blueback hips from first strike, throbbed in the darkness, beating a rhythm into his poor head. He remembered he was hit, he fell, he rose, he was torn, he rose again, he fell, he … his toes. It took them? He reached down and felt one foot then the other. Yes, she took all the left ones. Yes.

Harlan rolled over in his sleep mumbling something about bad smells, some muddled point of hygiene and fell quiet. He breathed deeply. He closed his eyes. What a light hold we have on our toes. If Dana saw him toeless, half assed and blue black, would she still love him? Did she love him? She said she did. He said he loved her but he didn't. He only said he did. He would love her now without toes. Dana went with him to Andy's wedding at Grace Episcopal in Providence. Sat with Mom while he seated people. Susan was beautiful in her grandmother's wedding gown. Andy was a porker, pure and simple. Dad didn't have a lot of faith in Andy's future. He liked Susan though. She was a good girl, no doubting that. She'd look after the porker.

Dana cried at the reception. Jackie got drunk with the Duke and Ricky Hoborth and some other ushers. Afterwards, as Andy's Mustang pulled away dragging shoes and cans, Dana told him she loved him but he was crass and cold and forbidding in the way of tall muscled athletes and that if they had a future life, he would have to stop, just stop that arrogant swagger. Dana loved him. She told him so. She even gave him her copy of <u>Love Sonnets of the Portuguese</u>. Dana loved him. Maybe. Jackie took the book of Sonnets tenderly into his powerful hands, kissed her, then tweeked her right breast. See. Like that. That's what she meant. So crass. Dana tells him he is loved. Gives him poems of loving and what does he do? Tweeks her breast.

Jackie winced as lion pain roared ass high, oddly feeling toes where none were. The door to the hut opened. He could not see who entered. A tall figure squatted at Harlan and felt his head then moved to Jackie. A cup of water was held to him. He looked past the cup into Mada's face. He took the cup, drank it, leaned forward, kissed her warrior mouth and tweeked her breast. She took the cup from him, dabbed her fingers into the water and sprinkled it onto his eyes and lips. She smelled his wounds. She rose to leave.

"Dana, I love you," Jackie said softly.

"Yes, yes. Rest."

"I love you without my toes."

"I love you too," Mada said. "Rest."

"I didn't really love you before, Dana."

"Yes, yes," said Mada laying him onto the mat.

Jackie sank into himself. He drew his knees to his chest. She rose and he grabbed her wrist. She knelt down beside him. He held her hand to his curled stomach, laying there like the unborn, clutching the umbilical of life, sleeping again.

★ ★ ★ ★

"Dana?"

"Yes."

"Dana?"

"Who is this?"

"Jackie."

Three thousand miles and silence.

"I called your house. Your mother's house. I got your number. I called you."

Silence.

"Dana?"

"Who . . . is this?"

"Jackie Nef."

"I wanted to call you. I got your number. It's hard to call. I thought it would be easier. I lost my toes."

"Who is this really?"

"I wasn't sure I loved you but after the lion took me down I got sure. I'm sure now but I get so tired and my hands are so hot, almost on fire."

A distant slamming of receiver. He sat alone in Andy's den looking at the phone. Tom walked in and sat staring at him.

"Hello Tom."

"Hey."

"What's up?"

"Daddy says you can't walk on water."

"He's right."

"But I saw you. At the pool you did it, I saw you."

"Maybe you saw me in the shallow end. I've been in the pool for exercise. I've been swimming."

"I won't tell."

"People shouldn't walk on water."

"It's okay. I won't ever say anything. Only do something else."

Jackie reached over and touched Tom's hand, huge hands, a child's version of grandfather hands and ran his fingers through his close hair.

"Life is good Tom."

Tom smiled his wild savage smile. Jackie smiled also. He stood up walked to the television set and turned around facing his nephew. Slowly Tom's eyes, the joyful heathen's eyes jumped in ecstasy. He clapped madly and bounced in his father's chair. Jackie had floated to the ceiling.

"Our secret Tom," said Jackie spinning.

"Secret. Secret. Secret," shouted Tom.

Jay Craymore stormed dramatically into the outer offices of Smiling Jack's suites at Peakskill Films, saw Andy talking with Gene and shouted across the room.

"You see this?" he yelled, holding up a copy of the Hollywood Reporter. "Where the fuck does he get off offering Milo to some nobody? Read the contract. I direct, I cast. Period. I mean what is this shit?"

Andy took the trade paper and read the section underlined in red pencil. 'Jack Runyon has tapped an unknown to co-star in his eighty million dollar epic. A stage actor of astonishing potential but yet to make his first film. One observer on the stage scene calls the mystery man the greatest craftsman of his generation.'

Andy looked up and passed the paper to Gene.

"Okay, look," said Jay. "He might be the greatest stage actor ever but my god, a lot of stage guys have . . ."

"He's not a stage actor."

"What?"

"He's not an actor at all."

"Then what the fuck is he?"

"Look Jay, Mr. Runyon did offer him the part. He turned it down."

"Turned it down?"

"That's right. The article is bullshit."

"Well," said Jay after a moment, "if he didn't turn it down I'd have fired him. Nobody is going over my head on <u>The Last Prussian</u>. I've put in too much time. Too much energy. Too ..."

"Jay," said Gene, proper and soft, "Mr. Runyon has put in all the money. Money, Jay. So if Mr. Runyon desires to put some vagrant into the lead you'll still do it and learn to love it or he'll grab you by the balls and throw you back into summer stock. Thanks so much for stopping by. Don't forget your article."

Jay skulked from the room. Gene sipped coffee and said, "Why did he turn it down?"

"Did you see him? My brother, my brother used to be what, I don't know, what God meant people to look like. Jackie was perfect. He hasn't got any toes on one of his feet. They broke him good."

"Who?"

"One day, I'll tell you."

"Anyway, 'The Smiler' was serious. He wanted him."

Smiling Jack appeared at his office door and pointed to Andy. "C'mere."

Leonie heard the music also.

"Let it carry you. Flow with it. C'mon," the dance instructor breathed. "Go, now hang down, up and go. Arms. Arms. More arms. Prancing and we go."

The roomful of men and women in tights and sweats pranced and went. To the left, now right. Watching the instructor's feet and hips and arms. Catching themselves in the wall to wall mirrors.

The long number ended.

"Walk around, shake it out, c'mon," ordered the instructor.

They rose shaking arm and leg, neck and head, moving slowly from one wall to the other, checking hips and thighs, breast and waist. Here they all are. Tight. Wanting to be tight.

Leonie pulled on jeans and got a drink of water.

"So?" Judy Bott asked.

"So nothing," smiled Leonie.

"You been up on the new Alan Hunter movie?"

"No, but I heard he was doing one."

"I love him."

"Me too."

They walked out of the dance studio and strolled along Sunset.

"Where you parked?"

"On Fountain."

"I walked. I had to get away from Tony. I think I might move out."

"I'm sorry you guys are having trouble."

"Me too, but what ya gonna do."

They walked to Fountain.

"See ya Friday," said Judy.

"See ya."

Sister Margaret's engine fluttered for several seconds but at last the old girl turned over and chugged Fountain for Oogles. Leonie changed into her mini, served drinks til six, had a wonderful dinner of calf's liver and onions, and energized, tackled the remaining three hours.

Dennis came in ten minutes before Leonie's shift was up, ordered a beer.

"I think about you."

"Dennis . . ."

"I was thinking maybe we could drive up the coast this weekend."

"I have to work on Saturday."

"Sunday?"

"Dennis, I like you. I really do."

"I like you. I think about you."

"It's just that I'm not looking for an actor. I want to find somebody that's not all . . ."

"Fucked up?"

"Right."

"But Leonie, everybody's fucked up. The whole world has got . . ."

Somebody signaled her, ordered a drink and paid. She looked across the room to Dennis, still watching her, still holding his thought on the edge of his tongue. She poured him a beer and brought it over.

"On the house."

"Thanks. The whole world has got fucked up. Everybody wants and nobody gives."

Leonie was taken aback.

"Say we were business people. Maybe I'd be a child molester or something and nobody would know, just that I was a respectable businessperson. People don't say 'all business people are fucked up.' No. But actors? Sure. We're all gay, all stupid, all sex fiends, all drug addicts, all alkies. Right?"

Pretty good Dennis. Pretty damn good.

"But inside, inside we're people trying to make a connection. You want and you need and you give, so you try to find some one other person who also wants and needs and gives. I think about you."

Leonie sat down and looked at him.

"Dennis that's … wait a minute. Wait a minute. I've heard that before. That's Jess in <u>Country Boy</u>."

"Took me two days to memorize. I'm going to do that for my audition tomorrow. <u>The Last Prussian</u>. You up on it?"

"I have to go now Dennis."

Sister Margaret refused to turn her engine.

"Leave it. I'll give you a lift. C'mon for God's sake. You can get it fixed in the morning. It's late."

Dennis' smug face filled her side window.

"C'mon."

Leonie followed him to his five year old Corvette, purchased by careful allotment of his unemployment insurance, and got in.

"You're over near East L.A., right?"

Leonie sighed.

"What are you thinking?" asked Dennis.

"The Sierras."

"Pretty?"

"In the summer in the real hot weather we'd go to this place where a little stream would form a pond, we'd swim."

"Water must have been cold. Mountain stream and everything."

"Yeah, woke you right up."

"Nude?"

"What?"

"You guys swim, you know, nude?"

"Left here Dennis."

The Corvette pulled into the parking lot.

"Thanks."

Dennis followed her to the steps.

"Hey, okay, I'm sorry. What I say? C'mon."

"Night Dennis."

Dennis started to speak but was interrupted by a man at the top of the stairs.

"I need some soup. I think I overdid it again."

They looked up at him.

"It's good, isn't it? People walking on the sidewalks and children playing somewhere. Hear them?"

Leonie walked up the stairs and took him by the hand.

"What kind of soup?"

"What was the kind ... before?"

"Vegetable."

"I need it."

"It's good for you."

"I need it then. I do."

★ ★ ★ ★

"*Three letters. Three letters* to them and nothing to us. They do not give. Two hundred days and Electric Boat does not give. Let them go."

Lumpapa furrowed his brow pensively.

"Two hundred days," she said again.

Lumpapa stood, head down in thought, and walked to a corner of the room.

"Koro?" he asked not looking up. "What do you think?"

Koro thought rice cakes and goat milk.

"I think we should do what revolutionary people should do."

Lumpapa turned and smiled. He pulled his manifesto from his shirt. He walked to Mada and boldly read.

"It is better to ransom the world than to take a backward step."

"So we kill them," she said.

"We kill no one," he snapped.

"Oh?"

"Oh, ho."

"The black one will die soon. He is already talking to himself. He is crazy."

"He is crazy," agreed Koro.

"He pretends to be crazy," corrected Lumpapa. "Old trick, old trick."

"Electric Boat does not care," Mada persisted. "Let them go."

"A bird in hand," read Lumpapa.

"I do not want to kill anyone," said Suni, the tall boy, quietly. Mada walked to him and put her arm around his shoulder. She glared at Lumpapa.

"Let them go."

"No."

"We are not killers."

"We are the people. We are good," said Lumpapa. "We are too good for them. We have them now. We will get what we want."

Mada and Suni walked together from the revolutionary hut to the schoolhouse. They sorted out the bread dough and gave it to the listless children. Suni's stomach cramps had lately become so severe he could not eat. He took only tiny sips of water. She watched him closely. She rubbed his distended stomach in small soft circles. He closed his eyes and lay on his side.

★ ★ ★ ★

When he was sixteen and wheeling racks of furs around Seventh Avenue, he had this habit of carrying a tiny screw driver with him to unscrew the other kid's rack wheels. It was one of a large assortment of tricks he used to make himself the number one rack boy on the street. For setting the standard for foul play and low competition he was awarded the title 'The Scuz' from his contemporaries. As the years went by, through good times and bad, rising and falling and rising up the ladder again, he remained consistent with his nickname. When Andy answered the door that Saturday afternoon he did not see an elderly gentleman in a pink leisure suit smiling at him, but Sid 'The Scuz' Morris in all his dangerous splendor.

"Mr. Morris?" he asked stupidly.

"Who the fuck else," he laughed, making a feigned grab at Andy's privates. Andy doubled up and fell back into the room. "Gotcha. Heh. Heh. Heh."

"Can I get . . . coffee or anything?"

"Coffee's bad for you. What the fuck you pulling? Trying to kill 'The Scuz'?"

"I just . . ."

"Gimmee cup. Black."

'The Scuz' walked through the house to the deck and slid the glass door.

"I'm a movie guy." In the high sun his still red hair shined. His sweet, round face wore a permanent tan.

"Yes, sir."

"What's the Sir, shit. Come fucking on. No Sir shit."

"Sid."

"Scuz."

"Scuz."

"Now you are wondering why 'The Scuz' is here. Right Tony?"

"Andy."

"I ever meet you before?"

"At Green Glen. I was with Mr. Runyon."

"I thought it was Tony. So sue me. The Green Glen huh? I don't remember, but what the fuck. Hey, swear to god. You got to watch Jack. He's a good Mick. The fucking best. But he's a prick and should be dead. Fuck him. What you doing, growing the coffee beans? C'mon."

Andy poured a cup, and took it to 'The Scuz'.

"Smells good. Rots your bowels but what the fuck. Okay. C'mon."

Andy followed him through the sliding glass doors onto the deck.

"You hear about my film <u>Sunday Dawn</u>?"

"Sure."

"Great film. I mean it's gonna be a great, great fucking film. Commercial but just artsy, fartsy enough."

"I wish you good luck with it."

"Don't ever say that. Don't ever give me that shit. That's the kind of shit 'The Smiler' comes up with. You're too young to remember <u>Side Glances</u>. Almost made it in fifty two. Shitty decade for films. One day I get a script, <u>Side Glances</u>. Picture now. Woman. American. Big tits. Sitting at a coffee shop gets this, what, obsession for the short order cook. He's got a family, kids. She don't fucking care. She's got it all, clothes, tits but not him. Long Story Short. She goes crazy, big car accident, guy's wife and kids fucking squished, they meet again in another coffee shop, another time, only what? Guess.

"I . . ."

"Only she's the short order cook and he's sitting there ordering food. They see each other. She's on hard times. She got this outfit on that don't show off the tits – they fall in love. The end. Fuck Jack Runyon and everybody. 'The Scuz' got a hit. Only I don't get a hit because this perfect broad, this bitch I was gonna make into a star gets the flu and fucking dies. Like that. Dead."

"So you never made the picture?"

"The tits died," 'the Scuz' sighed. "Fuck Jack Runyon. You know what that potato eater did? He murdered her. They had lunch one afternoon, bastard was trying to steal her away, gave her the flu. Gave her the fucking flu. Fuck."

"I'm very sorry."

"Hey, don't think about it, I don't. Anyway, darling listen here. I go to Althea's funeral, a beautiful woman by the way, fucking guy killed her, sucked the life out of her, ruined her heart but that's another story. I'm there 'cause you go to funerals and, of course, Jack is my very, very close friend and I notice this wonderful man being offered a role by that dumb Mick. And not just a role but a pretty goddamn good one."

Andy arranges his face in concentration.

"I give him this. He can pick 'em. He don't live in that pink pussy palace for nothing. I say to myself this guy at the funeral has got it. It's in the eyes. I know that much. My guy Deeds tells me he's related to you. You know Deeds?"

Andy nodded.

"I always tell Deeds he got a broomstick up his ass. Talks too fucking soft. I guess he's afraid of me. Smart guy. Anyway, this guy related to you?"

"My brother."

"So? What's the . . ."

"Asshole," screamed Tom.

Jackie, Jr. ran laughing to the table and squatted behind his father. Tom appeared at the door holding a plastic baseball bat in one hand and a book in the other.

"Asshole," Tom reiterated rushing at Jackie.

"Tom, your language," said Andy.

"He took a dollar from my book bank."

"I didn't take his dollar," lied Jackie.

"Liar," screamed the heathen, connecting a major league stroke of plastic to Jackie's head. The older beast went down in a heap but when Tom moved in for the death blow he found Jackie had lured him close and now, uninjured, applied a vice-like head-lock on the caveman. Andy leapt to separate the combatants. Suddenly a shrill whistle brought the battle to a halt. 'The Scuz' was sitting confidently at the table holding a crisp fifty dollar bill in each hand.

"Fifty big ones each. Now hit the road."

The savages darted to 'the Scuz', ripped the fifties from his pink fingers and bolted into the house.

"Nice kids. They turn on you though. Mine hates me. I give them. I always give them. They turn. I got one, listen, boy about forty-five, lawyer. He comes home tells me I gave him too much. He says 'I'm unhappy 'cause you gave me everything.' Know what I said? I said, 'Fuck you.' So what?"

"What?"

"What's it gonna take to get him in Sunday Dawn?"

"I ..."

"Okay, <u>Sunday Dawn</u>'s going to front Rocky Horn but I can offer the second lead. He's a range rider, Horn's pal. It's a star maker."

"Mr. . . . Scuz, my brother told Mr. Runyon that he wasn't interested and …"

"Sure, sure, sure."

"He was serious."

"Serious? Look Tony …"

"Andy."

"Sure. I know the game. I made the fucking game. I come by to say <u>Sunday Dawn</u> is interested."

He stood up and walked into the house. Andy followed. At the door 'The Scuz' turned and looked hard at Andy.

"I know the game. Remember. <u>Sunday Dawn</u>."

He opened the door, stepped out, then said over his shoulder. "Six to eight weeks tops. Second billing, nine hundred fifty thousand."

Andy went to the bathroom and splashed cold water on his face.

Outside, Henderson Anderson, a private investigator hired by Jack Runyon noted the license on the blue limo of the man in the pink leisure suit, and called it into his office.

"I got a nina, a two-a, a three-a, a C as in Carl, B as in Bat and P as in Pecker. That last one's for you darlin'."

"My hero," snarled Marlene at the office.

Henderson lit a Camel and leaned back. Runyon said the guy was about five foot ten, skinny and sick. He'd find the guy. He closed his eyes against the sun and continued drawing the smoke.

Ralph's supermarket was ice cold, air conditioner booming all night. Leonie pushed her cart through the juice section, turned onto canned vegetables and stopped at the peanut butter display. She looked to the other end of the aisle where Jackie walked slowly, head down.

There is that bubble under the breast bone that will tell us, if we listen when it comes rarely to us, to run and sing and jump. This is joy then? Under the breastbone? For Leonie? She trembled, hands onto the cold cart, tapping in Rice Krispies and parsley. Jackie had sat quietly last night and drank all of the soup. He did not speak at all except to say 'good, good'.

"Lions," he said wiping his chin with his hand.

"I love lions," she said.

"When they overdo it they find shade. They rest."

"More soup?"

"No, but it was so good. Lions do not like heat."

"I love them."

"I do too. I walked here. I remembered the streets. I came just to see you."

"I'm glad."

"I'm Jackie Nef. People thought I was dead."

"I'm Leonie Polk. I guess some people think I'm dead too. Last time you were here you fell asleep at the table. I didn't even get your name."

"Jackie Nef."

"Yes. Jackie Nef."

He rose, walked to her kitchen sink and turned the faucet on and off.

"Water."

He did it again. He saw the on and off flow of water. Life on command. He ran it onto his fingers then shook it off. He turned to Leonie and she saw the eyes wash over in tears.

"I'm better but I still get tired. Less tired everyday. I'll sleep now."

She took him to her bed and lay him down. He closed his eyes. She removed the tennis shoes and socks. The Lion's foot pointed to the ceiling. She touched it, then undressed him. Naked, his ribs were the strings of a guitar and the muscles and ligaments and sinews stared out in impossible connection. Leonie put a fresh sheet over him, undressed and got into bed. She moved close to him, put one arm under his head and held him with the other, rocking back and forth, cradling an enormous infant under the cool yellow sheet. Something was happening.

Rebecca Haycroft pulled into the Peakskill parking lot as the brown Hollywood sun was leaving. She'd been to the beach. Something kept telling her to call in. Gene looked odd. Eddie Burke's smug sneer was now a nervous twitch.

"What? You sounded hysterical," she said to Gene.

"Do you think we're overcompensated for what we do?"

"Of course."

"Well this is one of those moments when we earn our money."

"What? The Last Prussian? Oh my God. What?"

"He wants to see us in the office. Emergency meeting. He's a crazy man."

"Oh god, oh god," said the usually serene Rebecca. "Where's Andy?"

"Not invited," smirked Eddie.

"Stan?"

"Couldn't get in touch with him. It's just us three," Gene said. "He's waiting."

Eddie shook his hands and felt some tension release from his neck and shoulders. He relaxed. Big deal. He's seen crazy. How crazy could he be?

Gene knocked on the door.

"Come the fuck in."

Gene looked at Rebecca and opened the door. Furniture had been tipped over, an ancient vase lay in pieces on the floor. A pen knife stuck in the center of the priceless Persian rug. Several panes of glass were smashed and a portrait of Raymond Massey as Lincoln had been impaled on a coat tree.

"Good god," uttered Gene.

"Are you alright Mr. Runyon?"

"Did they hurt you?"

"Did who hurt me?" standing on top of his desk in his jockey shorts.

"Whoever did this," explained Eddie.

"I did it, you asshole. Where the fuck do I find these guys? So, I meet this little girl gonna be a star. Sometimes you can tell right off. Got to have the skin first. Her skin was milky, soft. Natural blonde. Well sandy, but nice, made it natural blonde for her, couldn't tell. Good kid. Smart. Had her play the nurse in Beamon Brothers in Bedlam. Those Beamons were funny guys. Where are my street clothes?"

Gene quickly opened the closet and got a pair of checkered slacks and a blue pullover and brought them to the desk.

"I came over sraight from tennis. Couldn't even shower. Too pissed to shower. Those Beamons. One tall, Lefty. One fat, Fatty. One short, Stubby. Funny. We did Beamon Bros. in Boise, Beamon Bros. in Brazil. Very funny stuff. I put the blonde, see, into those movies. Didn't talk, didn't have too. What happens? Sid Morris, who should have died with his mother at birth, gives her a part in this new movie of his. I ask you. Who found her?"

"You did," they sang.

"Fucking A. She takes the part. Broke my heart. Would you believe that night I went home, sat in my leather chair and wept for the girl with the big tits who had gone and gotten herself involved with the most insensitive scumbag in the world? I wept. Get my shoes."

Eddie, cum laude, Clemson, darted to the closet.

"Morris murdered her. They say she got a cold and died but I close my eyes and I see 'The Scuz' walked through tuberculosis wards looking for infected bread to give her. Fuck him."

Jack pulled on his tasseled loafers. Dressed now he stood on his desk.

" Now, I'm playing tennis. I'm winning. I get this call saying 'The Scuz' was over Andy Nef's house. Why, I ask myself? Why? Because he wants the brother."

"Mr. Runyon," began Gene, "I really don't . . ."

"I'm still talking here fuck brain. That so all shit cocksucking hard to see?"

"No sir."

"So why the fuck else? He wants the brother, and as far as I'm concerned there is no other actor in the country who can handle Milo but the brother. 'The Scuz' gets him, I'm fucked. I can't make the film."

'Smiling Jack' climbed down from the desk and strolled over to the shattered windows.

"I want the brother. I don't care how you do it. I want him on The Last Prussian or what Rebecca."

"Or else, sir."

"Heh, heh, heh. Look what I did to my fucking office. Heh, heh, heh."

★ ★ ★ ★

Lumpapa climbed into the hole first, followed by Koro and two boys. Lumpapa gestured with his rifle and the prisoners moved against the wall. Koro and the boys began shoveling the foul waste into wood buckets. Koro gagged and could not work for a moment. He turned away. Once a month, the ritual of cleaning Lumpapa's cave. Two new boys were chosen each month. Lumpapa came to think of the task as a kind of passage into manhood and a reminder to the village that even after this first year the possibility of salvation loomed in the hope of Electric Boat ransom.

Jackie watched detached, most days now passed in dreams. He had lost almost ninety pounds but was still not yet dry in the way the young boys were. Harlan laughed a crazy laugh, smiled his unnerving smile. Koro and the boys would not look into his face. He broke early. Who can say why? Only see how he wrings his hands, so hard that the skin has fallen away from the knuckles. His mind had drawn him now, out of the dry heat, the sucking emptiness of the desert, into a saving place with grandfather and Mack's candy store in South Louisville and open hydrants, cool and wet.

Thunder cracked and Harlan stood up. One of the boys, Suni, hit him in the stomach. Intestines vibrated through his body like coiled springs. He shit himself. Harlan reached out and grabbed the boy by the neck while the bald child swung wildly.

Lumpapa grabbed his wrist and Koro threw an arm around his neck. Suni thrashed wildly on the end of Harlan's bony hand. The tips of his fingers seemed to disappear into the sinew of the boy's neck. Harlan threw his head back and screamed for Sister Agnes. Lumpapa slapped his hands, Koro pounded his shovel against his legs but he could not let go. Suni flopped like a flag in the wind. Jackie, fresh from a dream of sailing, grabbed Harlan's face and turned it to him. He squeezed his cheeks. Harlan turned quickly to Suni and released his grip. Suni fell to the ground crying, rubbing his throat. Harlan now fell under the weight of accumulated blows. Lumpapa screamed something at him and helped Suni outside. It was more than six months before the hole would be cleaned again. You must cover it with dirt.

★ ★ ★ ★

Smiling Jack never mentioned the midnight meeting to Andy. The day at Peakskill trickled along. Both men seemed subdued. They reviewed Alan Hunter's percentage clause on the way to Green Glen, driven by the silent Wills.

"It comes to roughly eight percent."

"Ahhh," said Smiling Jack.

"We also agree to travel in Hunter Airlines between L.A. and San Francisco for the duration of the shoot. Stay at the Holiday Inn in Reno he owns, if we use any of that part of the desert for location, and Hunter Associates, the catering firm, must supply all food and beverages."

"Eight percent. Gross?"

"Of course, Sir."

"What are these guys? Jesus. I agree to give them eight percent of the gross and they take it. Don't they know I hide gross? They'll never get a dime. Dumb bastards. I love this fucking business so much. Hey Wills. You hear that? Dumb bastards."

Wills nodded.

"So what else?"

"That's about it on the contract. I can send it over today. It ought to be signed, sealed and delivered in a week."

"That it?"

"Yes, Sir."

"Nothing else?"

"I don't think so, Sir?"

"Wills, shut off the fucking speakers. I hate it when the whole world knows your business. People are so fucking nosey. It's one of the shitty parts of life. You like Hunter, Andy? Yeah, you told me, that's right. You think he's good. I tell you a secret. He stinks. Know what his last picture did? Zip. Fucking black hole. I tell you another thing. A Jack Runyon film never loses money. Never. Now sometimes it might take awhile to get back some moolah but I always get it. Heh, heh, heh."

"I know, Sir."

"Yeah, you know. I'm a winner is what I'm saying. I'm a big Mick winner."

Smiling Jack turned his eyes back to the window and missed them, suddenly, awfully, missed Philly and Robby and Ray-Ray and Les and Billy and especially Maury who laid it all down at Normandy. Just one more time. One more eleven year old afternoon.

"Just one more," he muttered.

"Sir?"

"Just one more."

Later, at the Green Glen Jack chased one of the Pro's lobs. A cabana boy brought a phone to the table.

"It's Gene. I couldn't say anything at the office."

"You alone?"

"He's on the court."

"He say anything about your brother?"

"Oh no. What? What?"

"He knows you talked to 'The Scuz' yesterday. He's pissed. We had a secret meeting last night. He wants your brother. Did Morris really offer him a part?"

"Nine hundred fifty thousand dollars worth of part."

Gene and Andy pause. Telephone poles swayed.

"What did he say?"

"I didn't tell him. He didn't come home last night."

Another pause, rustling wires.

"Nine hundred fifty thousand?"

"Yes."

"I got to go. Watch that fucker."

Andy ordered a double Martini. He never drank on the job. Rules of the trade. So much for rules.

They walked up Highland. Her red Volks had to be towed to Peterson Park garage. She didn't mind. A light breeze seemed to lift the maroon haze off the foothills. They walked toward them. One new day. An occasional filmed-through-gauze day. A good day for holding hands and they did. Leonie felt as though she had never held hands before. His fingers and knuckles did not seem so bony now. My magic soup, she thought.

"It is magic. I feel it in my blood."

She must have not thought soup. She must have said it out loud.

Across the street, in the shadow of Television City, Robbins Wholesaler called from rows of pants and skirts racked out on the sidewalk. Tables overflowed with socks and visors and sandals and ties. She spotted a white linen suit with a tie chord.

"Try it on. Please."

Jackie started to unbutton his pants.

"You have to go into a dressing room."

While he changed she picked a red Hawaiian shirt. Twenty minutes later, the model of rakish starved elegance rolled in toeless gate towards his brother's home.

"Thank you for buying me these."

She squeezed his arm. At Sunset Boulevard Jackie stopped at an old woman sitting on a bench.

"Your bags."

"My things."

"May I look?"

He released Leonie's hand, walked over to the bench and sat down. Leonie could smell the bite of stale urine.

"Owned a house, oh God, here, nice house with . . . William Brackridge was his name. Mine was Linda, only mine was Ricci. Linda Ricci. He had a house, him and me. Here."

The old woman reached into the bag and took a framed picture out. Her fingernails were still long and cared for. He held her hand as he looked at the picture.

"Every Sunday we would walk to St. Catherine's and he would whistle and, oh God, I can never make people see it, birds would whistle back at him. That is how sweet his trill. But we never married and we never had babies. Here's the house."

"Where is it?"

She raised her eyes and pointed across the street to Denny's Restaurant. He nodded.

"Where are you now?"

"I'm here. I'm here now and I was a beautiful girl."

He put one finger to the side of her head and she closed her eyes.

Leonie slipped fifty cents in the coin slot and pulled out the green bordered Variety. She leafed through it then put it into her shoulder bag. Jackie walked over and they continued toward the hills.

"People do not have very much," Jackie said after a moment.

"Some people."

"Most people."

They walked in silence.

Tom watched the black Buick from the hedges across the street. He didn't know 'The Smiler's' detective was on stake out, only that it had been parked watching the house for most of the day and the guy inside with the handlebar mustache and black sunglasses must be one of those child molesters his teachers and parents told him to be on the lookout for. The seven year old had indeed been on the lookout. Now he was sure he had one. He waved to Elliot who waved to Jackie. Jr., stationed in the Merrill's garage who signaled Richie DeVoe, ten year old son of Dodger pitcher Terry DeVoe and the unrivaled neighborhood nutcase. Richie walked over to the Buick.

"Hi," said Richie.

"Hello son," yawned Henderson Anderson.

"So, uh, how about a piece of candy or something?"

"What."

"You know."

"Candy?"

While Richie talked, Jackie snapped away with his mother's Polaroid camera. Tom tied clothesline cord to the fender of the Buick, pulled it around a tree and wove it back and forth several times until a web of rope anchored the Buick to the tree.

The detective handed Terry his last remaining Lifesaver. Terry reached out and took it, then yelled at the top of his lungs, "Got it?"

"Got it," screamed Jackie. Jr.

"Now," yelled Tom up to his baby brother. Elliot scampered to the phone, pushed 911, and slowly repeated his address over and over. Tom leapt up holding a gallon of oil based glossy yellow paint at the top and bottom and hurled it over the back of the car.

"Get him Tom," yelled Jackie.

The detective, dazed by the screaming assault and click of camera and throw of paint oozing down the rear window, thought to emerge from the car and defend himself until, to his left, he caught a glimpse of the horror running toward the car with a solid ash, 36" Louisville Slugger.

"Oh my God," he uttered. The nightmare had fallen. Small devils crawled from the earth. Beelzebub with a baseball bat.

"Get him, Tom."

Frantically he rolled his windows up and locked the door. The Buick struggled to turn over and finally did seconds after the first stroke shattered his side view mirror. He gunned the engine but only rubber turned. A second blow took out the passenger side window. The detective frantically held out his identification and pressed it against the front window. Bits of glass rebounded off his badge as Tom shattered the glass. He gunned the car again. It pulled and spun. The beast now had cocked the bat for the driver's side.

"Oh my God," the detective said. He pushed the door open as Tom swung for the wall. The force of the swing knocked him to the ground. The detective instinctively grabbed his gun from the compartment of the car and stepped out. He kicked the bat away, reached down and picked Tom up by the shirt.

Mr. Pollino looked out of his stucco house window.

An unmarked police car, with two bearded undercover cops, wheeled up crossing the detective's Buick.

"Drop it," one said as they both leveled their revolvers.

"These kids . . ."

"Police! Drop it!"

The detective dropped the gun. Tom pulled away for the safety of the police but as he did his elbow inadvertently popped against the right testicle of the man with the half yellow car. The police now calmly walked to the kneeling, gasping figure who raised his head and watched speechlessly as Jackie, Jr. handed his collection of Polaroids to them.

Smiling Jack sat in front of his Beverly Hills palace.

"I'm tired today."

"You played hard, Sir."

"Yeah, I guess. Oh yeah, you got to set up a screen test for Claire Guest's little asshole friend."

"Howard?"

"She's a bitch but a good kid."

"I'll do it first thing tomorrow."

"I'm not killing Milo. Milo doesn't die in the middle now. He's a winner Milo is."

"It's a great part like it is, Sir."

"Then why the fuck you being so shitty to me. You don't like me? I treat you bad?"

"No sir, you treat me very well."

"I trust you. I don't trust many guys. I trust you, you come through. Only Andy, what? I can't get him out of my head. I look at the fucking skinny brother I see Milo. Milo makes the movie."

"I . . ."

"Okay so I know 'The Scuz' been negotiating with you but what the fuck."

"Nobody has been negotiating. Mr. Morris came by the house. Scared me. You never see him in daylight."

"Fuck him."

"I've only seen him at that corner table in Ma Maison."

"All day long. He's a scumbag."

"He said he wanted Jackie for his new film. He offered, God, he offered nine hundred fifty thousand. I haven't seen Jackie. I haven't even . . ."

"One million, flat cash," 'The Smiler' deadfaced. He stepped out of the Rolls. "One million, flat cash. I been good to you."

He walked briskly to his front door. Andy sat, with Wills at the wheel, silently for ten minutes.

"Take me home, Wills," he finally said.

Elliot's hotwheels lay tipped on the sidewalk. Andy didn't bother to move them into the garage. He didn't take special notice of the bent maple tree sporting fresh rope burns or the shiny yellow street.

"We got one Daddy," Tom screamed. "We got a sicko."

"I called the police," chirped Elliot.

"They took all the pictures."

"But I got him. Bam."

Susan came into the room, kissed him, and relayed the police's story of how the boys rescued little Richie DaVoe from a child napper. Jackie had come home fifteen minutes earlier with a friend. Want a drink? Andy poured some Vodka into a tumbler, drank it, poured some more and followed Susan into the living room. Leonie sat next to Jackie on the couch.

"Andy, this is Leonie."

Andy smiled. Jackie was folded into the couch in his new white on red ensemble.

"We missed you last night."

"I missed you too."

"I mean we missed hearing from you. We wish you would tell us . . . never mind."

Andy lay his head back on the chair and closed his eyes for a moment, opened them and drank the new Vodka.

"Get me another, would you?"

Susan would rather not, tells him that with her eyes, but complies.

"So Jackie."

Jackie smiles first at Andy, then Leonie.

"Things are happening here. Things are moving."

Leonie glanced towards the kitchen.

"You're a hit. You're a hit. Did you know that?"

Jackie shook his head still smiling.

"I saw a woman today. About as old as mom would have been. She lives on a bus stop bench."

"Jack Runyon thinks you're hot stuff. Sid Morris, too. They want you."

Andy noticed Leonie's Variety at the top of her day bag. He reached over and took it out. Susan returned with his drink.

"Let me see, here we go. Page two. Sid must be slipping."

"What is it?" asked Susan.

He handed the paper to her. Leonie watched her expression. Leonie reached over and slid the paper from Susan's hands.

'Unknown Offered Near Million in Morris' Biggee.'

"I'm up for a role in that movie. I'm an actress," said Leonie. "I wonder who he offered it to."

Jackie stood up and walked to the sliding glass doors. Andy stood and watched him.

"Did too," Tom cried entering the room.

"Liar," said Jackie, Jr.

"Hee, hee, hee," chortled Elliot.

"Cannot," taunted Jackie, Jr.

"Can too," cried Tom.

"Liar."

"Hee, hee, hee."

"He offered it to him," said Andy.

"C'mon Jackie," said Tom running over to his uncle. "Fly."

★ ★ ★ ★

How can a country become so . . . dry? Does the driving sand, the static crack of air simply end at a fortunate border of heavy grass? Here is desert and now here is the end of desert? Suni shakes his head. These are very, very large questions. It is hard to think of anything lately. Suni tries to remember to tighten his jaw. Mada noticed he was often slack jawed. Suni tightens it. Two days ago, by the well, he sat in the dust and drank a wooden scoop of water, his back against the mud wall. He could not stand up. Koro waved from his hut and Oaka, sweet and brown who lived over Lumpapa's cave whistled at him. He looked always for her but he could not say why. He sat for six hours under the sun and only Mada, carrying water for the men in the hole noticed he could not walk. She carried him back to the shade of the schoolhouse and rolled some dough for him.

"She was growling last night," he said.

"I heard her too," said Mada.

"I hear the cubs now. They are getting big."

"Must be getting big, yes."

"One of those men was growling back at her."

"I heard him."

"Which one do you think?"

"Black one."

"He's crazy."

"Yes."

"He growls and cries and laughs. White one doesn't do anything. He's crazy too."

"Maybe."

Mada left Suni in the shade of the school hut and walked into the sun. She walked to the well and put the wooden ladle back into the water. She walked over to the prison hole. She felt him watching from the window slit. She knelt in front of it and slowly put her thin fingers through the opening. Five black boned appendages, delicately hanging in the window of the cave. A moment passed, day birds, frightened by a dog, flurried overhead. Hot wind threw sand against her legs. Mada felt a brush of air against the tip of her middle finger. She closed her eyes. Another brush, another finger, until all had the lightness of his fingers meeting hers, at the tip of the flesh before it descended to nail.

★ ★ ★ ★

Howard angrily threw the umbrella down and marched to the water cooler. He drank in silence, then returned to the corner of the studio where his long awaited screen test was being administered.

"It's bad enough, that I have to use a fucking umbrella instead of a sword and have to pretend this Bill Blass blazer is a Napoleonic uniform but to look around and see a platoon of stagehands shoving bagels into their mouths is just too, too much. Okay. Okay, I'm alright now. Okay. Fuck it. Let's do it."

Claire Guest huffed past the brutal grips and brushed the perspiration from Howard's eyes.

"There was a moment when I actually believed the umbrella was a sword. A rapier," she whispered.

"Before it opened?"

"Just before."

Manny Mageo, deputy of local 161 of the stagehand union admonished his cohorts.

"Alright, let's all ditch the food, put the coffee down. Sorry."

"It's very distracting to him."

"Yes ma'am."

"Anything that distracts his concentration is taboo."

Manny nodded. Howard took his position on the set and breathed deep.

"Don't waste tape on the bastard," Manny whispered into his mike to the control booth.

"Stop tape," the booth whispered.

"Okay sir," smiled Manny, "we're ready for you."

Andy dropped Leonie off at the transmission shop. Jackie climbed from the back seat, kissed her oddly on her fingertips then sat next to Andy. She watched his face.

"I'll see you then?"

"Yes."

"I will won't I?"

"Yes."

A light rain began to fall. Andy turned onto Santa Monica. Andy lit a cigarette.

"Want a cup of coffee?"

"Okay."

The boys and girls who sell themselves huddled under a Safeway's awning. Jackie noted the mascara streaming down one child's face.

"Anguished."

"Sick fuckers. You got to wonder what kind of people let their kids run around like that. Jesus."

Andy pulled into Barney's Beanery and took a table by the window. Andy ordered a Mexican beer and Jackie some tea.

"Get a beer. C'mon."

"I like tea pretty well."

"C'mon."

"Okay."

The waitress placed the beers in front of them, looked at Jackie and left. Andy raised his frosted mug.

"To . . . you."

"To . . . me."

The lost brother. Foam dripping down his chin and onto his red Hawaiian shirt. He reached over and dabbed Jackie's lips with a napkin.

"Jesus, what am I doing?"

"It's okay."

"You can wipe your own chin."

"That was a nice thing."

"See, I'm used to wiping everybody's face. The boys. They're like little animals sometimes. I don't know."

"The boys are truly amazing."

"They're something alright."

"You're very lucky."

"I'm lucky huh?" said Andy draining his beer and ordering another. "If I'm so lucky why ain't I rich?"

"You're not rich?"

"I'm well-off. Rich is another thing. Another thing altogether. Pop would say I was rich."

Jackie smiled.

"Pop would say, 'My God, boy, look at that house'."

Jackie put his glass down and began drying the table with his napkin.

"Anyway, I'm not rich. At least not in the way you're going to be rich."

Jackie gazed out the window. A tall black woman was walking by. The rain soaked into her pant suit.

"Now, you know I love you."

"What?"

"You know I love you and . . ."

"I love you also."

"Sure, I know that. And you must know because I love you I would never let anyone or anything hurt you or compromise you in any way."

Jackie leaned across the table and kissed his brother on the lips. The waitress looked up. A man with half an enchilada hanging from his mouth stole a sidelong glance.

"Anyway, you have two firm offers on the table by two very reputable producers who are both very, very determined that Jackie Nef perform in their film. Now it may appear that I'm being self-serving by recommending that you accept Mr. Runyon's offer of the role of Milo in The Last Prussian. Money aside, even though Mr. Runyon's offer of one million dollars is substantially greater than Mr. Morris' offer, the main consideration has to be artistic. Morris is doing a schlock western. The Last Prussian has a genuine shot at being a memorable film and the part of Milo, a memorable role. So I'm going to strongly recommend you accept Mr. Runyon's offer to play Milo in the film, The Last Prussian . . . for . . . one . . . million . . . dollars."

The rain had stopped and the sun was beginning to peek through heavy cloud cover. Two boys powered skate boards by the window.

"I'm not an actor."

"Anybody can act. Athletes act and they have no talent."

"I'm not interested."

"Jackie ..."

"This beer, this beer is wonderful. Only I'm so full, I don't know. Remember how Pop drank beer? How? How much beer?"

"Lots of beer."

"Lots and lots and lots," laughed Jackie, drinking his.

★ ★ ★ ★

One morning Suni awoke feeling strangely refreshed. He stood by his mat and stepped to the door. His long, flat hand shielded the sun from his eyes and he felt a cool breeze from distant hills wrap around him. He smiled a tall child smile and his few teeth caught the early sun and glistened, shining like stars. He ran awkwardly to the village center, holding his arms out as though he could take flight in his birdweight. He laughed. Mada saw him from the school house and ran to him. Lumpapa also ran to him.

"Cool. Oh cool wind," he shouted.

Lumpapa reached for him but he fled to the edge of the village, the beginning of desert and lions, with Mada and Lumpapa and Koro and some children running after him.

"Cool wind, Mada," he shouted.

"Suni."

"From those hills. There. The cool wind comes from . . ."

Suddenly he dropped his arms to his side and tumbled to the dust. Lumpapa held him sobbing bitter tears. Mada shook him.

Here is another then, another dead child.

Reaching down she touched the top of Lumpapa's hat. His animal eyes turned up to her, red eyes, and turned back to the dry child. Koro called to several of the boys to bring shovels from the revolutionary hut and started for the rise above the school house which held the piled stones of Suni's mother and father and brothers and sisters taken by a cool breeze of their own.

Koro dug for two hours to the rhythm of Lumpapa's wails, his rocking of the child. Finally Mada pulled Lumpapa to his feet and together they carried the corpse to the grave. Rocks were piled high to keep the wild dogs from the body.

Suni awoke to a cool breeze and two hours later was under the dust.

Lumpapa stayed until the heavy afternoon sun drove him down the rise and into his hut. Mada watched him from the school house. Stumbling on the slope, falling, sobbing. Mostly a fool, Lumpapa. Mostly a loud, small, flailing, strutting fool with a dream of water sweet and clear. His pain was in the bonding of the village, like a mother and a child. It was as though he died with them and was resurrected every morning. It was as though he went into the darkness with them. Mada did not go to him. As in the past he would be inconsolable. When her sister Absa died it was she who tried to comfort him. Her own sister. She held him and before God felt him becoming smaller. Mada truly believed if enough of the village died Lumpapa would simply disappear.

When darkness came, Mada dipped weary fingers into the water and ran them over her lips and eyes. She stood by the well, a part of the stillness, then walked slowly to Lumpapa's cave. She knelt by the window slit and winced at the smell. She lowered her ebony arm into the window and felt his fingers brush the back of her hand.

"Dead then," Jackie whispered dryly.

"Yes."

"A child?"

"Suni."

His hand held her delicate fingers and kissed her arm. She closed her eyes against the searing smell.

"It's alright."

"What is alright?"

"I'm with him now."

"With who?"

"Suni."

The stars twinkled perfectly in the sky. Mada raised her free hand to her face and pinched her nostrils.

★ ★ ★ ★

"Stan shot himself. He's dead."

"Shot himself?"

"Put the gun inside his mouth and blew the back of his head off. Just like that. Boom. No head."

This is how Gene greeted Andy at Peakskill.

"Apparently despondent over, you know, all those paternity suits, he goes home calls his wife into the kitchen and just like that. Boom. No head."

"You mean she saw him do it?"

"Boom," Gene putting a finger into his open mouth for effect. "No head."

"Jesus Christ."

Eddie Burke sauntered into the office and picked a bagel off the coffee cart.

"Stan shot himself. He's dead."

"Shot himself."

"Put the gun inside his mouth and blew the back of his head off. Just like that. Boom. No head."

Eddie stopped spreading the cream cheese and chives across his bagel.

Rebecca Haycroft came out of 'The Smiler's' office.

"He's hot today. He just set up a meeting with Alan Hunter

and Jay Graymore. He took one look at their script revisions and just about went through the roof."

"Aww fuck," said Eddie, "some weekend then, huh? Some fucking weekend."

"Could be worse," said Gene, again putting the finger into his open mouth. "Boom."

"Boom," said Rebecca with the same gesture.

Mookie knocked on the door and Susan answered it. "He here man?"

"I'll . . . get him."

Mookie grabbed Jackie's arm frantically. "C'mon man."

They descended the outside stairs to the red Chevy below. Pedro was behind the wheel. Chaca was stretched out on the back seat.

"He's hurt bad, man."

Jackie got into the back seat and touched his head.

"Better?"

"Yeah, better," smiled Chaca.

"You have to get to a doctor, a hospital."

"It's a bullet. I go to the hospital, I go down."

"Who shot you?"

"Nobody."

"Who shot him, Pedro."

Gang silence.

"Truth is everything."

"Old Man Santiago shot him. Motherfucker threw a slug into him when we were running out," Mookie finally said.

"Got him good," said Pedro.

"Fifty lousy bucks, that all we got," said Mookie.

Jackie turned to Chaca who looked away. "You robbed him?"

Gang pause.

"You robbed him?"

"His store. He got a little grocery store. Everybody robs him. He stays. He knows what's coming. He got me good."

"He got him good."

Jackie got out of the car, walked back up the stairs and returned a moment later. They drove to the closest hospital which was Garden Crest and took Chaca into emergency. Mookie stayed with him while Pedro drove Jackie to the Bank of America at Sunset and Fountain. The pair then headed into the Barrio and Old Man Santiago's Grocery Store.

"Mr. Santiago?"

"Roast beef good today. Plenty of Planken too. Take it home, fry it up, Amigo."

"You shot a young man the other day."

"You a cop?"

"No, I'm a friend."

"His or mine," Santiago said edging behind the counter.

"Well, I'm his friend and I'm your friend."

Old Man Santiago pulled a small handgun out from under the cash register.

"You got problems with your friends. You got good friends then and bad ones. If I'm your friend you got good ones, if that animal I shot is your friend you got trouble. This is a registered gun."

Jackie reached for the side of Santiago's head.

Santiago slapped his hand away. "I been on this corner twenty-six years. I never hurt no one. My wife and my kids and me we'd be up four-thirty polishing apples so they look pretty. Santiagos only know work. The animals don't know work. They laugh at it. They hate it. But when the working's done they want money. Twenty times I been robbed. Twenty bucks, fifty bucks, bags of food. Am I made to work for the animals? This last time I have this gun."

Jackie looked a moment at the old man, then walked down the counter, looking at the shelves of food and the glassed meat display case. He breathed deeply through his nose and smelled the open bags of beans and garlic, tea and onions.

"Your store smells so good."

"It's all fresh. I don't sell bad meat. I keep the garlic and onions out for the smell. My wife loved the smell of garlic."

"It smells wonderful . . . garlic."

"My Ines would put a bag of garlic by the meat and a bag of onions by the dried fruit. She knew, my Ines. My Roberto would polish the apples. He would look after all the vegetables. He's a doctor now in San Diego. Robert Santiago, M.D. and Jane, Ines named her Jane. My little American. She has five children and one husband and they work and I think are happy."

"But it's hard without Ines. So much of you went with her into the light. You can't help that. Parts of us have to leave. Still it's so hard without her smiling and the burritos at ten and the thick Mexican coffee."

Santiago put his gun down and stepped away from the counter.

"She would serve it in those small cups. Demitasse. I couldn't even get my finger through it and we would just sit behind the counter and talk about our Roberto and our Jane. My little Ines . . . here in this chair. So quickly and quietly . . . just gone."

Jackie reached for the side of the old man's head. This time Santiago just looked at him. His eyes closed to the touch.

"You see she is in the light then. You can see true she is surely in the light."

Jackie removed his fingers and placed some paper on the counter by the cash register.

"The one you shot is named Chaca. He is not in the light. Do you think you could forgive him?"

Santiago nodded. Jackie walked into the street. Pedro pulled up with the low-rider and they were gone.

Old Man Santiago ran his fingers through tight white hair and breathed deeply. He walked to the counter and looked at the paper Jackie had placed there. He picked it up, letting the stack flip beneath his forefinger and thumb, then slid the twenty thousand dollars under the register.

★ ★ ★ ★

"Jackie?"

"I'm here. I'm in the corner."

"I can't see you."

"I'm here."

"Move into the light for God's sake."

"I'm moving."

Jackie slides into the middle of the pit.

"Are you allright?"

"I want to talk. I'm back for awhile. I'm here now."

"I'm here too."

"I come and I go. I go <u>with</u> it, that's my . . . problem. Whenever it wants me I go. I go."

"You're shivering."

"Well, yes. Yes I am. I'm a cold motherfucker. I don't think about it. How long man?"

"Years I think."

"Years?"

A lioness roars in the distance near to where villagers bury each other. Harlan turns to the sound and smiles.

"She bored tonight. That's a sad little roar. She just yawning. I think about her. I wonder, you know, how she's doing. Sometimes I worry about her babies. I talk to her sometimes."

"You roar, man."

"I roar. I know."

Harlan and Jackie laugh. Another roar. Harlan stands and walks to the window. Jackie watches him but does not move.

"The boy don't have to hunt, you know. He can lie in the shade and the ladies got to bring the good shit to him. That's how it is with Lions. Those are the Lion rules. You like the Lions?"

"Yes."

"I see an arm sometimes come into the room. You touch it, Jackie. Whose arm?"

"Sometimes I'm sure of the arm. Sometimes I don't know."

"You kiss the fingers."

"I kiss the fingers."

"I hear you talking and I'm afraid of you."

"I'll still be Jackie. Don't be afraid."

"I see you turn. I've seen it. Is it good to turn in the air? Spinning? A man in the air?"

Jackie slides over to Harlan and puts his arm around him. The Lioness roars.

★ ★ ★ ★

Jay Graymore defended himself stylishly. He moved to the center of 'The Smiler's' office and turned dramatically.

"See Mr. Runyon. He sees her but she doesn't see him. He immediately keys in on her burning sexuality but because she doesn't get a long, hard look at him she is able to keep him at bay . . . for awhile. The scene will deliver. It's a hot scene. It's a . . . a . . . hot, hot scene."

'The Smiler' put a cigarette in his mouth and Eddie lit it.

"What's she wearing?"

"Oh you'll love this. I've got her in a French officer's uniform with basic blue and grey and a hint of silver flash. Real silver sword."

"Got her all decked out from head to toe huh?"

"With a hint of silver."

"Great."

"It's got those enormous ruffled cuffs with . . ."

"That's great. So here's a chicky with a four million price tag and you got her dressed like fucking Napoleon."

"But later we ..."

"Who gives the fuck about later? Know what she did in her last film? What was that?"

"Lady Destroyer, Paramount, Angel Dumas sir," Gene read from his clipboard.

"That's the one. She fucked guys and then she murdered them. Lots of them."

"But she can't fucking act for shit," added 'The Smiler'.

"Not for shit," chimed Eddie.

"When people look at this chicky . . . what's her name?"

"Sylvia Dupree," said Gene.

"Yeah. People look at Sylvia Dupree because she's got a great fucking body and because she's a little fucking dirty. Understand me?"

Jay understood.

"You write like a dead man. You write bad. Bad. I piss on your rewrites. I'll get somebody else to do the rewrites. See ya."

Jay fucking well understood.

"So where's Hunter? I wanted Hunter here. He did these rewrites with that asshole."

"Mr. Hunter wasn't available."

"Not what?"

"He wasn't . . ."

"He wouldn't come? He so big he wouldn't come? That asshole dick bitch shit prick bastard. I'll fucking kill that snot ..."

"Jack," smiled Alan entering the lair.

"Darling, we were just talking about you. Loved the rewrites just got to touch up a little and we're off. So how are you?"

"Great. Anxious to get started. By the way that was a stroke of genius getting Sylvia. She's a lovely girl. This'll really be a break out part for her."

"She'll break out."

"Jay's idea is to have her simmering in the movie. Always a pot about to boil over. Her sexuality under wraps."

"Interesting," nodded Jack.

"Jay thought we should tease our audience. Keep her in an officer's uniform. How are you coming with Milo?"

"Still in negotiation."

"I met him at Althea's birthday party. His brother works for you, right?"

"All in the family," winked 'The Smiler'.

"We had a nice talk. Something. We talked. Anyway if there's nothing else I think I'll go back to Malibu and tackle the rewrites."

"Great, great," said 'The Smiler' who gave Alan a bear hug, told him he was the greatest, and waved good-bye.

"Fuck him," said 'The Smiler', softly shutting the door. "I got an idea. Gene, get me the fucking script."

Elliot walked up to the old woman who sat acrid on the bus stop bench.

"What happened to you?"

"She's poor," explained Jackie, Jr.

"Hello Linda Pucci."

"Why, hello. Why, hello boys."

"I'm Elliot."

"I'm Jackie, Jr."

"You smell bad," said Tom quietly. "My eyes hurt to be near you."

"But I was a beautiful girl, child. People smiled at Linda Pucci – William Brackridge made her a home. There. Across the street. He was a wonderful man. Birds sang for me and I washed my skin in lemon water, a flower in my pretty hair."

Jackie held out his hand and Linda walked over to him. The boys grabbed her bundles, her bags and grocery cart. They walked to the corner and down Sunset. Tom walked up beside her and held her other hand. No one spoke.

The silent procession stopped in front of the Anna Ide Adult

Home, a pink, two story stucco, flanked by two enormous palm trees. On the porch were several older men and women whose eyes lit at the sight of children. Tom strolled over to an ancient man in a wheelchair.

"Look," he said to Elliot, "this is what's gonna happen to you."

Jackie and Linda were met by a matronly looking Spanish woman who led them to a small back corridor. On one room door was the name 'Linda Pucci.'

"This is my name."

"Si."

"It's a room with my name on it."

"It is your room."

"But . . ."

"William Brackridge loved you," said Jackie.

"Oh, I was loved. I was loved."

"This room is from William."

Jackie touched the side of her head and turned to walk back to the street.

"I was a lovely girl."

"Yes Linda. Very lovely."

The four walked quietly out to Sunset and toward home.

"Is that really gonna happen to me?" asked Elliot.

"Just like that only your ears are gonna fall off too."

"People get old," said Jackie.

"I don't want to talk about it," said Jackie, Jr.

"They get old and die and get put in a box and put in a hole and people throw dirt on them," said Tom.

"Shut up," yelled Jackie, Jr.

"Or they bake them in ovens until nothing's left."

"Asshole," screamed Jackie, Jr.

★ ★ ★ ★

The grey Land Rover stopped by the well. Three soldiers emerged and drank. A white man in a t-shirt and khaki slacks slipped out of the front passenger seat and drank from his western canteen. He stretched, rubbed his lower back and walked to the center of the village. Lumpapa watched from his window. He slid the revolutionary weapons under some cooking supplies. He hid his uniform under his blanket. He stuffed his revolutionary book of proverbs into a hole in the crumbling hut wall and pushed some dirty stucco in after it.

The village children ran to the chalky stranger an army of tiny beggars. Lumpapa burned with rage at the sight. He would discuss self-respect at the next children's revolutionary council meeting. The man yelled in English to the soldiers to give the children something. They looked back at him. Finally he pushed through the children, took a canvas trail sack out of the vehicle and gave them each some precious item. A box of raisins, crackers, Slim Jims. Mada watched from the school house.

The man walked again to the center of the village. Lumpapa walked toward him smiling cautiously. The man also smiled.

"I'm looking for someone. A man. A tall, thickly built man. I traced him from South Africa. He was seen around here. Years ago. He worked for Electric Boat. Do you know Electric Boat?"

"Boat?" laughed Lumpapa.

The Bakwanes yelled for him and climbed back into the Rover.

"Those children are awful sick."

Lumpapa stiffened at the remark but smiled through it, thinking: Have I not been a good shepherd? All for the children so White men with trucks full of Bakwanes animals and raisins can feel good for a second in the disposals of goods?

"Yes," he smiled, "many are sick."

"No Electric Boat?"

"Oh, ho, ho, no boat."

Lumpapa stood in the village center and watched them drive over the rise. Mada joined him. Under the single large tree, by the piles of black stones marking the passing of generations the family pride of lions lay in the shade, the male-boy at the center. They stopped the Rover. The driver walked around to the front. The White man joined him. A shape of a man lay with them. Perhaps they killed him in the night and carried him to the tree.

"I think that's how lions live," the driver said.

"Jesus," uttered the man.

"See a man, eat him. Now shit mister, we never going to see this boy of yours. We going back to Monton."

"I paid you."

"We looked."

"I paid for a longer look."

"Too bad."

"Which one of you is going to tell that boss of yours, that Lani Sec, you cheated me."

The Bakwanes do not like to be called cheaters. But they are cheats and often proud of it. Lani Sec was not a Bakwanes. He was not of their noble tribe. They looked at one another.

"Another village like this one if we drive west awhile."

"Then drive."

"Okay son of bitch, but remember," the driver said shaking his fist at him, "you gave away your lunch."

Mada and Lumpapa watched them leave the burial ground, small against the red sun.

"You should have told him."

"Then what would we have?"

"What do we have?"

"Electric boat . . ."

"They will never pay. They do not care. My God I'm so tired."

"Get out of the sun."

"It is not the sun."

"You argue woman. You fight me. I am tired too."

The woman of the family who lived above the hole, oblivious to the odor, joined them.

"My husband was not home last night. He went to pile more stones on baby's grave, then was not home."

Lumpapa looked up to the rise.

"It was dusk. I told him to wait. He was worried about the dogs."

★ ★ ★ ★

As far as rainbows, Hollywood's combination of smog and natural inversion serve to heighten the reds, dull the blues and completely wash out the delicate shades of white. A Hollywood rainbow is essentially a fiery arc. Andy sipped his morning coffee and watched it from the kitchen window.

Dragging himself into the kitchen, Tom said, "I want waffles."

"Cereal this morning."

"I want waffles."

"Can't make waffles. No eggs."

"I'm not going to school then."

"You have to go to school."

"Why."

"It's your job."

"Bull . . ."

"Language pal or you're gonna spend after school in your room."

"What kind of cereal do we got?"

"Do we have."

"What kind?"

Andy opened the cupboard above the fridge.

"Honey Oats, Raisin Crisp, Fudge Crisp, Corn Crisp, and Cheerios, are your brothers awake?"

"They're assholes, Fudge Crisps."

Andy got the box down and poured them into the troll's bowl. He poured milk.

"Too much milk, you ruined it," Tom screamed.

"Go to your room," Andy screamed.

"Okay," Tom screamed.

"And don't come down until you can act like a human being," Andy screamed.

"I'm never coming down then," Tom screamed.

"Then don't," Andy screamed.

"Good morning," Susan said.

"Good morning," Andy screamed.

"Fudge Crisps getting soggy."

Andy sat down and began to eat them.

"It takes a real man to eat a bowl of soggy Fudge Crisps."

"I don't believe we buy this shit for the kids. Is it my imagination or is Tom turning into a complete savage?"

"He's only seven."

Susan drank her coffee in silence. Andy mashed the fudge balls silently against the roof of his mouth.

"When we were kids, Pop would make bacon and eggs and fried tomatoes. Then he'd soak up the bacon fat and juice of the tomato with a piece of toast. I don't know why I'm thinking of that."

The rage of reds dispersed. Hills became visible, a slight breeze moved the smog toward San Bernadino.

"We were normal people, at least normal for Rhode Island. We had normal friends and Pop was in the Masons and Mom belonged to Eastern Star, me and Jackie were Scouts. We had a clear view of things. You know? Because really and truly that's all that matters when you stop and think about it. Things that matter. Know who your friends are. Believe in God. Know the fastest point home. No gray areas. Everything clear. Does that make any sense?"

Susan shouted, "Let's go you guys. School bus in twenty minutes."

"Now though, I don't know. I'm eating fudge crispies, I have absolutely no idea who my friends are, I don't believe in God and I still can't find a nice route home at night. Nothing's clear. What do you think? Midlife crisis? I don't think so. Something's up. I got to go."

"Who represents your brother?" Gene asked jogging across the outer office towards him.

"What?"

"What's his full name?" Rebecca shouted.

"Why?"

"Hunter's out. Your brother's in."

"Rebecca's polishing the offer sheet. We've been going all night. Eddie's with Hunter's lawyers. Graymore is out as director. Norm Rector is flying in from New York. It's big. Norm Rector. Unbelievable. Three academys. 'The Smiler's' pulled out the stops. Who represents him?"

Rebecca walked toward them with a five page stapled document.

"We got the line here. Want to hear it?"

"Maybe his agent should . . ."

"He . . . Jackie doesn't have an agent."

"I guess his brother will just be forced to negotiate for him." Rebecca smiled.

"It kind of looks like that."

"What's ten percent of fourteen and a half million?"

Andy sagged against the coffee cart.

"You alright?"

Rebecca poured some coffee.

They were silent. The coffee burned against his lips like the steaming cocoa his Nana would bring him, early morning, the room icy, window frost, and Andy under that lavender goose down comforter. Nana opens the door and brings the cocoa and puffs the pillows. Nothing too special for the boy visiting his Nana and if in the night his dreams woke him, Pa would lumber in, still big, tough, and rub the top of his forehead and big grandfather voice singing 'Derby Town', and chasing away the critters of the night.

"Darling," called Smiling Jack Runyon, standing in the doorway. "I got some un-fucking-believable shit to throw at you."

★ ★ ★ ★

Above them a child crawled across the thin floor. Night fell, with it clear air, cold air, flew in from the distant hills of Nambia so agitating the pride on the rise that the restless boy reached out his paw and took off the head of a dog, watched it roll, then strolled away from the carcass in disdain with his mother swatting at his rear.

Koro entered the cave and aimed his assault weapon at the withered men who squatted against the far corner, eyes dimly opened. Lumpapa entered carrying two large, torn blankets.

"Cold," he said, tossing one to Harlan. "Cold and terrible. Blankets."

Lumpapa regarded them, lumped into the corner and he was not without pity. He turned to Koro.

"Tomorrow we will clean this prison. Mark down for boys and shovels."

He turned back to the lumps and half smiled kindly.

"Tomorrow we shall have a clean prison and as you can see we have given blankets to you. The cold is miserable but it means water will soon be falling in the hills."

Harlan struggled to his feet, letting the blanket fall onto the ground. He had lost over one hundred pounds and what remained of body fluid and sinew, stretched painfully across his shoulders and hips.

Koro leveled the rifle at him and Lumpapa took a step back for Harlan was a hard sight and a terrifying mirror of men.

"I'm home Mama. I got to say it, Daddy is dead. I went down like you told me and a brother in a white t-shirt took me downstairs into a cold basement where all the walls were grey and the floor was painted grey and they had them maybe twenty tables and people on the tables and Daddy was on a table. Dead. Brother in the basement say he lucky he got shoes because most of them get found without shoes. When it's cold. What they do, he say, is drink the wine, feel fine, drop the dime, forget the time and do the crime. Do it to themselves. Friends steal the shoes. But Daddy had his shoes, Mama."

Harlan stopped talking. Jackie stood, moved to him, put his arm around him and looked at Lumpapa.

"Koro, out," said Lumpapa. Koro moved back and disappeared.

"You have blankets," said Lumpapa softly. Then, wanting to say more, "It . . . it will rain in the hills soon."

Lumpapa hesitated a moment, then left.

Harlan could stand no longer and sank with Jackie still holding him, to his knees. Harlan's heart beat through his arms and shoulders into the veins of Jackie.

"You burning man."

"It's true."

"I see you talking, turning, now I see you, feel you burning."

"It's good."

"It's warm, man."

Jackie raised his hand, palm up, in front of his face and they both looked at it. Veins pushed through alabaster flesh, converging in the center, below the mound of thumb muscle. He closed his hand leaving one long-bone finger protruding. Harlan watched it move slowly to the side of his head and there followed a darkness and a sensation of flight, an utter glide through blackness toward a lighted room. He circled a man in a chair laughing easily and twirled at the smell of cherry pipe tobacco, the familiar aroma of Daddy. The man looked up to the top of the room at the soaring Harlan and reached, gently rubbing his fingers against the floating child. Harlan turned again and passed into the shadow, watching the room fall into distance, then complete darkness again, then the cold cave and the warm arm of Jackie.

"You see then," Jackie said quietly. "You see then he is surely in the light."

"The light! The light," laughed Harlan.

"The light," laughed Jackie spinning in the air.

★ ★ ★ ★

Leonie treaded water. He circled slowly in his floating chair. His cigar smoke descended upon her in a pool-size inversion.

"Mr. Morris, do you think we could move down to the shallow end?"

"You want the shallow end? You got the shallow end, and Darling, I tell you and tell you. Call me 'Scuz'."

Larry Deeds, 'The Scuz's' assistant, had been waiting for Leonie at her Wednesday morning dance class. He presented his card and invited her for a barbecue at four at the home of Sid Morris. She said she'd try to attend. Larry Deeds needed assurances. He was almost hysterical over the possibility of her not attending. Leonie noted how his voice rose in pitch and vibrated in a clarinet whine. To calm him she promised she'd be there.

"See," the 'Scuz' said, paddling over to the three foot marker. "See, like I told you, I find out about you being an actress and I say, 'Scuz', what about <u>Sunday Dawn</u>? My new picture. You hear of it? A wonderful pic. Gonna be wonderful. Anyway there's this part. It's one of these . . . Jesus . . . Hey Deeds, what part?"

"Uh . . . that's, that's, Rosalind, sir, one of the dance hall girls."

"Rosalind. And she's a beauty of a part. 'But wait,' I say, 'Rosalind's got to be gorgeous, she's got to <u>have</u> it.' What to do?

Then I find out about you and, swear to God, the sirens are going off. You and <u>Sunday Dawn</u>. Huh? Huh? Huh?"

Leonie swam away from 'The Scuz' and stroked a clear crawl the length of the pool and back again.

"Nice stroke, fabulous stroke. You see that stroke Deeds? Fabulous."

"Fabulous, sir, very … fabulous."

"Hey Deeds, your fly's unzipped."

Larry Deeds quickly turned and grabbed for the zipper but it was zipped.

"Heh, heh, heh," enjoyed the 'Scuz'. "Seriously, you got a fabulous stroke, swear to God. Deeds, write this down. Some swimming in <u>Sunday Dawn</u>."

Leonie returned to the shallow end as Deeds scribbled furiously.

"Okay."

"Okay what?" smiled the 'Scuz'.

"Okay, I'll take the part."

"Hear that Deeds? Hear that? Lorrie is set for What's-her-name."

"Rosalind," said Deeds.

"Leonie," corrected Leonie.

"Of course. Now darling, darling, girl, now that that's settled let me share with you some of the problems, tribulations even, that confront big time, rough guys in the upstairs part of the movie game."

Scuz took a long sip from a Tom Collins in the arm holder of the floating chair and re-lit his cigar.

"Complexities. That's today's word, darling. Remember it. Complexities. Every move in the game is covered by some rule, written or unwritten. Every wheel has got to be greased and I'm not talking slipping some fucker – sorry –"

"That's okay."

" – some fucker a truck load of cash to bump your project ahead. No, I'm talking about the one part of the game where big bucks don't count. Know what counts? Packaging. That's where you begin, then all the shit they put you through is worth it 'cause you got a lock on it. You like cowboys, darling?"

"I . . ."

"See, there's the handle. I know we're all waiting for a good old fashioned, top quality, mind you, Western. That's what <u>Sunday Dawn</u> is. Now there is an audience for this, saga. They're my people out there. I never lost touch. I love those bastards. People who drive trucks and stuff. Anyway I got this beautiful story and the package was great only I need a greater package. Are you following 'The Scuz' darling?"

"Yes, but I . . ."

"I hear things. You can't keep it quiet. I hear things. Hell, I hear everything. One of the things I hear is that Jack 'and I pray to see him laid out in a wooden box' Runyon is unloading Alan Hunter from <u>The Last Prussian</u>."

"Firing Alan Hunter?"

"Out baby. Hunter is history. Persona getouta. He got an offer out to the guy he wants as the new Prussian or whatever the fuck. And do you, darling, darling girl, know who that could be?"

Throughout this monologue, 'The Scuz' had inched back over to the eight foot end of the pool, pulling Leonie, treading breathlessly, with him.

"It ain't Deeds. That's a clue. Hey Deeds. Are you the new guy starring in <u>The Last Prussian</u>?"

"Oh, gosh, no sir, I'm not."

"That's a good clue. 'Ain't Deeds'. Another clue. You know this guy. He's . . . interesting."

Leonie's leg starts to cramp.

"I'm talking in circles here. 'The Smiler' wants Jackie Nef. I know you know this guy. I just know, see. What I'm saying is I seen this guy, this so-called producer devour young actors. Give 'em a shot. Then shoot 'em down. That's his style. He's a pig. Murdered his own wife, I'm sure of it and a lovelier woman you could not find. Deeds! What's that offer sheet?"

"Mr. Runyon's?"

"Jesus darling, I pay this man to be an idiot. Of course you prick bastard."

Larry Deeds frantically looked through his notes.

"Here it is Sir. Uh . . . fourteen point five million and no percentage clause?"

"What?" asked 'The Scuz' incredulously.

"Fourteen point five."

"No percentage clause? Well Jesus Christ on a crutch isn't that just like Jack 'good-bye, so long, good riddance' Runyon. No percentage clause."

'The Scuz' turned to Leonie struggling to keep her face above the tide of chlorinated water. "That," he said firmly, "is a sin in the eyes of this producer. A man puts himself to the front of a film, name blaring coast to coast, he should be in line for some reward if and when said film pushes into the black. Now darling, darling girl. My new . . . Who?"

"Rosalind, the dance hall . . ."

"Rosalind. I would like you to take a message to your Jackie Nef."

"Mr. Morris?" she gargled.

"What darling?"

"I think I'm drowning."

Leonie grabbed hold of the floating chair and 'The Scuz' paddled to the three foot mark.

"Better?"

Leonie nodded, as her cramp subsided.

"Fifteen million even, and selling point, selling point, three big percentage points ...gross."

"Gross, Sir?" asked Deeds, writing a verbatim transcript of the conversation.

"Yea, gross," answered 'The Scuz' taking a long suck on his cigar and turning crotch first to Leonie. "Gross baby," he wheezed. "Gross, gross, gross."

Susan double-parked in front of the Bank of America at Sunset and Highland. Jackie sat, knees pulled up, in his white linen splendor on a small bench adjacent to the public computer, midway down the hall of finance. He stood when he saw her.

"They called you?"

"You didn't come home again last night. Your brother was frantic. You know how he gets."

"He's a worrier alright."

A tall young woman walked over to them.

"Is this your sister?" she asked walking the thin line between pleasant and unpleasant.

"I'm Susan Nef. I'm his sister-in-law."

"Do you have an account with us?"

"Yes."

"For how long."

"Seven, eight years, I guess ... what's going ...?"

"Would you step over to my cubicle, please?"

They followed the woman.

"Please sit down."

Jackie and Susan sat, the woman swiveled in her chair,

showing her back to them as she importantly studied a document and typed the pertinent information into her computer. She swiveled back to them.

"Mainly, it's a problem of identification or at least that's one of the main problems. You are who?"

"I am Jackie Nef," he smiled.

"That's right and here's your account on my screen, only often it is not enough to simply say one is who one says one is."

"He's Jackie Nef," said Susan pointing. "Believe me."

"Oh, but it's not even a question of belief or disbelief, it's a question of procedure."

"I am Jackie," he smiled again.

"Well, alright, we'll call ourselves identified. It's unusual but we'll put that problem off the books and call you Jackie Nef only here's another problem. Large transactions usually require several days notice."

"Before I took . . ." began Jackie.

"Yes, you did. Forty thousand."

Susan looked quickly at Jackie. The woman continued.

"Now I realize on my screen you received same day withdrawal. That's unusual enough but for the sum of four hundred thirty thousand, it's unheard of."

"How long would I have to wait?"

"Four hundred thirty thousand?" asked Susan. "What can you possibly need four hundred thirty thousand dollars for?"

"Approximately you would have to wait fifteen days to close out the account."

Jackie stood up and smiled.

"Okay."

"Jackie, I don't understand."

"Well, that was painless wasn't it? Now do either of you have any other questions, if not I'll get the withdrawal form," she said exiting the tiny stall.

Jackie turned to Susan.

"Susan. Can you see? It all burns me. I'm burning."

He raised his hands.

"My hands. My hands."

"It's alright Jackie."

"No, no. I mean my hands."

He held them out higher, palms up. Almost as though they were a child's, inspected before dinner.

"What about your hands?"

"Something." The right one burst into blue flame, then the left. "Something about these hands."

★ ★ ★ ★

Mada lay on the hard dirt. After an hour of sleep she rolled from her back to her side. Unmoving except for the flick of lid across her open eyes. A fly landed a few inches from her and she meditated upon its fearless flitting side to side. She blew at the creature and it fled high over her head. She rolled upon her back again, watched the fly and closed her eyes.

Unable to sleep she stood in the center of the room and tried to clear her head. She had been constantly with Aina, Koro's wife, for the past three days and nights, at first dabbing at the open sores breaking through the walls of her flesh below the breastbone. Then later, holding, rocking the dying woman from day into night, then into day again. When Aina called out on the third day, screaming to anyone, everyone, to bury her deep, pile rocks high against the pull of wild dog, Koro in his grief, wedged himself into the corner of his hut and raked at his eyes with his fingernails.

Mada laid a mud pack onto his eyes. She ordered the children to gather stones and dig a tiny hole while she wrapped small Aina in a rough black garment and carried her, followed by the usual sobbing, destroyed Lumpapa, to her grave. Within an hour a large mound of rock covered the body, and the children and Mada started down the hill. Lumpapa, having fallen onto the mound, heaved huge sobs into the sky and earth. The dogs watched, waiting.

Suddenly Lumpapa, pompous and small, ripped his shirt off and screamed at the dogs. Mada and the children turned. He pulled at his pants raging a tribal oath at the gang of creatures. In an instant, naked, he ran towards them. The largest animal, brown and black, with a trace of spittle oozing from his black lips, turned and leapt away from the charging man. The other seven followed. Lumpapa, picked a stone and flung it ferociously, catching a dog in mid-pack, on the neck and knocking him down. The naked man stood over the stunned dog and held it down with his foot. He picked another large stone and bashed its skull, again and again. Mada and the children watched from below. The other dogs watched from the rise. The warrior screamed powerfully to heaven and was running at them again, flinging rocks, his little warrior gate impressive, even to Mada. The largest dog again led the others away, tripping up dust, never taking eyes off the wild man.

"Come down," Mada yelled as the children stared and smiled. "Come down, little man."

Lumpapa ignored her. His hysterical run had now leveled into a hunting lope, the movement of a million warriors. He stooped and picked up a long stick. He moved again into the footsteps of ancient tribesmen. Around the rise he followed the dogs as they moved in an almost perfect circle, never letting the graves from their sight. At the shade tree, the lone, grey tree, they widened their circle and quickened their pace. The warrior moved to cut them off, cutting straight and close to the tree, back bent, stick-spear hanging low in his right hand, head down against the sun.

The Big Boy stood quickly, an amazing rise of beast on his four long, dirty legs.

Between the lions again, thought Lumpapa, stopping. "Here I am between the lions."

Koro had labored to restore his AK-47 assault weapon for several years. It lay at the foot of his mat, as always, wrapped against the dust, a magazine already placed into the chamber. Mada grabbed it.

"How does it work?" she shouted.

"What? What?"

"I need to shoot it. How?"

"Just aim," he said sadly, "and pull the trigger."

Mada ran from the hut to the edge of the rise. She saw Lumpapa facing the beast, growing more tiny with every passing second. She raised the weapon to her shoulder and squeezed the trigger.

Lumpapa and Big Boy both turned to the small explosion and to the woman lying unconscious on the ground, blood pouring from her shoulder and forearm. Lumpapa screamed and again ran down the hill crazily only this time the Big Boy did not follow. He turned to the scene below. Children ran crying toward the fallen woman, the warrior screeched steadily down the hill and a blinded howling man, face packed in red mud, lurched from his hut in the direction of the blast.

The Big Boy turned his huge head slowly towards his mother and sisters. A smile danced across his eyes.

★ ★ ★ ★

"What?"

"I've written it down," Leonie said, looking through her purse.

"See I was finishing my dance class, I take modern jazz over at the Alhambra Studio, and this guy . . . uh . . . Deeds . . ."

"Larry Deeds."

"Larry Deeds. Anyway this Deeds guy just walks up to me and invites me to a barbecue at Mr. Morris' house. I was suspicious, of course, but the man was nicely dressed and had a limo and driver and I certainly knew who Mr. Morris was, so I went."

Andy looked out of his kitchen window at the murky sun dropping behind the hills.

"It's all so unbelievable. He wants Jackie for the starring part in his new film. I came right over here because . . . I . . . haven't, he hasn't called me or come by or anything. I'm a very nice girl, woman, and I'm easy to talk to and a good listener and I thought he . . . I wanted to relay the message. Here it is. I wrote it down. Fourteen, my God, fourteen and a half million dollars and three percent of the film."

"Gross?" asked Andy turning away from the window.

"Very."

"Gross is bull shit. They all hide gross."

He turned back to his view of the hills, now shimmering from the reflection of a thousand swimming pools.

"I'm forty today," Leonie said suddenly.

"What?"

"I'm forty. Today. I'd forgotten. Today's my birthday."

"Well, Happy Birthday."

"Forty. Jesus. Forty."

Henderson Anderson watched her leave the Nef home, get into a red Volkswagen and drive away. He put his rake down and pulled a small tape recorder from his pocket.

"Woman leaving Nef home in red bug, license Cal. 60032. Approximately three-twenty."

He clicked the machine off and slid it back into his pocket. The light khaki shirt ripped under the arm pit when he bent to retrieve his rake and the straw hat irritated his forehead, but he had to admit, paying off the Pollinis' Asian gardener was a stroke of genius even if he did say so himself.

"Where's Tiski?" Angela Pollini asked, from the kitchen window.

"Who?"

"The regular gardener."

"Oh, he wasn't feeling well today so he asked me to cover for him."

"He weeds by hand."

"What?"

"He never uses a hoe or anything. He weeds by hand."

"Me too," lied Henderson Anderson.

Mrs. Pollini ducked out of the window and Henderson raked his way out of sight, behind a large palm tree. He looked again at the Nef house.

Across the road, Tom Nef threw a plastic model of the U.S.S. Intrepid against his bedroom dresser, and watched it shatter into untold pieces. Tears of rage and self pity welled up into his terrible eyes.

"My model," he screamed. "My model's broken."

"I told you, you had to spend ten minutes cleaning up your room and you went and destroyed a perfectly good model. You ought to be ashamed," barked Andy standing in the doorway to his bedroom. "Now you can just stay here an hour."

Andy slammed the door. One hour, Tom thought. O black heart of fathers. O shattered aircraft carrier. He flung himself onto his knees and tenderly picked up the flight deck. Dead plastic men, tiny, on their faces, lay strewn across it. They were the lucky ones. They would never be confined. Jailed. O unhappy hour.

The prisoner stood, then slumped into his chair by the bay window. He sadly viewed the free world. Cars moved by, mailmen walked, children played in after school joy. Across the street a dog sauntered around the Merrill's garage, and the Pollini gardener was . . . Wait! That's not the regular Pollini gardener. The regular gardener was a Japanese man. The man who always smiled and who bought two cups of lemonade from their summer stand. Always two cups and always paid extra. No, this was not the regular Japanese, lemonade swilling gardener.

Tom ran into Jackie, Jr.'s room, pulled his binoculars from a shelf and charged back into his bedroom. He pulled his shade and peeked the glasses out from a corner of the window. He focused sharply onto the face. The straw hat pulled low. That face. Familiar.

Henderson Anderson was enjoying the stake-out. It offered a chance for reflection on his long and partially propitious career. Everyone should have the good times he's had, he thought. The moments. The moments are what it's all about. How many operatives end up in non-fiction accounts of real crimes? He did.

"Pretty slick," he said to himself, removing his straw hat and running his arm across his sweaty forehead.

"Oh boy," said Tom.

He walked slowly along the shaded sidewalk, west on Sunset, his sagging shoulders swaying. Occasionally he would raise his head, open mouthed to breath deeply. Drivers would look. Passengers would point. He walked, centuries racing in his amazing skull. A breeze fluttered down from the dusty hills. He shivered, goosebumps rose over his hide. He crossed the street to continue on in the sun.

A mile past the UCLA field house he slowed, feeling suddenly exhausted. He walked through a thick hedge and onto heavy blue grass. Kneeling, he pushed his hands into the soft manicured lawn, rolled to his back, and slept the sleep of the just. The sleep of the voyager whose sun now poured lavishly upon him.

★ ★ ★ ★

Noah Mesala imperially doled out ten new rands into the waiting hands of the policeman and stepped from the Rover, followed by his wife, who gingerly descended the vehicle weighted down with both of their traveling bags. He told the policeman to return in three days, gave him another shiny rand and watched him roar off in the direction of Monton.

Several young children ran to the prosperous stranger in the red, yellow, gold and green gown and pulled at his sleeves, holding up empty hands. He looked at them a moment then swatted at them with his swagger stick. As soon as they had retreated to a safe distance he turned and swatted gently at his wife who dropped the traveling bags and ran to the well to bring a drink to Noah Mesala, Ndebele headman.

"Ahh," as the ladle of water poured into his mouth. "Ahhh."

Lumpapa crept from his hut.

"Ho," he shouted, unsure.

"Ho," shouted Noah Mesala.

Lumpapa walked across the village yard to the fat stranger.

"I am Lumpapa," he said in English.

"I am Noah Mesala, headman of the Ndebele, husband to fifteen women, owner of land, breeder of goats."

"Ahh," said Lumpapa. "South Africa."

"We are recently resettled," shrugged Noah.

"Ahh."

"Koro then," smiled the headman, "we would talk to him."

Lumpapa gestured for the two travelers to follow. Noah swatted at his wife who picked up the baggage and fell in behind them. As they passed the hut that sat atop Lumpapa's hole, Noah's eyes burned.

"What?" he demanded.

"What, what?"

"That smell, that air."

"What smell?"

"The smell of shit. The shit smell. My good God. Now simply my good God. You must cover it. You must cover it with dirt. I will tell them."

"No, no. I will tell them. That is a wonderful idea. I will say, 'Cover it.'"

"With dirt."

"Of course."

"Cleanliness must begin in the hut. Occasionally we are judged by cleanliness alone."

"Ahh," replied Lumpapa, his teeth gnashing in his head. Judged by whom?

They entered Koro's hut. He lay miserably against the wall and pushed himself into a more upright position at the sight of them.

"Here he is," pointed Lumpapa.

"You are Koro then?" Noah Mesala asked pompously.

"Yes," he nodded at the fat man through blurrily returning vision.

"I am Noah Mesala, headman of the Ndebele, husband to fifteen women, owner of land, breeder of goats. This is a wife. Her name is Kaina, sister of Aina. She wishes to see her sister Aina and to visit as though they were girls again in the Krall of their father."

Koro stood and looked at the sturdy Kaina. "This is what my Aina would have been had she stayed with her father in the Krall of the Ndebele."

"Aina?" smiled her sister nervously.

Koro looked closer into her eyes and could not speak.

"Dead," Lumpapa said.

"Ahh," said Noah Mesala. "Dead," he repeated in his tribal tongue.

The wail began deep and bubbled up to her mouth, flooding the hut, the yard, the village, with grief.

Koro wept with her.

Lumpapa, of course, also wept.

Noah Mesala swatted gently with his swagger stick, against the legs of his wife. When it became clear to him that their common grief had a certain lasting quality and would continue unabated for a time, he exited the hut and stood under the low sun.

"My good God," he uttered to himself. "They might have resettled us, but at least there are veldts of grass and water. This place. My good God."

"What?" a tall woman asked.

Noah Mesala regarded her as if a dog had suddenly spoken.

"You were talking, I wondered if you were talking to me."

"No," he hissed at the woman who would speak directly to the headman.

"There is no one else here. Did you think there was someone else here?"

"Woman," he shouted, "I am Noah Mesala, headman of the Ndebele, husband of fifteen women, owner of land and breeder of goats."

Mada looked at the fat man and smiled.

"Ahh."

"I am here for Koro then, with the sister of his wife."

"Ahh," said Mada, turning to enter the hut.

Noah noticed how her left arm seemed dead at the shoulder and hung like a soft, black slip of rope. He turned back to the dry yard and shook his head in the recent memory of his veldt with his tall grass and water.

The musical wail of his Kaina, rose and fell, throaty and full, a saga of mourning. From across the yard another wail, wanly made its way to her, sharing in the passing.

Noah listened to the mysterious siren and moved to it.

★ ★ ★ ★

It rang as Susan entered the house.

Through the window she saw Andy standing by the pool.

"Andy, Gene."

"I'll call him back."

"Gene can he call you back? Just a sec."

"Andy. Urgent."

"Tell him I'll call him fucking well back, goddammit."

She opened the sliding glass panel and walked to the pool.

"Where are the kids?"

"They're around."

"Are you drunk?"

"Do I look drunk?" All the buttons on his double-breasted forest green Bill Blass suit were fastened. A quart of vodka rested in one pocket, a quart of orange juice in the other. He swayed side to side with his eyes closed.

"Couple of drinks. Sue me."

"Know where I was?"

He stepped onto the diving board.

"Know where I was?"

"I give up. Where were you?" he answered bouncing lightly.

"I was at the Bank of America. They called me down to verify that Jackie was who he said he was. It's not often somebody with-draws four hundred and thirty thousand dollars."

He bounced higher.

"He picks it up in fifteen days."

Higher still.

"Then he lit his hand on fire. Lighter fluid it looked like, blue flame. So how was your day?"

Andy bounced full in the air, rebounded into a forward side twist and plunged into the cool of the pool.

★ ★ ★ ★

Harlan died in late August, of the sixth year. Straightened himself from the hips, for he could not stand, and took a short, sand paper breath. He sat as he always sat in the center of the room. Laying on his side, Jackie watched him grab the stale air and swallow it through the tiniest opening of his desert lips. The sixth year. Cataracts layering his eyes, no longer diving for the tiny meal.

"Mama", falls from Harlan's mouth.

An hour passes.

"Maaaaaa . . . Maaaaa?"

Jackie rolls slowly to his left side and rises onto hands and knees. He can stand. He stood a week ago. He crawls to the center of the room and lays back onto his side. Food is matted in his beard and he pulls at it. He watches Harlan then closes his eyes, and says, "Here. I am here."

"I hear you."

"I'm here."

"I like it you're home and I'm home. I like it you makin' the good cookies. Daddy hit you again?"

"No, I'm fine."

"Why don't he hit me? There's a sickness there. He got it."

Outside of Lumpapa's Mada moves to the crack and passes

the long ebony arm into the darkness. She waits and feels nothing aginast her fingertips.

Harlan tilts forward and curls into himself. They lie on the dirt together.

Hearts stop. Jackie had his hand over Harlan's when it did. Jackie moved his hand from Harlan's chest to his forehead, his fingers brushing tenderly against cinnamon skin.

Harlan turned full to the light. He was new. The light was the truth and whatever waited did not make Harlan afraid. So death was the unlocking of the impossible secrets. He turned closer to the light and saw Jackie moving away saying, "Go."

Mada withdraws her arm and leans against the hut.

"You are in the light now," Jackie shouts. "You are surely in the light."

In the Village, there is silence. Suddenly Lumpapa sobs.

★ ★ ★ ★

4:00 A.M.

"So?"

"Huh?" Andy held the receiver.

"What the fuck?"

"I . . . Mr. Runyon?"

"Question. You acting as his representative?"

". . . No, I . . ."

"Who?"

"No one, I guess."

"He needs somebody. I don't want to screw him."

"I know that."

"I'm not 'The Scuz' you know. I'm not Sid 'go die' Morris. I don't want to go around screwing people."

"I know."

"I don't want to screw myself either."

'The Smiler' waited.

"You dead? You fucking die or some such?"

"No, no."

"You won't believe. I'm sleeping. Two, maybe three. I wake up. No security alarm. Nothing. On the end of my bed. Who? Guess. No, don't guess. Too fucking unbelievable. The fucking 'Scuz'. I look up at this fucking lizard face. I say, 'What the fuck,' he says 'Good fucking morning.' I'm lying there, that dry shit in my eyes, my dry mouth and he starts in. This fucking venom filled scum bag, about how he's gonna beat me to this kid and how he's gonna see to it I go the way of 'The Elder', who got what he deserved, and then he says, that he got the kid's signature and he waves the contract in front of me."

"He waved the contract in front of you?"

"You fucking deaf? Read my lips. He waves this contract, or deal memo. 'Jackie Nef' he says. 'I got it,' he says. I'm lying there, half-up, half-down. I'm rubbing my eyes and the lizard is looking and laughing and he's waving this paper 'here it is,' he says, 'I got it' he says."

Andy stood and pulled the phone cord around his arm. He listened to 'The Smiler' gasping into his ear as though his entire diatribe was performed in one breath.

"Wait," Andy mumbled.

"Wait? Wait?" bellowed 'The Smiler', but Andy had already put the phone down on the carpet and was heading for the bathroom. He brushed orange and vodka from his teeth, took three Alka-Seltzers, a Tagament, two Tums and gargled. He dry heaved twice into the sink and gargled again. He jogged back to the bedroom.

"Honey?" Susan grogged.

"I got it. It's fine. Hello? Hello, Mr. Runyon? I'm . . . No I'm . . . I had to . . . Sir? Sir? SHUT UP!" Susan sat upright. Career pause. "Sir? Sir. Can you hear me? I'm sorry I said shut up. Can you hear me?"

Moment to moment. Lives in the balance.

"Yeah," he answered miserably.

"Are you alone now?"

"Yeah."

"Are you in the bedroom?"

"Yeah."

"Where is he now?"

"I don't know. He said, 'fuck you' and he was gone."

"You're sure it was Mr. Morris?"

"I know him forty-five years."

"I mean . . . sometimes if I eat something that doesn't agree with me . . ."

"You think 'The Smiler's' losing it?" he asked, genuinely hurt.

"No, Mr. Runyon, I don't. No. Absolutely you're not losing it but you have to ask yourself how could he possibly invade your home, given the security you have?"

"I pay two hundred thousand," 'The Smiler' said feebly.

Andy looked at Susan and closed his eyes. "I can come over if you'd like. Keep you company."

"Jesus, shit, c'mon. You got kids. You got wife. What the fuck you need to keep me company for? I'll just stay here alone."

"If that's how . . ."

"Oh course we could probably review some of that contract together. That Jackie Nef thing."

"I'll be over in about forty-five minutes."

Andy hung up the phone and stood looking without seeing.

"Honey, are you alright?"

"I'm not sure."

Andy pulled into the circular driveway and went to the front door. He knocked several times. A touch of sun rose over the roof. A man and a woman jogged by on the street outside the hedge, their feet slapping softly against the damp pavement. He rang the bell. Still no answer. Followed a slate path through the gate, back to the pool.

Quiet. So quiet. He checked his watch. Five-thirty. No lights. He turned back to the front. He had driven over. He had buzzed and called. He was in a state of beyond the call of duty.

"What do they want from me," he mumbled.

"Andy? Andy?"

"Mr. . . . Runyon?"

"You come alone?"

"Yes, I . . ."

"What time you got?"

"Five-thirty. Mr. ..."

"I'm almost seventy years old for chrissake."

"Mr. Runyon. Where are you?"

"Here. Up here."

'The Smiler' had climbed out of his window, edged around his drain ledge and was sitting on some tiling directly over Andy's head.

"There's got to be a fucking ladder somewhere, huh?"

Andy ran around to the pool cabana but it was locked. He managed to find one of the gardener's ladders leaning against the front hedge.

Wills pulled the Rolls into the drive, parked it behind Andy's new BMW and followed the frantic ladder bearer around the back.

"Wills . . . I . . . what are you . . . I've got to get this around here."

Andy unfolded the ladder into its large A-shape.

"What this?" 'The Smiler' demanded, no longer whispering.

"It's the gardener's ladder."

"It don't fucking reach. Who's that?"

"It's Wills."

"What the fuck are you doing here? It's ... fuck. That's right. Tennis with Claire. Bitch wants to play at six-thirty."

"Mr. Runyon, you're going to have to reach your foot onto the very top step. We'll hold the ladder and you hold the ledge."

'The Smiler' took a deep breath and eased his feet onto the step. Wills held the ladder from one side, his expression as unflinching as his clenched lips, Andy held the other.

"That's perfect. That's very good sir."

Delicately, like a fading tightrope artist 'The Smiler' pushed himself away from the ledge standing rigid atop the eight foot A-frame ladder. On top again. At long last alone on the top rung.

Andy moved his eyes from 'The Smiler's' amazing act, and looked down at his shoes and chuckled. Wills watched him. 'The Smiler' danced an uncertain dance. Remarkably balanced. Andy raised his eyes to Wills. He saw something.

"Did you say something, Wills?"

"What? What?" shouted 'The Smiler'.

Wills shook his head slowly.

"I . . . I thought you did."

"What?" screamed 'The Smiler'.

"Nothing Mr. Runyon. Step onto the second rung."

"I got to get steady first."

Andy felt the ladder teeter then stop.

"Just a second," 'The Smiler' shouted, holding out his arms. The morning birds grew still and quiet. Wills and Andy stared from opposite sides of the ladder.

"Cool breeze."

"Sir?"

"Cool breeze. Got it in the face. Old days, East Hundred and Ninth street. Hot. The old man told us no matter how hot, somewhere around there's always a cool breeze just a little over our heads. Things work like that. Yeah."

'The Smiler' closed his eyes again, swaying slightly.

He descended the ladder and stood silently. Three on the dewy manicured bluegrass of a big deal place. Andy felt somehow simpatico. A quiet communion. He felt the old mogul had transformed, in the throw of cool breeze, into a man more commonly approachable, accessible, even tender. A miracle then. Andy felt the change. The easiness in 'The Smiler's' eyes. He reached out and placed a reassuring hand on the new man's shoulder. 'The Smiler' turned to him and smiled.

"I want to say, how glad I am to be here, Sir."

"Well, thanks," said 'The Smiler', "and I want to say, if your brother signed with Morris you're out on your ass, you bastard you."

It glistened. From the basement burner that replaced the ancient asbestos furnace, to the second floor lavatory newly grouted and polished, to the third and fourth floor, where the smell of freshly sanded oak stamped the aroma of success upon the renovation. Across the street, in the immaculate playground of St. Peter Claver Roman Catholic Church and Parochial School, Father Nicky Lombardi watched the daily progress amid cries of tartan uniformed girls and little boys strangled by blue ties, firing kick balls at each other.

The Benedictine brothers patrolled the fenced playground like Marines on point duty, scrutinizing every outsider. They never rested, never relaxed until the last one had been turned over to a parent and even then visited any home with a literal vengeance at any slight, real or imagined, to their precious charges. They were made for this. Father Nicky sighed. They did not need ordination to know they were ordained for this. They never wondered. Father Nicky was always wondering. Wondering about old friends, wondering about old girl friends, wondering how it had come to this at twenty-nine. Replacing Father Giscard, St. Peter Claver's assistant pastor, who was gunned down in his car at the Maplewood Pizza Emporium. Why would anyone kill Billy Giscard? Why was he out of collar? What was he doing getting pizza at one-thirty in the morning? His last assignment had been in North Hollywood. The Holy Rosary. He got there when he replaced Father Tom McGuint who was stabbed outside the Farmer's Market. Three a.m. Go figure. So Father Nicky also wondered what it was about him that every time some priest gets bumped off the call goes out: Get Father Nicky. He'd have it made if a bomb went off in the Bishop's car: Get Father Nicky. Jesus.

A ball bounced off his shoulder and Brother Moriarty, who took kick ball officiating seriously called interference and ordered the eight year old back to the plate. Robbed of at least a double the boy glared angrily at Father Nicky. So did Brother Moriarty.

"Father, you're right in the field. The kids can't play the rebound if you stand there."

Father Nicky looked stupidly at them a moment, then nodded and moved away. The boy waited until he was well out of reach. Shook his head as if to say, "Dominicans. Jeez. Can't live with them, can't live without them."

"Play ball," screamed Brother Moriarty.

Outside the fence, trash mounted. Abandoned cars, stripped to the chassis, lined the curb. Weeds grew vibrantly in the adjoining lot snaking around rusting washers and bald tires. Broken glass was everywhere. The Brothers had valiantly assaulted the piling refuse but while St. Peter Claver mirrored order and cleanliness the ten square blocks of despair reflected doom. They could not dent it. They fell back and became smug, even hostile to the surrounding environment. 'Look at St. Peter Claver', they would say. 'Now look at everything else.' They loved the children though. Blindly. They loved them without equivocation and the children knew it. While the local public school board admitted to a sixty-five percent drop-out rate, St. Peter Claver's was practically nil. The children understood from the beginning what was expected of them. The wishy-washy approach of public schools which included such educationally destructive devices as due process and students' rights had no place in 'The Great Plan' as Brother Emery was fond of saying. Simple rules. Homework was assigned each morning to all grades and done after school was dismissed at three. Three to four. One hour. Homework completed and passed in. No books, no pencils, no paper ever left the confines of Peter Claver. The Brothers were watching and, surprisingly, the children liked it. No one had watched them before, no one absolutely, positively knew, <u>knew</u> their great capabilities and demanded they live up to them. They were not treated fragilely but they knew they were unwaveringly admired and respected. The Brothers were proud of them.

"Hey Father. Hey Priest," shouted a voice across the street.

"Me?" asked Fr. Nicky.

"What do you think," said Chaca, gesturing to the old building and its rapidly growing new façade.

"It looks great," shouted Fr. Nicky over passing cars.

Chaca wiped the dust from his hands and crossed the street to the fence. Brother Emery watched him. Brother Emilio watched from the study hall.

"Used to be a school. Old school," Chaca said, wanting to talk. "Then used to be a warehouse, then truck-farm depot. You know what man? Still smells like a school. I'm Chaca."

"Nicky Lombardi."

"You replaced the pizza guy."

"Yes."

"My mother goes to church, so she knew about it. She was pretty upset. Priest Killers."

Brother Moriarty picked up the kick ball.

"Why are you fixing it?"

"Oh man," smiled Chaca, "the dream, see, is to get everything under one roof. Fill the rooms. Kids in the gym, you ought to see, it's hot man. Then maybe a couple of neighborhood doctors, some lawyers, social workers, people who can let the downtowners know we're here man, and from here we can get that lot picked up and get it together. It's gold man. There it is. It's tomorrow."

"Is there a problem, Father?" asked Brother Michael, an enormous black man with a shaved head and a tattoo on his neck, below his right ear. A tiny dagger from another life.

"Hey man," nodded Chaca uneasily.

Brother Michael fixed him a look.

"A problem, Father?"

"No, no," answered Fr. Nicky quickly.

Brother Michael turned and stared at the renovation. Chaca and Fr. Nicky fell silent. Chaca had attended Peter Claver until sixth grade when he just stopped coming. A thorny statistic. Brother Michael had gone to the apartment maybe ten times. Cajoling, then pleading and finally threatening but Chaca's mother stood firm in the resolution that he was one they had all but lost.

"Pedro and Mookie with you?"

"They're working, Brother Michael."

"There?"

"It's gonna happen man. We got the bread to make it happen."

"Drugs?"

"No. Swear to God. As God is my judge," answered Chaca busily crossing himself.

Brother Michael looked hard into the eyes of his ex-student. Chaca returned the look fiercely.

"Got time to give us a tour?"

"Yeah, oh yeah, man. C'mon. Oh man."

Brother Michael strode to the playground gate.

"Come on Father," he said.

Leonie quit in the middle of jazz class. Quit. Lost her point of ref-
erence. She stood patting her stomach in the middle of the thirty
member class swiveling and reaching and swaying into the afternoon. The hopeless feeling bubbled again. It was there alright.
It snuck in during stretching to Errol Gardner's 'Concert by the
Sea,' and by the time the dance captain threw on Lionel Hampton
and the others were loose and sweaty and hurling themselves into
the open spaces, she had a stomach ache.

She slid to the mirrored corner and grabbed a towel. Her
knees buckled and she grabbed hold of the exercise bar bordering
the room and pulled herself to the door. Her clothing was in a
neat pile on the floor. She slipped on her jeans and carried the rest
to a small waiting room. Voices, quiet, carried out of Gary's Nest,
the small, partly glassed enclosed office of Gary Evans, manager
of the dance studio. The usual vibrant Gary had slid into a deep
depression after the death of his partner and his manner with staff
and clients alike was gruff, even cruel. This grief had put him in a
corner where his once great hopeful spirit filled the studio, now it
cowered in a corner of his office.

Leonie stood and moved to the door, carrying her exercise
bag. The voices gently bubbled into a laugh.

Leonie opened the office door and peered in. Gary had, weeks
ago, pushed his desk to the corner of the tiny room so no one
could see him from the waiting area. He was sitting in his low
swivel chair, his eyes closed laughing.

"Gary?" she said.

He opened his eyes and looked at her.

"Where are you?" a voice asked Gary, from an opposite corner. Leonie's eyes moved to the voice. She knew.

"The light," Gary smiled.

"The light," Jackie said.

Gary rose and walked over to Leonie. "Thanks, thanks, for coming into the office. Nobody does anymore. It's okay though, I understand, but thanks."

Leonie put her arms around him and held him. He shuddered as a cold child. She released him and looked at Jackie Nef moving toward them.

"I love you," she said.

"I do too," said Gary and he kissed the bony hand that had moments before rested against his temple.

"I've been waiting for you Leonie."

"He has," chimed Gary happily.

"Waiting here so we could walk outside and down some street and hold hands."

Sunset Boulevard, ten blocks in a sweet breeze. Quiet blocks. Leonie felt a squeeze, a tightening of his hard fingers around hers.

"I love you, too."

★ ★ ★ ★

He watched from his hill. Sad eyes opened and closed in slow motion. The woman with the dangling arm emerged into the light from the largest hut and with her, children on stick legs, holding one another's hand as a living chain, weak and brittle. Stopping, she assembled them, boys on one side, girls on another. The little, blackest man joined her from a hut. He appeared to be sobbing and another man in a filthy khaki uniform helped him move along. Behind them several men carried a board covered by a blanket. The group turned to the hill and took several steps toward it until the smallest child pointed to him, watching from the rise. They stopped and watched. They raised their eyes and said nothing.

Big Boy turned purposely, his huge head with its perimeter of long hair waved back against the warm breeze, and gazed at his mother, ill under the trees. She could not stand and had had no water in a day. She raised her head when he faced her under a billowing cloud. Her Big Boy. He turned away again, back to the villagers, and shook his head against the tiny African flies. One of his sisters, lying about on the far side of the gigantic tree, whined for him. He sighed long and hard.

They moved again up the hill, the children divided on either side of the men carrying the board. Lumpapa led. His wails muffled and far away. At the graves, near Aina and Koot and Reena, near Moora and Ati, they cleared a space and the men pulled at the rock earth with trowels and hoes.

Koro leapt into the ready grave and placed the end of the board in one corner of the hole. He nodded to the men and Harlan's tiny body slid into his rest. They removed the board and began to push the dirt and the stones onto the body. Lumpapa sobbed again. Harlan's stiff hand tilted up and remained, after the first throws of dirt and rocks, the only visible part of the young man from Louisville and Electric Boat. It remained spidery and oddly beautiful against the continuing puffs of desert earth.

The young children ceremoniously took stones, one at a time, and laid them onto the grave, piling them again, as before, high, for the wild dogs were watching, swaying back and forth, dreaming of meat.

Where Big Boy napped with his sisters a small bird pecked at one of his hind lice. He rose angrily and stamped the dust like a child. The mourners quickly gathered the children and descended toward the huts. He padded quietly over to his mother. She lay dry and dead, eyes closed as in sleep. He nudged at her with his head but he understood she was gone. He stood over her a moment then moved to the new grave. Harlan beneath the stones and the hand forever pointing.

★ ★ ★ ★

A cool damp breeze blew through the screened window chilling him. He sat straight up and in the darkness was, for a moment, disoriented.

Leonie turned in her sleep and crinkled herself against him. He looked at her and gently pushed the hair away from her nose and cheek and tucked it behind her ear.

"Here is sleep then," he whispered.

He left the bed and went into the bathroom. He let the faucet fill his palm with cool water and then rubbed it into his eyes. He filled his palm again and sipped.

A lion roared and he dropped the water to the floor. He moved to the bedroom and saw she was still asleep, then into the kitchen where it surely waited. It roared again, hollow and toothless and trailed off into the darkness. He flicked on the kitchen light and the Big Boy rose sharply by the flowing curtains and disappeared into the light filling the room. He moved to the window and a huge truck roared below. He stood at the lion window motionless, the breeze raising goose bumps over his naked body. A man with a lunch bag and a newspaper walked below, two women worked busily in the bakery on the corner filling the window display, their voices carrying up to his window.

A boy sauntered arrogantly down the street, his gang colors

and earring catching the street light. He paused and lit a cigarette, letting it dangle dangerously. At the bakery he stopped and
admired the window display.

His head spun.

And a hand brushed gently across his back.

"Come to bed."

He turned slowly to the eyes of the woman.

"C'mon, it's still early," Leonie whispered.

Jackie, not quite conscious, followed.

Norm Rector had completed the rewrites Sunday night, cop-
ies were made, collated and bound on Monday, and a solid cast
assembled in the conference room of Peakskill films for a first
read-through of The Last Prussian, now titled Prussian after toy-
ing with Prussian Lust, A Soldier's Desire, and Prussian Hearts.
Sylvia Dupree would read Miranda and John Agat, the T.V. star,
who lacked 'Big Screen Pizzazz', would fill in for the elusive Jackie
Nef. John Agat did the reading in the hope that all things equal
and people being people, if this new sensation failed to show, he'd
have an inside track at the role himself. John Agat did not know
that he lacked 'Big Screen Pizzazz'.

The cast assembled around the oblong table. A glass of water
and a package of five flavor Life Savers rested to the side of each
script. Behind the chairs were a circle of still more chairs for Norm
Rector, his staff and 'The Smiler's' mob.

Rector entered the room with 'The Smiler', looking cheerful
and vigorous despite fifty-odd years in the film racket. He rubbed
backs and kissed cheeks and settled into a rather moving background of the Napoleonic wars. The cast listened with rapt attention. Seven of his films had won Oscars. Three times his directorial
skills were honored with that same prize. He represented, in a

business of technology, a glimmer of human command. In a realm of middlemen and phonies, a proven artist. Unafraid to fail and unafraid to succeed. A throwback.

After he ended his historical perspective and told a humorous anecdote of a recent lunch with Larry Olivier, they were off. Everyone, cast and observers, alike, turned to the first page. Jackson John, Mr. Rector's assistant director and longtime companion read the staging directions and camera angles. He cleared his throat.

<u>Prussian</u>
formerly
<u>The Last Prussian</u>

The camera sees light, tiny yet significant. A slow pullback reveals
an eye, then another eye and nose and mouth until a lovely angelic
face of a five year old peasant child . . .

"And Norm, it doesn't say if the child is a boy or a . . ."

"It really doesn't matter Jackson darling, I may make it a goat."

The room delivered the compulsory chuckle. Except 'The Smiler', who had come to hear the script.

"C'mon," he uttered, half pleasantly.

Norm smiled lightly, then sat down, nodding to Jackson John to continue. Why hadn't he become one of those hotshot Producer-Directors, he asked himself? That's what he should have done. He knew that now. If he had, he would be in charge right this instance and not nodding pleasantly to this scary entrepreneur. But he was seventy-four years old. He needed this job. Another shot. Bigtime. Hollywood Reporter. Variety. Academy dreams. Norm Rector, at the very least, one of film's three greatest directors, screwed tight his shit eating grin and listened.

Norm Rector had chosen Buck Durban to read the pivotal role of Karl's father, Herr Warner. Buck had been around a long time and as a side to his acting talents, had raised his abilities as pompous boor to new heights. This trait infused every character he played with those little accents and innuendos that condemned his roles to one dimensional land. Flattened out by arrogance. Every syllable he uttered was delivered as though he had won a Nobel Prize he could not accept, or accepted an Academy Award he did not want, or callously turned away and implied he had earned it, should have accepted it, deserved to win it but chose to remain . . . clean.

Eddie Burke sitting to the right of 'The Smiler', tried to look interested but soon the acting duo of Agat and Durban, as Father and Son, had rendered him nearly comatose. Rebecca Haycroft nudged the little lawyer into alertness.

"At least look interested."

"Bite my big Irish banana."

"I'd need a tweezer and microscope to find it."

"Fuck off."

Half an hour later Sylvia Dupree entered the work as the peasant girl. Her lovely blond hair cascaded over her shoulders and a few wisps lay gently over her breasts. She wore a formless grey sweatshirt in the way beautiful women, confident of body, lean to comfort instead of style. She wore no makeup and Andy, behind 'The Smiler', was amazed at how large her face was and how the glasses that pinched the edge of her nose gave her an almost professorial air of intensity. It was hard to imagine this pleasant young woman as The Lady Destroyer. Looking at her Andy smiled as he remembered the movie trailers that announced:

'They destroyed her family
they destroyed her love

But they could not destroy
The Lady Destroyer'

This was Sylvia then. This girl who sat twirling her silky hair
and playfully elbowing that porker Buck Durban over a scene
where he discovers her in his son's bed. This is the actual Sylvia
that 'The Smiler' was convinced was 'a little fucking dirty, you
know, slutty in a nice way'. Andy watched her closely. Men, he
imagined, must all watch her closely. Not that she's perfect or
even desirable but . . . almost the girl you don't want anyone else
to touch.

But she did seem a bit naughty . . . and smart.

Andy marked how in several of the more sensuous scenes with
Karl and with two British generals, she would giggle and look over
to 'The Smiler' with the slyest little grin as though they shared
some small moment. And how the beast would grin back obvi-
ously eating it all up in daydreams of starlet sex. She played him
like a guitar. She did not use cymbals or bass or drum.

At midpoint in the script Norm ordered a break. He looked
over to Jackson with a shrug that said he wasn't really sure how it
was going. So many scenes to visualize, so much history to uphold.
Most of the crowd ambled over to the coffee. Sylvia sidled up to
'The Smiler'. Gene Moniz, Rebecca Haycroft and Eddie Burke
surrounded Andy.

"We'll all fall," was all Gene uttered.

"What does that mean?" asked Eddie.

"Shhhh," whispered Rebecca.

"Who's shouting? Just what does that fucking mean?"

"Have you spoken with him?"

"I can't find him."

"Could he possibly have already signed with Morris?" asked
Gene.

"No. I mean I don't think so. I'm not sure."

"Fuck," said Eddie. "Fuck, fuck, fuck."

Rebecca looked across the room to 'The Smiler', leaning against the wall, nestling close to Sylvia.

"This is his last one, I'll bet. He's more serious about this one than any other film. If he doesn't get what he wants, he'll start ripping. Remember 'The Elder'."

"Oh shit," said Eddie, "he'll get us all."

They looked across at 'The Smiler'. Understanding the beast was easy. He played to win. He played to kill. He had eaten all the raw meat he needed thirty years ago, it was habit now. They watched him in awe of his sheer capacity to hide his fangs.

"He seemed to be enjoying it, especially the tender moments," said Norm Rector, sidling up.

They turned to him and slowly, as people ten days in a lifeboat or twelve yards in front of an avalanche do for inexplicable reasons, they began to laugh.

Old Man Santiago wrapped his big hands around one side of the washing machine and Mookie grabbed the other. They straightened it and pushed-pushed it the twenty-odd feet to the dumpster.

"Couple hands over here," Old Man Santiago shouted.

Brother Michael and Chaca jogged over, each grabbed a side and hurled the rusting relic into the bin.

"That's the last big piece of junk," observed Chaca surveying the lot.

Brother Michael smiled and shook his head. Across the lot, by St. Claver gate, Father Nicky and Pedro filled a cardboard box with broken glass and cans.

"I've got to get back to my store," said Santiago. "Tomorrow, again, twelve to one."

"Thank you, Amigo," smiled Chaca.

As Santiago cleared the lot and turned down the street toward his grocery store Brother Michael said, "A nice old man. Hard worker. Where'd you meet him."

"He got me man. He got me good."

Mookie laughed.

Brother Michael smiled.

"Vatos locos."

"That's us," shouted Chaca happily. "Crazy guys. Hey. Pedro. Vatos locos."

"Vatos locos!"

At one-thirty Peter Claver's tower bell bonged the end of cafeteria and signaled Brother Michael back to class.

"Got to go."

"Hey man," said Chaca, shaking his hand.

"Look man," said Brother Michael seriously, "look what you can do. Look at the things you can do."

Chaca smiled and nodded and felt a rush of joy as Brother Michael strode away on massive legs, his black robe, sashed at the waist. Father Nicky walked over and emptied the contents of the box in the dumpster.

"Just the little stuff now," he said wiping his face with the back of his hand.

"We'll plow most of that under," said Chaca.

"Plow?"

"We're getting dirt," said Mookie.

"See," explained Chaca, "we gonna get ten truckloads of dirt, good dirt, and I got a guy gonna mix all the dirt up with his tractor. I got this guy he's coming Tuesday morning. We got this chart see, and we made thirty little squares for people in the neighborhood to plant stuff. The people been coming by and putting their names down."

"Corn and shit . . . stuff, I mean," added Mookie.

"That's okay, I say shit too."

"Yeah?"

"Anyway, this is gonna be a place of gardens and flowers gonna be everywhere. I told you man. We gonna get it moving from our Center. It's beautiful."

"He'll like it man," smiled Mookie.

"Oh yea, he'll like it."

"When do you think he'll come."

"I don't know, man, but he'll come."

"Yeah, man, he'll come."

"Who'll come," asked Father Nicky.

"The man," said Mookie.

"The main man."

★ ★ ★ ★

Mada sighed and looked toward Lumpapa's cave and back to the little man who was no longer a funny little man. He had become too small to laugh at and she found herself wanting to cradle him and comfort him in the way of small children. She turned and walked slowly towards the school hut.

"He died. I don't know," he said.

She stopped but did not turn.

"White?"

"No, no. I mean the Black. He died. I just don't know . . . why?"

She shivered and turned to him.

"I know he died. I thought you meant . . . Are you alright?"

"Oh the hill, where he lies, is possibly the hill he should be on. Did he look Bangwatse?"

"He was too brown. There was white blood there," interrupted Koro.

Lumpapa turned to him suddenly and shrieked, "He was Bangwatse and on the hill he belongs."

"Oh yes. On the hill he belongs."

"He would call to the lion. Remember Koro? He would keep you up."

"I remember."

"He would answer the Big Boy."

"Yes, yes."

"Only Bangwatse would do that. It is right and good for him to be sleeping up there. It was his fate to be here and I was only an instrument of that fate."

Mada walked to the amazing shrinking man and thought of Harlan's long and beautiful fingers and how they clung to the day even in the grave and she reached around him with her long thin arms and drew him close. He sagged against her, then straightened himself and looked into her eyes.

"Will you go to him again?"

She looked at him a moment and her dead arm flopped back to her side.

"Will you? Do you know how foolish you look pushed against the wall with your stupid arm inside the hole? What does he do to your arm. It is intolerable."

Mada turned and walked toward the school hut. She felt old and dying and sorry for herself.

"They laugh at you," Lumpapa yelled after her, tears in his eyes. "I have heard the children say, 'There she goes again. There goes her arm into the prisoner's hole.' No more. Do you hear? I forbid you."

Much later, after sleep, she sat up and looked at the children scattered about the room. She imagined them thrown from the sky like so much debris. Sleep is ignorance, she thought, and that is why it is so important. An ignorance, luxurious and without reproof.

She left the hut and stood in the center of the village. She often stopped as she moved, for no reason, except to wonder or look. This night, Mada looked at the stars and at the perfect kettles several groupings of stars made. She smiled to herself and continued to the hole. At the wall she nestled against the window slit and although she tried to think she thought only of what Lumpapa had shouted, seeing herself against the stone with derision. She slowly weaved her hand, her good hand, into the slit and down into the cold cavern. It is an odd ceremony, she knows. If she were a child and she saw a woman against the wall, hand disappearing into stone, she would also laugh. People are made to be laughed at. God must laugh at us. All of us reaching into stone. Mada closes her eyes. She finds perfect lean of head and rests it onto a flat stone.

★ ★ ★ ★

They had scrambled eggs and sausages and wheat toast and lots of grape jelly.

"Want some more?" smiled Leonie, holding the coffee pot and looking morning beautiful in a terrycloth robe with a rose on the back.

Jackie nodded then rolled a sausage into the jellied toast.

"Know what this is called?"

"Sausage sandwich."

"Nope. It's called 'sausage buddy'. You can make it with bacon only then it's 'bacon buddy'. In Rhode Island anyway."

Leonie poured coffee and sat down again at the small table.

"My father used to have a great talent for breakfast. It was . . . what? I suppose artful," said Jackie.

"Artful?"

"No matter what time we woke up you'd smell the meat. The bacon or sausage or sometimes ham. Like an alarm clock."

"You never mentioned your father before."

"I'm remembering things. Things were good. He worked hard. He threw the ball around. I remember playing games well and knowing it and being proud of it."

"I was a cheerleader."

Leonie took a bite of the sausage buddy.

"Good?"

"Mmmmm."

Jackie took a bite. It was the largest bite she had seen him take. A true bite. No flea nibble there. He kept his eyes open when he chewed. She had never seen him do that, either.

"Your eyes are open."

"They are?"

"You close them when you eat."

"I'm remembering things. I'm trying harder to remember. There has to be a balance."

They looked, for a moment, out of the window to the parking lot below. A man caught in a word.

"Who?"

"What?"

"Who told you there has to be a balance?"

Jackie smiled at her and slowed his chew to a slight circular motion.

"A friend. Dear friend. Being able to tell him. Telling him . . . sustains me."

Jackie reached over and brushed his fingers against hers.

"I love you."

"You keep saying that."

"I love you," he laughed.

"I never thought I'd be this happy."

He lay his elbows onto the table and held her face.

"Think only of now and the light will always come. And be kind. And never turn from anyone. Turning away is the callous part of us, because we are smaller than you can ever imagine and almost unseen but wondrously valuable. Remember, any pain is a pain to all of us but never turn away, that is the most important."

He smiled and swallowed his coffee and held up his cup.

"Beans," he said, "who ever thought beans could give that."

"Beans," she said smiling and confused and overjoyed.

"We have a lot of people to see today and we're going to see them all. How's your car?"

"She's fine."

"C'mon," he said, "let's go."

And they did.

Henderson Anderson was roughed up in the holding cell. His shirt collar was torn off and a small bruise had begun to discolor his cheek by morning check when the officer released him. He walked several paces behind the policeman and stopped at the booking desk to claim his wallet and keys. Bob Kemp, who had paid bail, waited impatiently, then both walked out of the precinct.

"Thanks Bob."

"You look awful."

Henderson let out a sigh.

"What happened?"

"Some fucking asshole had a ..."

"No, how did you end up stealing a car?"

"I didn't steal a car."

"You were driving a stolen car."

"I was set up."

"Who set you up?"

"Some . . . Jesus . . . kids. I'm not sure. Look, I've been in this line of work a long time. Okay, mostly divorce shit but I swear to God something crazy's going on."

They got into the black Lincoln with the Trayco Detective Agency crest on the driver's door and pulled into traffic. Henderson lit a cigarette and fiddled with an eavesdropping device, a long, cone-like object that could center in on any conversation up to a quarter-mile away. He plugged it into the cigarette lighter to save its battery pack, aimed it in the direction of the car in front of them and slipped on the earphones.

"So what kind of trouble am I in over at Trayco?"

"Boss' pissed."

"What's new?"

"Borkman broke that slasher case he was working on."

They pulled into traffic, moving west of Pico, towards Doheny and the Trayco offices. The route skirted close to the Barrio and Henderson Anderson lowered his window and spat.

They pulled into a Gulf station.

"Fill it," Bob ordered. Then to Henderson. "This station is three cents a gallon cheaper than anywhere else and it's Gulf."

"Whoopie-fucking-do."

Bob paid the attendant and pulled back into the flow of cars.

"One day you'll pull into a station and say 'fill it' and some guy will say 'can't, no fuel, that's it.' Just like that. People just walking away from their cars."

"They'll never run out. Don't be an asshole."

"I guess you're right."

Henderson Anderson sighed at the great injustice of it all.

Yet light can break through and even the darkest late afternoon can have its clouds pierced. Saving, for awhile, the day.

"Jesus H. Christ," he said again. "Follow that fucking car."

"What car?"

"The red one. The Volkswagen."

"Then just say, 'Red Volkswagen'."

"Just follow the fucking thing," screamed the near apoplectic Henderson.

Fr. Nicky got into the St. Peter Claver parish car and headed into the Barrio. Two blocks from the church he pulled over and parked against the curbing. He stared ahead and weathered a rush of doubt, a wave of 'anywhere but here, anyone but a priest'. This was not the first time he found himself exhausted by confusion, breathless and sweaty. Nicky knew it for what it was. Classic anxiety. Modern man. Nicky struggled for a deep breath and finally felt oxygen roll slowly into the bottom pouches of his lungs. He leaned his head back and closed his eyes.

"Hey man? Hey, hey Father Nicky? You okay?"

Nicky sat up.

"I thought you were dead man," Mookie said.

"No, I . . . I . . . I just got . . . tired all of a sudden."

"Dirt's here."

"What?"

"The dirt. Load of dirt's all delivered. Garden's getting set up. Block party tonight."

Mookie hopped around to the passenger side and got in.

"Let's park this sucker."

Nicky turned on the ignition and pulled around the corner to Claver's gates.

"You coming to the block party?" Mookie said, getting out.

"Oh . . . yes, sure, I'll be there."

"Later."

Mookie ran across the street to the new community center. Nicky watched him, then moved the car through the gates, parked it behind Msgr. O'Brien's station wagon, and went into the living quarters. There is no way into the home except through a large pantry-like hallway of ancient birch to get to Msgr.'s Piano Room. Often, in the evening when a superior or a parishioner would phone with a problem, Mrs. Bacca, Peter Claver's housekeeper would answer and say, 'Msgr. is in the Piano Room, I'll get him', which, after all, is a good deal better than 'He's watching the Raiders and drinking a beer.'

"Hello Father," Mrs. Bacca said cheerfully, dusting the already immaculate room.

"Hello Mrs. Bacca. Msgr. around?"

"I think he's in the office."

"Thanks."

The door to the parish office was open and Nicky stood in the frame. Msgr. O'Brien lay on his back on the rug in front of his desk, with his legs crooked at a ninety degree angle and his rear-end pushing flat against the floor. Nick watched the shoeless priest grunt, hold position, release, grunt again and repeat the process. Msgr. rolled over and propped himself up on his hands and knees, seeing his young assistant as he did.

"Back exercises," he smiled, sweat balling on his forehead and above his upper lip.

"I'll come back."

"No, no, come in."

He performed three or four cat-backs, arching his spine high and then dropping it into a sorry sway.

"Cat-back," he called out. "I do these everyday. If you don't your back revolts. Learned them at the Y. They've got me pretty much out of pain."

"Lower back is tough," agreed Nicky.

"Tough," he said, standing and reaching high into the air.

"Finger reach."

"When he finally released his body from the upright stretch, he shook his hands lightly by his side and slipped on his black loafers.

"Did you see the weekly? I've got you down for morning mass four times and eleven o'clock on Sunday. Is that okay? Ralph wants to drive to Needles Saturday night and see his mother."

"That's fine," Nicky said, and it was, only he had to admit, old Ralphie pissed him off royally. Fr. Ralph Amarado was the Associate Pastor at Peter Claver. At fifty years old, even in formal collar and jacket, he looked like a man with a used seventy-one Ford to sell. He played every angle, worked every possible scenario he could to ensure a lighter work load, a longer vacation, a larger portion at supper. He had more ill relatives that needed attendance 'out of town', had more attacks of hay fever or 'general malaise' and downed more second helpings than Nicky believed possible.

Msgr. moved around the long table that served as his desk, straightened a pile of parish newsletters and sat down.

"So . . . have you been having any more attacks?"

"I am sorry about that."

"That's fine. It was hot in the confessional."

"Thanks for taking over. Mrs. Ogilvy about stroked out on me. Right in the middle of her confession it just came to me. I couldn't breathe. Pretty embarrassing."

"Fine, it's fine. Have you had any more?"

"No, no more," he lied.

"See. It was the heat."

"Actually I just had one," he said feeling redeemed, "I had to pull the car over to the curb. It's pretty disconcerting."

"It's warm out today, isn't it?"

"No, it's quiet nice really. Breezy."

"Ahh."

Nicky picked up a paperweight. Inside the clear glass casing was a small maple leaf. He held it a moment and put it down.

"I got that in Canada," Msgr. said. "Toronto I believe. It's very cold up there."

"I think what it is, is I have to rethink the priesthood. I've been suppressing the internal dialogue with self. I've barreled over any cognitive reasoning at all, hoping that once these attacks go away everything will be okay only they can't simply go away without rational discourse. Know what I mean?"

Msgr. tilted his chair back onto the rear legs.

"I've been . . ." he began but his chair almost went over backwards and he caught himself.

"I hate when that happens. Yes, I know what you mean . . . I think."

Nicky waited a moment hoping Msgr. would take his thought further. Tell him tales of other young priests in crisis.

"Did I mention I put you down for Sunday Mass at eleven? That's alright isn't it?"

"Yes, that's fine."

"Fine."

Msgr. opened the large window behind his desk a crack. Nicky left the room

Andy had just stepped out of his car in the Peakskill parking lot when he saw them rounding the corner on foot heading for Wills and the Rolls.

"Start the fucking car," offered Jack 'The Smiler' Runyon.

Rebecca Haycroft dropped some papers and Gene Morris left the swift procession to help her pick them up. Eddie Burke kept jogging behind the beast. Rebecca and Gene caught up to them as they entered the car. Wills squealed out of the parking space and came to a halt in front of Andy. 'The Smiler's' window rolled down and his red face filled the space.

"Fuck," he explained, "Fuck, shit, double and triple fuck."

"Mr. Runyon?"

"Andy," said Gene, finding a tiny piece of window space to speak through. "Mr. Runyon. . ."

"Fuck, fuck, fuck."

". . . Mr. Runyon has just received a call from one of his . . . sources. It seems your brother is meeting with Sid Morris . . ."

"Prick bastard."

". . . He's with him now at his home. You'd better get in."

Andy squeezed into the back seat between 'The Smiler' and Eddie Burke. Gene and Rebecca sat across the wide expanse of luxury auto and looked at them. Wills turned the Rolls west on Sunset for the short drive to the Morris estate.

"What do you know about the Morris lawyers?"

"What do I know about the Morris lawyers?" stammered Eddie. "They're sharp sir. Very . . . sharp."

"Problem here is they got to him and now they're selling. And they're warm, and they're friendly and slick. But it's money. It's money."

"You're offering a tremendous package," comforted Gene.

"I am," 'The Smiler' said, turning poutingly to Andy. "A tremendous package."

"It really is," added Gene to Andy.

"C'mon Andy, it's tremendous . . . just . . . tremendous," chimed Eddie.

"Look I never said it wasn't a tremendous package."

"Aim the air conditioner on me. I'm dying," croaked 'The Smiler'.

"See," said 'The Smiler', "it's a game of money. Now your doctors, your priests, your . . . I don't know . . . socialists, they don't give a fuck. A rat's asshole. They just don't care. Money is nothing. See, those guys are getting something else out of it. Rebecca, you got a doctor friend, yes?"

"A pediatrician. Thank you for remembering."

"Here's a guy . . . what?"

"Pediatrician. Children's doctor."

"He don't want the money. He's out there with the kids. Now that is something. There's a guy fixing kids. You fucking this guy?"

"Why, yes I am."

"There it is. He's fixing and fucking but no money."

"He does well."

"Fuck well. I piss on him. What? He doing three million? Four million?"

"Oh no."

"He's fixing but no money. Now this brother of yours. He's no doctor, no priest . . . so what? Bucks. Money. Cash. Dollars."

"Good point," Eddie agreed.

The Rolls pulled behind Henderson Anderson's car parked across the street from Sid 'The Scuz' Morris' heavy metal gate.

"Fucking gate. See? Big deal guy. I piss on him."

Henderson moved to the Rolls. Jack and his entourage stood on the grass next to the curbing.

"You Runyon?" Henderson asked.

"Fucking 'A' I'm Runyon."

"I'm Henderson Anderson with Trayco. That's Bob Kemp in the car. Another operative."

"Operative?" mumbled Andy dumbfounded.

"We were returning from a . . . stake out . . . when the suspect's car cut in front of us in a red Volkswagen. It was a 'made to order' tail."

"Where the fuck?"

"In there," Henderson said, pointing to the Morris house.

"Who the fuck?"

"That Nef guy and his little chicky. We laid some sophisticated audio surveillance on them while we were following. Guy was speaking gibberish."

"Gibberish?"

"Guy sounded like a Zulu," said Bob.

Gene walked over to the gate and pushed the call button. He waited a moment and pushed again.

"I know they're in there. C'mon"

'The Smiler' reached for the wall ledge.

"C'mon."

Eddie leapt forward and grabbed the sole of the beast's shoe, straining to elevate him. 'The Smiler' peeked over the wall.

"The coast is clear. Let's go."

He threw his right leg onto the slanted brick wall then the other and rolled off the other side.

"Jesus," yelled Eddie.

"Mr. Runyon? Mr. Runyon?" Rebecca called.

"Fuck . . . I'm . . . aw shit. Landed on some fucking compost pile. C'mon."

Eddie scrambled to the top of the wall like a zealot springing into the arms of the Lord.

"Sir, now just a second," said Bob Kemp, Trayco professional. "We are bound and obligated to obey the laws of the State of California and to work only within ..."

"You know who the fuck I am?" said the wall.

"Huh? Do you?" added Eddie perched on bricks.

"Yes sir, you're . . ."

"Fucking loaded, powerful, big deal guy. I'm talking fucking millions and millions."

"The man's got a point," said Henderson Anderson, leaping for the wall and inadvertently pushing Eddie over onto the compost pile of leaves and grass and Jack Runyon.

"You fuck," screamed 'The Smiler'.

"I'm sorry sir. I'm so sorry."

"Fuck you where you breathe."

Henderson disappeared over the wall followed by Bob. Gene, Rebecca and Andy quietly watched the last Trayco representative drop from sight and looked at each other.

"Come fucking on," the wall shouted.

Only a wisp of a cloud was in a sky so utterly blinding and blue.

"Listen," said Andy, "no airplanes."

"Rare," said Gene.

"I don't ever remember not seeing a plane," said Rebecca.

They searched the sky a few seconds and headed for the wall.

'The Smiler' and his band of nouveau commandos stayed low behind a tall thicket of rhododendron. They circled towards the cabana house following the perimeter of the wall. Once at the cabana, 'The Smiler' eyed the rear of the house.

"There it is," he said to no one in particular. "There's the house. C'mon."

He darted, remarkably quick, across the perfect lawn, around the pool, to the rose garden and squatted behind an exploding flower. Henderson and Bob followed immediately. Eddie Burke turned to Gene, Rebecca and the shell shocked Andy.

"I'm not really a lawyer."

"What?"

"I did a couple of years at Fordham. Secondary Education. I made up the Clemson Law stuff."

Eddie turned back towards the house, took a deep labored breath and followed 'The Smiler'. Finally the remaining three of strike force, duck-walked across the lawn.

"This is an All-American Beauty Rose," 'The Smiler' whispered. "You can tell by the tightness at the base, the crimson color, and how it tips out here. See? These outside petals? Some guy made this kind of flower. Rose used to be small and flat. They'd call them Antique. My mother knew these in Belfast."

"Beautiful. Wow," dribbled Eddie. "Smells good too."

"Movement," whispered Henderson. "C'mon Bob."

The two professionals slid to the corner of the garden, bounded upstairs and disappeared behind an ivy covered corner of the house. Suddenly the sound of a latch and voices.

"It's a beautiful day. There's not a cloud. There's blue. Hey Deeds, we'll take the coffee out here."

'The Scuz' walked to the white round iron table at the edge of the patio, three feet directly above 'The Smiler' and his horde.

"There's the pool."

Leonie smiled and nodded.

"This girl. Like a mermaid. Like Esther Williams. Esther Williams swam in that pool. Tallulah, Carol, Loretta. The same pool. They would come out here. They'd swim. Chaplin was back here. Chaney too. True story, Chaney loved to mow lawns. People'd be swimming, drinking. Chaney'd be off somewhere pushing my mower. Big smile. Everybody smiling. Today? Who can say? This pole here?"

'The Scuz' walked over to a fifty foot flagpole. White. Enormous at its base.

"There's nothing now, but all them houses, Chaplin's over there, Dougy's, West, all of them had the poles and we'd send signals. I had a red flag for pool party, white for dinner party, white with a black 'T' for white tie. They'd come over. Right here, right here on the patio Nelson Hardwicke shot Sandra Castle. Right between the eyes. Who knew? They were always at each other like alley cats. One night, white tie, I'm over here, I remember because, I mean Jesus Christ. I'm here against this wall talking to Consuelo Frame. My God you remember things like this. Her breasts were magnificent. We're chatting when all of a sudden. Crack. This tiny little explosion and Sandra is just standing there, looking disgusted, with an itsy little hole right here. She says 'Oh great.' Exact words then down she goes. Nelson puts the pistol back in his pocket turns to some young lady and says 'alone at last'."

Larry Deeds came nervously onto the patio followed by a short round Hispanic woman carrying coffee and rolls.

"Coffee and rolls. I hope heaven has coffee and rolls. What do you think?"

Jackie smiled at 'The Scuz' and looked over at Leonie.

"I think yes."

'The Scuz' looked at Jackie for a moment then reached for some butter.

"<u>Sunday Dawn</u>. A 'Tour de Force' of the West. Not the way we want to remember it but the actual way it was. Tent towns, and mud and cowshit and whores and all that kind of stuff. Only here's this man. Alone. Bright yellow horse. He understands the way of everything so we're gonna look at everything through his eyes. Shay Rucker. That's the man. That's you."

Jackie looked down into his hands, connecting his thumbs and small fingers into a figure eight.

"Oh and guess? Guess? We've been doing some great work on the part for Laurie."

"Leonie," Deeds corrected.

"Leonie. That's what I said. Take the shit out of the ears. Jesus. Swimming. There's swimming for ... this girl here, this lovely girl."

Jackie rose up and shuffled to the far corner of the patio.

"What?" 'The Scuz' asked Leonie. "I say something?"

Jackie stared out past the pool into the thick Rhododendron. So thick he could not see the far wall. It was as if the plants descended into heavy brush. Lush. Pushing out towards heart-land. Distant hills. Jungles. Blue sky.

A grey bird approached the patio, then banked off towards the pool. A cat stretched beside the cabana, climbed onto the armrest of a chair, bunched itself and looked out. Jackie turned back to the table.

"I'm not an actor. I'm not any kind of an actor."

"Baby, you don't have to be an actor. All you got to have is stuff. You got the stuff. We'll get you a coach. It'll be fun. Millions."

"Fuck," uttered 'The Smiler' from his hidden position.

"I'm not an actor. I would feel I'm doing something under false pretenses."

"Fuck false pretenses. You told me. You said, 'hey, I'm not an actor.' So even if you landed on your face in shit ... and swear to God you won't . . . but say for argument you stink . . . What? . . . I'm gonna say 'hey, I can't believe it?' No Jackie baby. The risk is all on 'The Scuz'. Not to worry."

"There must be wonderful actors out there."

"There are. Wonderful. But see, they don't have the stuff. The big picture as I see it. If you got it, you're safe. You don't have it, you're fucked."

'The Smiler' in the bushes had to nod quietly in agreement, giving 'The Scuz' his due.

"Take that Lance Paul. Remember?"

"Those old college beach party movies?"

"Lance Paul. <u>High and Dry</u>. <u>Hanging Ten</u>. <u>Beach Bunnies</u>. Those films made a bundle and Lance got good bucks for it and for awhile was safe. Kid grows up, you know, little pot belly, and what? No more <u>Malibu Luau</u>. No more <u>Fighting Surfer</u>."

"No more <u>Devil Surf</u>," said 'The Smiler', who had produced the Sandy Epics. "No more <u>Sandy and the Surfer</u>."

"Who wants a forty-five year old guy 'walking the nose'. So he's fucked. I'm in San Diego, I'm on business, I pull into this deli I like and I often go to and by the way if you enjoy a healthy slice of beef, the roast is especially good, I go in and bussing the tables is who?"

"Lance Paul?" asked Leonie.

"Lance Paul. One day the world is his smoked salmon and the next day he's clearing it off a table in a deli in San Diego, and point here, main information, the man who made millions on this beach guy, who lived off the fat of the profits, until the kid got fat himself and he cut him loose, was who?"

"You?" asked Leonie.

"Me? Me? What the . . . ? I . . . Jesus God now . . ."

"Oh not Mr. Morris," tooted Deeds, "Oh no, oh not Mr. Morris. He would never do such a . . ."

"Shut the fuck up Deeds. Now girl, I am going to say a name. I am going to say a name I think you've heard of and I'm sure this outstanding young man of yours has heard of. A man who destroyed the career of many, many beautiful young people including a young lady who I had cast in my film Side Glances only she was devoured by this vampire in the prime of her life. He happens to be a close personal friend of mine so I know about what I'm talking. A guy ..."

'The Smiler' popped up in a rage.

'The Scuz' fell back over a cast iron chair and into the hard rolls. Before he could get up 'The Smiler' had mounted the stairs and hurled himself onto his fallen counterpart.

"What the hell," screamed 'The Scuz' as 'The Smiler' groped for his neck. "Deeds. Deeds."

Deeds could not move. He stood paralyzed at the door. Andy pushed past Eddie and ran to the two-biggie pile-up.

"Fuck, Fuck," screamed 'The Smiler'.

"Fuck," screamed 'The Scuz'.

Andy reached into the swirling mass of mogul and attempted to break 'The Smiler's' dangerous grasp from 'The Scuz's' neck but 'The Scuz' in his panic pulled him into the pile up.

"Stop it," screamed Rebecca tactfully. "Someone is liable to get hurt."

'The Scuz' was now, conservatively, a minute or so from deal cutting heaven.

Gene moved around the pile and seeing no opening decided to grab a leg and pull.

Jackie walked to the dust ball of executives and observed the way men roll and the various sounds that come from the hollows of the body. The gut, the chest, the narrowing windpipe. After a moment he began to reach for 'The Smiler's' fingers.

Henderson Anderson wheeled around the corner of the patio planted his feet a yardstick apart and screamed, "It's going down Bob."

He raised a large caliber hand gun, leveled it at Jackie's chest, and squeezed the trigger.

★ ★ ★ ★

Big Boy was alone now, except for the awful dogs, and that was very alone. At first he would not allow them to trip near to where his sister lay, dead with her cubs, but after several days he moved over the graves and turned away. He knew they would clean the space under the tree and in his way suffered from the thought. There was also his need for shade, so he turned from her completely and in the Lion way forgot and thought only of his aloneness. He moaned rough and low. Watching and listening for something.

Koro swallowed and the water rolled down his narrow esophagus like a ball, stretching the passage until it thumped into his stomach. It hurt to drink but he did not remove his watch from the Big Boy on the rise. Mada crossed to him. Her eyes leaping a bit inside her hollow face.

"Look," she said holding a small, stone-hard root. "Water Lily roots."

"Water Lily roots?" Koro said, dropping his eyes from the beast.

"I dreamed last night the river bed still held the Lily roots. The children and I dug them. There are many, many."

"Very hard," Koro said holding one. "I don't know."

"We'll boil the roots."

"Yes?"

"Boil them until they are soft."

"Soft?" barked Lumpapa from his hut. He took a sustaining breath and half strutted, half drifted over to the well. "Who is soft?"

"Mada has found Water Lily roots."

"The children and I."

"She dreamed they were in the river bed."

"Riverbed?" questioned Lumpapa.

"I dreamed it last night and today we dug and look."

"Hard."

"Yes."

"Water Lily roots?"

"We'll boil them. We'll boil all of them."

Mada ran from the well to the school hut and grabbed all of her precious pots. She ran back to the well and what little moisture there was in her frail body burst onto her ebony skin. For a moment neither Lumpapa nor Koro could speak, then slowly, tenderly Lumpapa reached for her forehead and pushed the sweat in front of his palm to her hairline. She looked at the little man then dipped each pot one by one into the brown water.

"Fire," she said passionately. "Fire."

Koro, now excited by the thought of tender mushy, stomach filling root, headed up towards the Big Boy's shade tree.

"Koro," barked Lumpapa, "take your weapon."

"No bullets."

Lumpapa watched him climb, then with a damning utterance followed him up to the rise. The Big Boy's rise.

The two circled past the graves never removing their eyes from him. Directly under the shade tree they rose the last fifty steps until they stood on the dusty plain of the rise, made flat by

generations of lions. When Lumpapa saw the dogs, the black lips
deep into the rotting corpses, he was sickened, only he did not
reach for stone. Only the Big Boy could move them once they had
tasted the bloody flesh. It was good the dogs were stupid. When
they were finished they would leave and forget the tear of meat
but now it was best to leave them. The two men turned to the tree
and began to gather sticks from underneath it. Long and oddly
shaped and brittle, they pulled the pieces of ancient tree down the
rise and into the village, away from dogs and Big Boy, to where
Mada waited surrounded by pots of water covering Lily roots.

Mada laid a large fire on the hard packed dirt in front of the
school hut and it flamed high for several hours until a roasty bed
of red coals raised the temperature of the entire low lying village.
The water boiled. The roots turned somersaults, rising and falling
out of sight in the dark, and the children, somehow energetic,
scooted back and forth from the well, refilling the pots. Laughter
popped here and there. People moved to the well, to the pots.
Songs were sung.

Later the woman moves her stiffening legs through the dust of evening to the hole, the window slit. She had not been to the window
for five days. He no longer touched her fingers. For two months
she had come and lowered her arm and spoken and threatened
and wept yet within the hole nothing stirred. He sat unblinking.

She lowered her arm, pressing her cheek against the flattest
stone.

Dogs growled at each other in the distance. She raised her
head enough to look for a moment at the heavens and the kettles
of stars twinkling and thought how shapes are formed and cast
and have order and isn't that why she still loved the stars.

"They bloomed blue in the night," he said.

Inside the hole she flailed her long thin arm about until he touched her hand and held it against his face.

"Nymphoea Caerulea," he said. "Some bloom at night and some at daybreak."

"The river has been dead for a hundred years," she cried. "I dreamed . . ."

"Yes. The Tubers."

"They were hard. Too hard. We boiled and boiled."

"Egyptian Lilies. White and Blue. They were ... sacred."

" Too hard."

"Yes."

"Too old."

"It's true."

Mada felt his lips upon her fingers. She looked at constellations.

"Can you feed us?" she asked softly.

Mada tried to point to each grouping, to Crow, Enser, to Southern Crown, until she laughed and fell back onto the flat stone. A star blasted across the sky, then another. He took his hands, his fingers, his lips from her.

"No. I cannot feed you."

"They will die then. I mean the children."

She remained quiet and unmoving.

★ ★ ★ ★

The explosion stopped them. They looked up from the pile to Henderson Anderson who stood looking at the gun in his hand.

"What the fuck?" said 'The Smiler'.

"What did you do that for?" whined Bob.

"I thought he had a gun. I thought he had a gun."

"Your knee is in my balls," 'The Scuz' complained.

"Swear to God, he was going for something."

Jackie Nef reached into the pocket of his white jacket and pulled a candy bar out.

"Energy," he said. "Snickers."

"Well shit, I thought it was a gun. Sorry."

Beside Jackie, the plaster lion head he had rested his arm on, lay shattered on the patio's slate floor. Leonie ran to him and held him. Deeds came forward and began to sort out human tangle like a magician. He helped 'The Smiler', then 'The Scuz' to their feet. 'The Scuz' walked slowly over to the lion head and stared for a moment. Then moved his eyes to Jackie where Leonie held him.

"You will notice, you nice young man held by this lovely girl here, you will notice that until the bullet that crushed my lion head, and by the way, Jack Warner gave me that, gave me all the lion heads around the patio, you will notice that until a certain horrible individual and his gang arrived, armed and dangerous,

no one tried to kill you. I only mention it as a selling point to
<u>Sunday Dawn</u>."

"I thought he had a gun," moaned Henderson.

"Darling," started 'The Smiler', "I can't defend the schmuck
with the gun. It's true he is presently in my employ but let me say
if I had a meatgrinder I would grind him up."

Henderson looked miserable. 'The Smiler' continued.

"If I wasn't pulled down on the cold stones I would have, and
I know this sounds big deal but swear to God, strike me down, I
would have stepped in front of the bullet before I let some piss
brain shoot such a young and lovely man. Now I have heard
lies . . ."

"Fuck you," uttered 'The Scuz' darkly.

"Fuck you," retorted 'The Smiler' also darkly.

"Now I have heard lies about certain of my dealings and even
my dear and Irish rose who is in heaven and I know it . . ."

"Did I say she wasn't in heaven? If there's a heaven, okay, of
course, she's there."

"Lies pure and simple such as me killing my dear and lovely
wife of thirty-seven years and other pure fictions."

Jackie turned his back to the company and counted the
patches of Daylilies puffing about the grounds. He walked the few
steps to the slate landing and walked across the grass.

"Are you okay?" Andy called.

He paused in a dream that was not a dream at all.

"Lost," he called back. "Lost, lost, lost."

Leonie started to follow him. "Let him be alone awhile," said
Andy not feeling completely stupid. "Let him be alone."

Leonie watched him cross the wet grass and disappear into
the thick Rhododendron.

—

Norm Rector took a red pencil and delicately drew a line under the word <u>grand</u> on page 59 of <u>Prussian</u>.

"Say no more," nodded Georgio de Soto production set designer. "You want Grand baby, you got Grand baby. I'm seeing colors. I'm seeing moments of gold. I'm looking at, in my mind, swirls of silk drapes that cascade, actually cascade down the . . . image of a waterfall and just tremendous good things. Grand. I'm saying what is a ballroom without Grand? Say no more."

While Georgio drew madly in his sketchbook, Norm turned his attention to publicist Ginny Styles.

"Alan Hunter called again," he said holding up his coffee cup and saucer. Jackson John whisked it out of his hand and moved to the kitchen of their rented beach house.

"Coffee? Anybody else?" he sang out.

"No thanks," Ginny sang back. "He's still angry over the casting?"

"I would say he's hurt more than angry."

"I was definitely getting Alan's hurt," confirmed Jackson, delivering the cup to Norm.

"Thanks love," smiled Norm. "Anyway Ginny darling, do try to let him down easy, press releasewise."

"I'll write something sweet and call you with it before it's positioned."

"You're a sweet bean."

Jackson checked his wrist watch. "Ten a.m. Time for you know who to do you know what."

"Oh groan and moan," sighed Norman.

"None of that. You get into your sweats and I'm going to throw these guys out. Georgie. Norm <u>must</u> exercise."

Jackson laughed, mothergoosed Ginny and Georgie out the door and went to his room. He changed into his gym shorts and T-shirt, laced up his Reebok hightops and jogged to the living room.

"I hate this rented furniture," he shouted towards Norm's room, jogging in place.

"I hate it too," Norm yelled back. The door opened and Norm also jogged out, positioning himself in front of Jackson.

"Hands by your side," Jackson lightly instructed, "and shoulder pats and one and two and one and two and come on Mr. Greatest Film Director of All Time let's touch those shoulders and one and two and . . ."

Twenty minutes later they stood sweating by the deck of the house and surveyed a long expanse of the Malibu waterfront. After a quiet moment, Jackson sang very loud.

"I'll take Manhattan
The Bronx and Staten
Island, too"

"Me too," said Norm. "Me too. Something depressing about being old in Hollywood."

"Look what I've started. Sweetie, we'll be back in New York before ..."

"What do you think of the script?"

"Prussian? There are moments of such . . ."

"Jackson?"

"Well, yes. It is shit, but darling man, what was Rio Commancheros? Classic? You made it a great film."

"I wouldn't call it great."

"Then you're the only one."

"Actually I'm more concerned about this fella playing Karl."

"Jackie Nef."

"Here's a guy no one has heard about playing the lead in a seventy-five million dollar movie."

"He's not playing it yet. They haven't signed him."

"Jesus," Norm sighed again and looked back over the beach. A young man and woman jogged by. A little boy and his mother walked toward the water holding hands. The child held a pail and shovel and when the sand flattened into workable moist mush the boy dropped to his hands and knees and dug.

"Castles," said Norm smiling.

"What?"

"Castles."

Henderson Anderson had sulked off the patio, Bob Kemp in tow.

"Good thing you missed," Bob said as they headed toward the front gate.

"I didn't miss. I was aiming at the lion statue."

"No."

"Right between the eyes."

Andy and Leonie walked to the grassy point by the pool where Jackie squatted and sat quietly with him. Sid 'The Scuz' Morris and Jack 'The Smiler' Runyon watched, their staffs milling nervously nearby.

"Maybe . . . ah shit," uttered 'The Scuz'.

"What?" asked 'The Smiler'.

"Nothing. I was going . . . 'ahh shit' to myself."

"I know what you mean."

"I been 'ahh shitting' fifty years."

"You're not that old."

"Since the dawn of time."

"Jesus Christ."

"Anyway," 'The Scuz' remembered, "Althea was a tremendous woman . . . person."

"Thank you, Sid. Thank you very, very much."

"But I never got a chance to say 'Althea. Sorry you're gone.'"

"Thank you, Sid."

'The Smiler' looked down onto the back of the head of Jackie.

"It's not the money."

"Jesus," agreed 'The Scuz'.

"The money is just around."

"All around."

"How much is enough?"

"Who can say?"

"Not here though," said 'The Scuz' gesturing toward Jackie.

The three people below sat like baboons in the morning, staring at water.

"Maybe we . . . could deal," 'The Smiler' said turning to 'The Scuz'.

"Maybe . . . who knows. . . . Let's go inside. By the way, see these slate tiles? Chaplin laid these tiles. Loved to lay tiles."

They sat on the ground on either side of him. No one spoke. Jackie looked into the pool. Leonie stared over the cabana. Andy pulled at the grass, studying the square blades and green stain on his soft hands.

"La Salle Academy," he said wistfully.

Jackie remained fixed upon chlorinated water.

"Jackie was a running back in high school and every year, our school, that was East Providence High School, we'd play our Thanksgiving Day game against La Salle Academy . . ."

"I didn't know you played football," said Leonie, to Jackie who stayed with the water.

"He was the best. Weren't you? His senior year he carried the team. That last La Salle game was the only one I could make it back for. Sat with Mom and Dad. The whole game that La Salle coach, a priest, Fr. something, he's pacing up and down yelling at Jackie. Screaming. Insults. Trying to shake him up. But Jackie's just out there doing the job. La Salle kicks it. Now E.P. has the ball on their twenty. By now we got maybe 20 seconds left. We're on the forty. Everybody's on their feet. They hand off to Jackie and he's all alone, racing towards the goal."

"Wow."

"Now the Priest is running alongside of him screaming names and insults. Really unbelievable things. So here it is. Everybody standing, stamping, screaming. Go Jackie go. He stops."

"What?"

"Stops. Complete stop. He's not one foot from the goal. He wings the ball off the head of the priest."

"Jackie?"

"Not one foot from the goal."

Clouds in the shape of a bird cut between the sun and the whole yard was shaded. A light breeze disturbed the glassy pool. Jackie spoke without moving his eyes from the pool water.

"I was alive and they did not know it. If they had waited. If they had . . . I shouted when I saw them but the waterfall made too much noise. They did not wait. I had to follow."

Andy stared at his brother, then at Leonie. "Do you understand that? Do you understand any of that? If you understand any of it do me a favor will you? Don't tell me. I don't want to know. Just tell him for me that if he doesn't do <u>Prussian</u>, I'm out of a job. Tell him he doesn't owe me a thing. Tell him the way it is, that I'll be out and that's as for sure as tomorrow's coming."

Andy stood up and plunged his hands into his slacks. He looked down on his brother and envisioned him as a pipe-cleaner bent angular in the shape of a man. Jackie rubbed his bony hands together and continued studying the pool. Andy turned and walked to the house.

Leonie walked to the edge of the pool.

"That friend you mentioned, that friend you told me about this morning. The one you could talk to? Who helped you? Can he help you now? I don't think I know what to do or say."

Jackie rose and shook himself like a wet dog and shivered.

"There is a cold you cannot believe. Who would take me to the light I have seen but can never go to? Only Jackie can save me. Cold ache in the heart. Who would love me?"

Leonie stepped back and fell into the unheated pool.

★ ★ ★ ★

They sat by the road for an hour until the bus appeared. He smiled and took his food and Nomali bowed. He watched her from the rear of the vehicle as it roared away. She remained by the roadside and became a speck in his eye.

What to say? How to say it? How to say it and become paid for it because it is right to say it? He must say exactly what he had seen, for it was not the way of things nor how things should be. At Monton, then, closest to the village of Kaina's poor dead sister, he would tell what he had seen, for surely the reward would be substantial and perhaps even enough to retain his home, his land and most importantly his own white lawyer. Yes. Simply say exactly what he had seen in the hole while the others wept. All of it. Except the spinning.

★ ★ ★ ★

Chaca was resplendent. Tight black slacks that flared at the ankle, high black boots, red silk shirt, white bandanna topped magnificently with his gang colors.

"Running out of burritos, man," yelled Pedro by the hot dog and burrito stand.

"Burritos coming," hollered Old Man Santiago.

Lines of light were strung from the tall fence of St. Peter Claver to the flagpole of the neighborhood center, and back to the fence. A grid of light illuminating not only the blocked off street and Mariachi Band and dance area but also the garden jewel, carved out of the empty junk lot, now black with raked and leveled loam and an intricate arrangement of planks that delineated the various garden plots.

"Father, hey, Father," Chaca said jogging to Fr. Nicky Lombardi. "You came, huh? You got here."

"I had some duties or I would have been here sooner. I've never seen so many people around. I didn't know the neighborhood was this large."

"Yeah, it's large, yeah, only people been afraid. You know? Druggies. Crazy guys. Now we got a place though. We got the city to send two doctors on Tuesday and Thursday to see the people and a full time lawyer."

"Must've cost a lot," said Nicky, admiring the gleaming façade of the center.

"Clean money."

"Oh, I didn't mean . . ."

"Hey it's okay. It's money so clean it might have fallen from the sky."

Brother Moriarty had organized the smaller children into relay races. Brothers Emilio and Emery sat by a table next to the garden lot assigning sections to anyone interested. They were going fast. Brother Michael happily sold hot dogs alongside Pedro. Mookie ran up out of breath and grabbed Chaca's arm.

"I took the bus and walked there, only the lady say he's gone somewhere."

"She says he's gone?"

"She don't know where. You told him didn't you? He knows?"

"I didn't tell him. Didn't you tell the girl?"

"No."

"No?"

"No, c'mon, no. Shit. Sorry Father."

"That's okay," said Nicky, "I say . . . I say that word too. Tell who?"

"He'll come. He'll know to come. Go help Pedro with the burritos."

"Can I have one, man, I'm hungry."

"Okay."

"Free?"

"Okay."

It was dark by the time he crossed Howard Street. He felt drained. Odd. He was slipping again. His stomach had felt wonderful for hours, better than he could remember, and the black spots that came and popped in front of his eyes, came hardly at all, until now. He had been full and now empty. Yet he was not at all hungry and he let his jaw drop a bit opening his mouth to the warm light. What can a man remember that will save him? He was slipping again. Yes. The deep pit. An economy of flesh where only spirit mattered. He stumbled as though something had pushed him, landing up on his knees. He remained on the concrete a moment. Quiet street. Lamp light throw. He rose and squeezed his hands into fists and released them. He continued on, thinking of birds. He crossed the street and rested against the storefront of Old Man Santiago. In the night he hears the neighborhood laugh at the end of the block. He straightens himself and continues on, toward the sound of the voices. His white suit. His Hawaiian red shirt, his dirty sandaled feet. He begins to cry. He sees the lights strung from St. Peter Claver to the center.

He stopped under the lights. A little boy chased his balloon toward Jackie and he reached up and grabbed it.

Jackie handed it to him. The boy took hold of the string and stood dumbly looking up at him. Jackie touched the boy's hair and moved into the crowd. They sensed him and turned to him and he boiled in their eyes, ashamed and glad at the exact same moment. A toddler wrapped his arms around his leg and held on.

"The man," Mookie said quietly.

Chaca ran hugged him, talking feverishly, with great emotion, about the center, the garden, the neighborhood. An old Mexican woman walked up and kissed his hand. He did not want kisses, yet he did want them. Another old woman, then another, then a man, young and rough, tenderly took his hand. Frightened Jackie pulled back. He could only survive if he looked past them, past the crowd, children, balloons. He saw the loam sucking light and went to it. He called within himself and his heart slowed, the pounding eased and he felt air fill his lungs.

Though he moved slowly and kept his arms by his side in a body language of coolness, they brushed against him and touched him and finally kissed him again. A little girl tripped and sobbed over her skinned knee. He picked her up and held her. She stopped crying and waved to her friends. At the gardens themselves he followed the board path, admiring partitions and speaking hopefully of beans, long and green and tomatoes with tight red skin. He put the child down and reached into the new spread loam and a shiver sped through him. His fingers flayed beneath the earth level and felt a plant, a part of the plant, needing water. His eyes closed tight. Dark as the night. Black as the loam.

"That dirt feel good man? Feel good?"

He opened his eyes and fires faded. Fingers still under the soft ground.

"Feel good?" Chaca repeated happily.

Jackie stood and the pieces of caked loam dropped from his hand. He faced Chaca and the neighborhood bore in close. The brothers drifted together under the burrito umbrella. Fr. Nicky Lombardi stood fixed between the stand and the garden. The whole block grew silent.

"We knew you'd come man," said Mookie finally.

"Want a burrito?" asked Pedro.

Jackie smiled and nodded. Mookie, walked closer and held his hand.

"We knew."

They pressed closer and overcome, he reached his long finger out and touched them.

Pedro wrapped a hot burrito in a napkin and danced back toward him.

"Who is he?" asked Fr. Nicky as the boy passed.

"Everything Man."

Susan lay in bed thinking Hollywood freeways, thinking New England Inns, thinking Pink Bermuda beaches. Andy finally made it home. She got out of bed and met him in the kitchen.

"You didn't have to wait up."

"I didn't. It's past two."

"Yeah. I don't know. I took 'The Smiler' home. Drove around."

"Want some tea?"

"I want a drink."

Andy mixed a screwdriver.

"I was thinking of Bermuda," she said.

"How are the kids?"

"Kids are fine. I was thinking what a good time that was."

"It was nice."

"I think we're about due for another trip."

"When?"

"Yesterday."

Andy laughed and fixed another screwdriver.

"What?" asked Susan.

"I love you."

"I love you too. What?"

"Just the way you decide things. It's great. I love you but let me share an interesting bit of information with you, sort of bring you up to date . . ."

"Don't condescend."

"I wasn't condescending."

"Okay."

"If I was I'm sorry."

"What?"

"The Prussian? The Epic Shit box? If Jackie doesn't agree to star in the film, I am out on my ass in the snow, or the sun or whatever the fuck is going on out there."

"He'd fire you?"

"He'd . . . Jesus . . . see to it I never . . . you know 'you'll never work in this town again'."

"You're overreacting."

They paused and the two a.m. crickets paused.

What is madness? What is madness if the madness is accepted and accepted as something other than madness? Perhaps even health. Is it madness only if it is perceived as madness?

Leonie opened her apartment door and stood in the dark. She flicked the light and looked over her tiny place as though seeing it for the first time. Brilliantly clear, pans leaped off the shelves, a drip of water smashed onto stainless steel sink, spaghetti sauce stains grew huge on the corners of the stove.

She sagged into a kitchen chair and dropped her face into her hands. They felt clammy, as if they had never quite gotten dry from the pool. Rain began to fall, in tinny bops. She sat a long time, the rain soothing her. She rose and stood in front of the chair stiffly. Tired and alone. There it is then. But this is too much to consider in exhaustion, standing in the kitchen over the Spanish market, she slides out of the light, and is sucked into the dark, listening to heavy rain. Moving toward hope she goes to the window and glances to the parking lot and the bouncing rain where he squats, fingers tracing a line of asphalt looking up to her window. He rises and holds his troubled hands outstretched and she is instantly at the top of the landing onto the steps and down, down to pavement, by Buicks and Chevys, by re-builts and low-riders.

"There are things that trouble me," he half shouted over the slash of rain.

"Me, too."

"What to do? What to do?"

"About the movies? The jobs?"

"That, yes," he said sadly, "and this."

Blue flame burst from his right palm, then from the left.

"And this."

He rose from the earth, several feet, spinning slowly like a burning top in the rain.

"What to do?" he repeated. "What to do?"

Leonie fell back a few steps to a yellow Corvair watching a man hang in the air, ringing himself in blue-red fire. She turned and ran to the steps. She turns again to a burning man hovering in a parking lot. What is madness? Is it all madness? Is it madness only if she believes it? Accepts it? Beneath him now she reaches above her and grasps the very air, the very thinness of his ankles. And her fingertips meet. She pulls him gently to the ground and holds him. His flaming hands flow through her hair and grasp at her back.

"These are things that trouble me," he uttered into her shoulder.

"Your hands don't burn me. I was sure they'd kill me."

"No. They only kill me."

Leonie held him by the hands.

"Then they kill me."

They moved to the steps.

Fr. Nicky said Mass at five-thirty in the morning for the brothers and several older Hispanic women in the neighborhood, grabbed a coffee from the rectory kitchen and sat quietly behind the small desk in his first floor office. A half-hour later Fr. Ralph Amarado walked in with coffee, balancing three heavily buttered croissants.

"How was Mass?" he asked, laying the croissants on the desk.

"Mass was okay."

"I was hoping to get down for it but . . ."

"You were scheduled to offer it. I couldn't sleep was the only reason we even had one."

"My mom got me this Oval Bridge Digital Alarm Clock which is supposed to be foolproof but . . ."

"Didn't go off, huh?"

"That's high tech for you. You'd think we could get fresh croissants at least. Bad enough we get the margarine. At least they could be fresh."

"You'd think so."

"Say listen Nick. I know I'm scheduled for the eleven o'clock on Sunday and then C.Y.O. basketball at five but . . ."

"Your mother?"

"My mother has had another relapse and the doctors think I'd better hot foot it to the Needles today. Rotten luck, huh?"

"Rotten alright."

"Not sure when I'll be back. Monsignor told me to clear it with you. Did you notice there's no jelly in the pantry?"

"No."

"There isn't any jelly. Zip."

"I mean no, I won't take Mass and basketball for you."

"Anyway I'll be hotfooting it right after breakfast."

"Wouldn't want to miss breakfast."

"Personally I can take it or leave it."

"Really?"

"I just figure it's my duty to chew the fat with those

Benedictines. Zealous group if you know what I mean. Did you say you couldn't take it?"

"No."

"Phew."

"I said I <u>won't</u> take it. I've got some thinking to do and somebody to meet."

"But Monsignor said if it was alright with you I could . . ."

"It's not alright with me. I've got things to work out. I've got to . . . meet somebody."

"But my mom . . ."

"I talked to your mother last night on the phone. You were off somewhere. She sounded great."

"It's an act."

"She was calling from her bowling club. Said she bowled a one thirty-five."

"My God! That's fifty points off her average. It's worse than I was led to believe. I've got to get down there."

"Look, Ralphie, level with me. My lips are sealed. You got a girl down there?"

"Now just a . . ."

"A boy?"

"Cruel. You're so damn cruel."

"Coach of the bowling team?"

"That's it," Fr. Ralph said running towards the door. "I'm going to tell Monsignor on you."

Nicky stood and walked to the window and stared past the playground to the new community garden plots. Was it last night? Why would you think he could help? Answer the unanswerable?

Fr. Nicky pulled a small paper from his pocket and glanced at the name and address Chaca had given him last night. Jackie Nef. He looked up at the clock. It was six-fifteen. He walked out to the hall and towards the rectory door in the kitchen. Fr. Ralph was margarining up another croissant.

"Last chance to take my Mass or I'm going to tell Monsignor on you."

"Aww fuck off, Ralphie," he said, and pushed into the early morning rain.

"So how close?" asked 'The Smiler'.

"Close. How close you?" asked 'The Scuz'.

"Close."

"Director firm?"

"Norm Rector."

"Rector?"

"Big man. You?"

"Tony Falls."

"Firm?"

"Firm."

"Got Sylvia Dupree."

"Mmmmmmmmmm."

"Cubby Phillips for cinematography."

"That's a package. That's a package. I got Jane Tome. I got Ferdie Nostacuff."

"That's not chopped liver."

"That's caviar."

"Jane Tome."

"Okay, so we package both Sunday Dawn and Prussian. Coup the Nef into both films and up the bucks."

"And fuck the lawyers."

"Bastards they are my friend."

"And they don't care," agreed 'The Smiler'.

"And they don't KNOW," added 'The Scuz'. "They only

know the green and the lines and the gross and the New York and the Chicago and the LA."

"And Houston now, and Denver."

"Now it's everywhere. It's Phoenix. It's fucking Long Island."

"But they know shit about movies."

"Dick."

"They don't know the packages. They don't know the stars," said 'The Smiler' grandly.

"They don't know. I got gifts from the stars. I got presents."

"Those stars knew you. They loved you."

"They loved you, too."

"I don't know."

"They did. Jesus, they fucking loved you."

"Cagney didn't love me."

"Well, no, no Jack, Cagney did not love you."

"I loved him. Mother loved him. The Old Man and all the other mick drunks loved him."

"Everybody loved him."

They paused in reverie and reflected on those they loved and who loved them and who loved them not.

"It's morning. I'm going."

"Tired?" asked 'The Scuz' placing his arm on his shoulder.

"Fucking beat."

"Me fucking too."

"So?" asked 'The Smiler'.

"We go. We go," said 'The Scuz'.

"They don't know."

"They don't know shit."

"WE GO," they yelled and parted.

★ ★ ★ ★

Brigadier Lani Sec lay down his book on the large desk and rubbed his eyes.

"How does he do it?" he said aloud in the empty office.

Amazing, he thought, a true genius. Bandits slice herds of goats to pieces, murderers kill sleeping policemen, buses are held up at gunpoint and Lani Sec's dreadful troops cannot bring him even one criminal, while Hercule Poirot, that cunning little Frenchman, has no trouble whatsoever cutting to the quick of the villain's heart. There is a policeman by God. There is a policeman.

He stood and straightened the light green uniform, adjusted the shoulder tassels and cinched the leather belt tighter. Much of his day was spent adjusting and re-adjusting.

The adjutant opened the door, stood at attention and announced that Mr. Don Lawton of the Peace Corps would like a word.

"A word?"

"Yes sir."

"Mr. Don Lawton would like a word with me? One word? Only one?"

"I don't know, sir."

"You don't know. You never knock. You should knock. I would say 'enter'. Then you announce visitors. But you . . . you never knock. Why is that?"

"I . . . "

"What can I conclude from this? Maybe I should conclude that you would rather not be my adjutant."

"I . . . "

"So?"

"Sir?"

"What will you do the next time Mr. Don Lawton comes to call?"

"I . . . will say . . . no . . . I will knock and you will say 'enter' and I will say 'Mr. Don Lawton to see you sir'."

Lani Sec stared hard at the young Bantu a moment then smiled.

"Yes. If you do that I can only conclude you are an excellent soldier."

The young man grinned broadly, saluted and turned to leave, then turned back.

"Oh . . . sir?"

"Yes?"

"Should I knock for every visitor or only Mr. Don Lawton?"

"I conclude you have the brain of a beetle. Send him in."

Don Lawton entered as usual, grim and determined.

"Mr. Lawton, good morning. What is it today with the Peace Corps? More goats stolen?"

"There aren't any goats left."

"Ahh. That's right. The last goat was taken last month."

"That community goat depot was a bold and innovative idea. I want you to know in Nigeria the Corps supplied goat's milk to over two hundred children a day."

"I've been to Nigeria. I stayed in Lagos. The Royalton. I dined on chicken."

"Mr. Sec . . ."

"Brigadier."

"Brigadier Sec. I met a man who has told me a very startling bit of information."

"Very good."

"He's traveled a good distance to bring this news and he wanted to speak with someone in authority."

"So naturally he came to you."

"And I'm bringing him to you," Don said gesturing to the adjutant.

Noah Mesala was ushered into the room. Lani Sec regarded him without speaking.

"Tell Mr. . . . Brigadier Sec what you told me."

Noah stared imperially at Lani Sec and began, "I am Noah Mesala, headman of the Ndebele, possessor of land, owner of many things. A sister to one of my wives lived in a small village near here until . . ."

"Bangwatse?" Lani Sec demanded curtly.

"My wife is Bangwatse, yes."

"And so," Brigadier Sec said raising one finger, "the village is also Bangwatse."

"I visited the village and it was not a happy visit. Kaina lost her sister Aina to the great starvation you have here."

"What starvation is this?" demanded Lani Sec.

"Jesus," muttered Don.

"Jesus?"

"The Kalahari's been in drought for twenty years. Now when rain falls at all it comes in floods and washes out the topsoil and there's the socio-econom . . ."

"We have the tools. We have the policy. Yet these backwards people will not avail themselves. Who can say?"

"The Kalahari . . ." began Don.

"The Kalahari has always been cruel," shouted Lani Sec.

Silence then, to be slowly filled with A.C. whirl and current.

"Continue," the Brigadier instructed, nodding toward Noah.

"Ahh . . . yes . . . when my wife's sister died there was a great mourning within her house. Sorrow is what they know. I left them and walked under the sun and thought how unlike my home this was. There are no fields of grass and water. No birds that I could see, only dust."

"There are birds," Lani Sec said curtly.

"I saw no birds," said Noah, "perhaps there were. I walked away from the house of Aina for their grief gave in to shrieks. In the middle of the village, as the sobs faded, I heard another sound. A sound such as wind makes when it bounces into the crevices of cliffs. But there was no wind. I followed the sound. A man. A prisoner in complete sorrow. I saw him but I could not enter the foul room. I fell back and away for surely I would be killed if they realized I know this."

Lani Sec was quiet for a moment, then said. "Who are we to judge how tribal leaders choose to punish? Maybe a goat thief. Adulterer."

"This was no goat thief."

"Brigadier," said Don Lawton, passionately, "even if a man were a thief, surely to be kept as a prisoner is not justice. I mean without a trial."

"Almost two years, Mr. Lawton, you have been in Monton almost two years and still reject tribal authority."

"I . . ."

"It is not for me to lay law for these people and certainly not . . ."

"A white man," said Noah loudly.

Another silence.

"White man?" Lani Sec asked.

"Filthy and dark but his hair . . . it . . . fell like this . . . down onto his shoulders and his beard was long and horrible."

"So you say these Bangwatse have taken a white man?"

"Yes. I say this."

"What is the name of this village?"

Noah took a breath and slapped his palm together.

"Well," he said, "well, well . . . the village then . . . it is . . . close by."

"Close by where."

"You see . . ."

"He wants money," said Don.

"Money?" shouted Lani Sec.

"I had thought that surely here was a man for which a reward was offered."

"Rewards?" shouted Lani Sec.

"Surely something."

"Perhaps if you checked back through your files," Don suggested.

"I demand to know this village."

"I demand a reward."

"To hell with your demands."

Noah Mesala turned angrily and left the room.

"Mr. Mesala . . . Mr. . . . . Brigadier please. If he's a European or American maybe there's some information on him."

Lani Sec regarded him for a moment then walked to the file bank.

"I will see what reports of missing people I have."

"Thank you."

"But I do not like white people. Let me tell you plain. White people are not my favorite things."

★ ★ ★ ★

The Rolls moved west on Santa Monica toward the sea. Except for an occasional produce truck or odd car the road stretched out in before-rush-traffic magic.

"What's the breakfast place? What?" wheezed 'The Scuz'.

"Wills," shouted 'The Smiler,' "there's a breakfast place somewhere. Red Roof."

Jack 'The Smiler' Runyon leaned into Sid 'The Scuz' Morris and added, "You'll love this."

"I been, I forget. Big fuck eggs."

"Big fuck eggs."

Andy squinched his shoulders tightly into himself, taking only enough air for life. They flanked him on the back leather seat like two electro-magnets, pulling the energy of his heart right out of him.

"Now darling," began 'The Smiler', "the family good? Your lovely wife?"

"She's fine thanks."

"The kids?"

"Nice boys," said 'The Scuz'. "I met them."

"You met them?" asked 'The Smiler'.

"Nice kids."

"Great kids. Now darling something has happened that is

unbelievable in the sense that if you were to walk into the Polo, or Chasens . . ."

". . . or the Beverly Wilshire."

"All those places yes. If you were to go in and say that a new company has formed for the express purpose of making two films . . ."

"Prussian, Sunday Dawn."

"The same, they would all say 'big deal'. Now darling, if you were to go in and say this company was going to merge two fucking legends of this heartbreak town . . ."

"And this town breaks hearts."

"But if you tell them that Sid Morris, that great man and Jack Runyon . . ."

"Another great. An Irish hero."

"Thank you Sid, were forming their own company, they would shit."

"Bricks."

"Hard and square."

Andy scrunched and hunched and emitted a shuddering breath.

"You're . . . partners?"

"Listen," said 'The Scuz', "SCUMILER PRODUCTIONS."

"I thought of that," said Jack proudly.

"That guy," smiled 'The Scuz' approvingly.

'The Smiler' coughed a deep rich hack, brought up the culprit into his mouth and shot it violently out the window.

". . . And the brother?" asked 'The Smiler', wiping his mouth with the back of his hand.

Andy did not hear, lost in the echoing SCUMILER.

"Darling boy. We are now talking brother. Two film deal. You got us over a barrel. You are some shrewd fuck. Sid darling. This beautiful fuck still works for me, money and such, and is selling the brother too."

"Beautiful," laughed 'The Scuz'. "He's got us. We're fucked. But you don't raise such beautiful children as those of yours without a head. You got a beautiful head, you fuck."

"Two picture deal," said 'The Smiler'.

"First <u>Prussian</u> then <u>Dawn</u>."

"Thirty two five."

"Thirty two million, five hundred thousand."

"Four successive equal payments."

"What," asked 'The Smiler', leaning dramatically over Andy toward 'The Scuz', "is the manager's percentile?"

"I believe twenty-five percent."

"And what is twenty-five percent of thirty two five? Deeds?" yelled 'The Scuz'.

His man turned around immediately, calculator in hand.

"That's . . . uh . . . that's eight million one hundred and twenty five thousand . . . dollars."

'The Smiler' leaned close to Andy's face.

"I believe I can speak for Sid when I say that the manager's fee should certainly be in one upfront payment."

"Upfront," agreed 'The Scuz'.

"Eight . . . million . . . one . . . hundred . . . twenty five . . . thousand . . . dollars . . . cash money," licked 'The Smiler'.

Wills turned into the Red Roof parking lot and stopped the Rolls in front of a row of newspaper vending machines.

"You got to deliver you fuck," 'The Smiler' said. "You rich fucker. Here we are. Let's go."

Fr. Nicky had her address. Chaca had given it to him at the block party and as he drove down the side street and pulled into a small parking lot behind the Spanish grocery store he tried to imagine what she looked like. He chose biblical black hair, olive

Mediterranean skin, smooth, perfect. He conjured deep black eyes, the thinnest of desert lips. He sat in the parish car and stared up the stairs. Was it too early? Were they even at home? Fr. Nicky shut off the engine, stepped out of the car and walked to the stairs. Halfway up he paused. He stared at his black leather shoes and felt a moment of oddness that welled up from his feet into his head and subsided as suddenly as it began. He knocked quickly without contemplation, convinced one thought would drive him back from the door, down the stairs, answerless. He knocked. Another odd wave which he fought off. He knocked again.

He was wrong. Not dark olive but light with wild blonde hair and forty year old hard green eyes. "Come in."

Fr. Nicky followed her.

"He's in the bathroom. You want coffee?"

"No," he said quickly.

"Good coffee," she smiled.

"Okay."

She filled a cup for him and refilled her own.

"There's milk and sugar on the table."

"Black's fine."

"I like mine black, too."

He sipped it.

"This is darn good coffee."

"Some kind of blend. Farmer's Market."

"Ahh," he said sipping again. "Mmmm."

Fr. Nicky turned and looked down the narrow corridor to the bathroom and bedroom.

"My name is Leonie Polk."

"I'm Nicky Lombardi."

"You're a priest."

"Yes," he said feeling at his collar.

"My Uncle Teddy is a minister."

"Oh?"

"Unitarian. Arizona. Pretty different from Catholic."

"Well, not really all that different."

"The Virgin Mary, I meant, and Transfiguration."

"Well, yes, it is different."

He sipped coffee, working to appear comfortable.

"How . . . how did you know I wanted to speak with . . . him?"

"Lucky guess."

Fr. Nicky nodded.

"It hurts him you know."

"What?"

"All of this. Jackie is hurt by this."

"Hello."

Nicky rose and faced him.

"I'm Jackie Nef."

He stood in his faded red Hawaiian shirt and white linen slacks. A new pair of white low cut Chuck Taylor basketball sneakers. His skin was not as white as Nicky had remembered under the lights of the block party and his blonde hair nowhere near as shockingly yellow, yet his eyes leapt blue and mad. Two crazy scribbles on an otherwise serene face.

Leonie walked over and kissed his mouth gently.

"Breakfast?" she said.

"Oh god," he smiled. "I do love breakfast. Toast and tea and sausages with those little red peppers that burn the inside of your mouth."

Jackie looked at Fr. Nicky.

"I . . . I usually just have a donut and coffee."

"Ahhh," said Jackie. "These sneakers are wonderful."

Leonie brought him some coffee and he sat at the kitchen table next to Nicky.

"It's good. It's very good. The smell of the bacon. The coffee."

"Nicky is a priest," said Leonie.

"Nicky?"

"I'm Nicky Lombardi."

"Priest?"

"Yes."

"Be careful then."

"What?"

"It's a lot of responsibility isn't it?"

"Yes it is."

"Yes it is."

Jackie sipped his coffee and fell into a silence.

"I . . . I saw you at the block party."

"Block party?" asked Leonie.

"They have done well, haven't they. They are beautiful children, all of them."

"What party?"

"You know St. Peter Claver?" explained Fr. Nicky.

"Spanish Mission?"

"Actually it was a mission. There's a small chapel off the rectory that was part of the original. I go there sometimes alone. I just . . . sit there. Anyway these kids from the area bought this old building and fixed it up. Remarkable really. Actually fantastic. It's a community center."

"Gardens," murmured Jackie.

"They built community gardens too. They gave away garden plots at the block party."

"Beautiful children, all of them," said Jackie biting into a piece of dark toast.

"Chaca?" asked Leonie. "And Mookie? And Pedro?"

"Yes, everyone," said Fr. Nicky. "Everyone."

Jackie smiled. Toast crumbs clung to the corners of his mouth.

"They gathered around him. Old women and kids and men,

everybody. They gathered around and touched him and kissed him."

Leonie and Jackie stopped smiling.

"I haven't . . . been assigned to Claver long but I couldn't help but notice how . . . I don't know . . . hopeful . . . alive people seemed. They all . . . you know . . . used to seem so . . . defeated. Have I . . . ? I'm sorry if I . . ."

"No, no," answered Jackie quietly, not looking up from the toast. "It is good for people to feel hope. It was good to feel their touch but they should never look to find it in other people."

"Find what?"

Jackie stared at him hot and long.

"I have to go to the bathroom."

He rose rapidly and strode down the hall. He closed the door behind himself and ran the cold tap. Several small drops of sweat trickled out of his hair line and rolled down his forehead and into the wild eyebrows. He cupped his hand and ladled the water onto his face. Water for the eyes and water through his matted hair and water, cool, for his tired lips. Jackie raised his head until he looked into the mirror above the sink. There he was then, here he was again. He turned to the tiny window stared into the sun and shook himself out of a dream of water.

The BMW squealed onto the residential street, grinding to a stop three feet from the curb. Andy leapt from the car and bounded up the side stairs shouting as he went.

"Susan . . . Susan . . ."

He ran from room to room.

"Susan?"

Empty house. Christ. Christ. Christ.

Back down he charged, down to the shiny blue BMW.

Al Merrill was in his garage across the narrow canyon street.

"Better pull closer to the curb."

"What?"

"Somebody's liable to come along and rip the side of that thing right off."

"You see Susan?"

"Nope," said Al, holding two large, long handguns. ".357 Magnums. Let's see some asshole come around now, huh?"

Andy fell into the car. He rolled silently, radio off, windows tight against the world. Scenes passed. The side windows became cinema. Grandmothers and children, and orange hair.

His heart stopped jumping, his breathing relaxed to nearly normal. Yes. It could all be so much dust any moment. Yes. Thirty two million, five hundred thousand? A commission of eight million one hundred twenty five thousand dollars upfront money? He looked into the rear-view mirror. Then turning onto Sunset he banged both fists against the steering wheel. He tried to line up some order of events but there was no order, and so his mind continued to leap and curl wildly as if flipping through the memory of a computer, hoping for some truth, some absolute.

He saw them walking, screeched to a stop and popped out of the car.

"Money," he gasped.

Jackie gave a tiny wave.

"Hi Andy."

"Money," he reiterated. "Money, money."

"Hi," Leonie said.

"Money, God Dammit. I've got responsibilities. I've got expenses."

"We . . . we're . . ." started Leonie.

"That's okay. That's fine, that's good, that's fine, that's wonderful, that's okay. I'm not saying whatever you do isn't . . . fine.

It's fine. It's okay. It's good. But I know this. Both of you know this. This isn't anywhere else. This is here."

Jackie smiled and nodded.

"It is here."

"No I . . . look. Money. I'm not making apologies."

"Don't apologize."

"I'm not. I'm saying I'm not. So here it is," he shouted. "Here it comes."

Here it comes, thought Leonie.

"Thirty two million five hundred thousand dollars."

"Thirty two million five hundred thousand dollars," nodded Jackie.

"That's real money."

"But . . ."

"I don't get it either. What are you? I don't mean 'What are you' but I mean, c'mon Jackie, what <u>are</u> you. You've never done a film. You're not good looking ... you're not young, you know."

"Thirty two million?" whispered Leonie.

"'The Scuz' and 'The Smiler' partnered up. Two films. <u>Sunday Dawn. Prussian</u>."

Jackie looked over to Leonie and smiled.

"I'm not an actor."

"So?"

"I don't know how to act."

"Nobody knows how to act."

"But . . ."

"Jackie," shouted Andy hoarsely, "what do I have to do? Do I have to beg? Okay. I'm begging you . . ."

"Andy . . ."

"Please. Please take the package."

Jackie did not smile. He looked at the brother and then at Leonie who had backed herself slowly into a thick, green hedge.

Pieces of twig pushed her hair up into a point. Birds watched. Jackie smiled again and shook his head slowly from side to side. He said:

"When the sacred mound of mud is open

to the flying soul of a man

How can we slip him easily into

The red earth if his hands are full?"

Andy looked almost placidly at his brother.

"What?" he finally said quietly.

Jackie repeated himself slowly, musically, singsony, letting his head accentuate his words.

"When the sacred mound of mud is open

To the flying soul . . ."

"Jesus, Jesus . . . Jesus," shouted Andy. "What the fuck are you talking about? I'm saying thirty two . . . Jesus Christ on the fucking cross."

Andy stumbled back to the car and kicked the tire, and kicked the door, and pounded his soft fists into the hood.

"Fuck!" he shouted and began to cry.

"Leonie, my brother is crying. Am I doing this? Am I?"

"No," she gently lied, "he's doing it to himself."

"I don't think so. I'm doing it alright. But there are people who have skills, who . . . act. I am not an actor."

"There are actors."

"Skillful actors . . . yes?"

"Acting," she said "it's . . ."

She remembered classes and playlets and sense memory, and circles of flowing energy and other things.

". . . it's . . . really hard to put your finger on acting. There are these thin lines in art, and dance is on one, and painting, sculpture is on one, singing maybe but acting . . . it's something else."

"It's something else."

"Yes." Finally, definitely.

He stepped over to Andy and put his hands on the back of his shoulders. He moved close and whispered to the back of his head.

"All right."

"All right," said Andy without moving.

"They're having a read-thru of the new script version and a press conference tomorrow at Peakskill."

"All right."

"It's a good script. Susan thinks so too . . . I lied. She hasn't read it. Want me to pick you . . . up?"

"All right."

"Well then . . . I'll . . ."

Andy walked rapidly to the car and slowly pulled out into the street.

"A man gets into a car and is off with others. So stark."

"Why?"

"So unmistakable."

"Let's go home. I'll make some soup."

"A hearty soup."

"With everything in it."

"Everything."

They walked hand in hand for a bit, then got the bus to the Farmer's Market and bought hamhocks and carrots and lentils and onions. A pretty young Black girl served them juice.

"Do I know you?" she said to the fading man.

"I don't know."

"I know you!"

"Maybe not."

"I know. You're an actor right?"

Two Hasidics deftly side stepped a skateboarder, balancing their coffee and rolls.

"Why yes," he smiled, "Why yes I am."

Later, by the sidewalk in front of the Spanish grocery, an old man pushed himself to a seated position and burbled at them as they passed, holding his empty pint of MD 20/20.

"What's it? What's it, boss?"

Jackie stopped.

"What's it?" said the old man again.

"It's . . . acting I guess."

"Better than nothing, Amigo."

Jackie reached for the side of his temple but the old man slapped his hand away. He reached again.

"Don't touch. Don't touch."

"The light," smiled Jackie, showing his long fingers.

The man pulled himself to his feet and fastened his belt.

"Is my cock out?" he said.

"No."

"I'm pissing."

"Ahhh," answered Jackie thoughtfully.

The man walked to the edge of the sidewalk.

"Money," he said.

Jackie reached into his empty pockets. Leonie handed him a five dollar bill.

"Money," he answered, giving it to the man who held it satisfactorily in both hands. He waved it at them and smiled.

"Fuck the light," he said.

"Fuck the light," repeated Jackie quietly, thinking how elegant a man is even in his despair.

★ ★ ★ ★

Lani Sec dramatically counted out one pile of fifty rands and then another. He stepped back from his desk, looked hard at them and after a very long time, looked up to Noah.

"One hundred rands. Tell me."

The old man, the head man of the Ndebele, possessor of land, husband to many wives, father to many children, stared contemptuously back.

"One hundred rands?"

"I will not count it again."

Don Lawton also looked at the money and wanted it. Wanted more than that. Thousands maybe millions and an office off the back of some fine old, perfectly renovated Victorian where he could do something and people would pay him and it would be nearby to Fenway Park, where he would descend occasionally to box seats behind third and watch his sweet Sox nail the Yankees. A rich man looking after himself. The hell with everybody else. Number one forever.

"Money isn't everything, Mr. Mesala," he said weakly.

"Not to you, of course," snarled the Brigadier. "Not when you are American and have the world handed to you like so much cheese."

Don Lawton thought of the trailer park, later the projects in Southy, the old man serving time in Waltham.

"So here it is, Ndebele. Take it."

"Not enough."

"This is all there is."

"Oh, of course," chuckled Noah, "in all this land there is only one hundred rands for Noah. I spit at one hundred rands. I laugh at it."

Don Lawton rubbed his eyes with the heels of his hands.

"I laugh at it," repeated Noah.

"Brigadier," a soldier said, entering the room.

"What do you want?" asked Lani Sec harshly, transferring his building rage to the teenager.

"We've . . ."

"I ask you 'what do you want', because I realize how utterly hopeless it would be to expect you to enter a room like a reasonably civil man. Politely. Orderly. No, you barge in, not knowing if I'm talking to a farmer or a Governor. It is little wonder this fabulous white fellow here concludes we are savages."

The teenage recruit shot Don a contemptuous look.

"Take it," demanded Lani Sec, "take it now."

Noah placed hands on hips defiantly.

"Brigadier," said the boy.

"What? What? What?"

"The helicopter patrol saw a truck from the sky."

"A truck?" asked Lani Sec.

"A truck?" asked Don Lawton.

"One hundred rand? Well, I'll take it," said Noah Mesala.

Without removing his eyes from the soldier, Lani Sec reached behind him and deftly scooped up the two piles of money.

"A truck then, seen by our helicopters. Interesting."

"What shall we do Brigadier?"

Lani Sec looked over to Don Lawton and then slowly turned toward Noah. He took the two packets of rands and made them one, then slowly and deliberately fanned the colorful bills.

"Let me . . . think."

★ ★ ★ ★

Sylvia Dupree was understandably edgy. After six hours of make-up and wardrobe haggling, the opening sequence of <u>Prussian</u> was already behind schedule. Aged to eighty-one years old, the countess reflects upon her youth and love for the astonishing Karl. The set was shrouded in secrecy. The Tower Room of the Countess was dark and moldy. Georgio de Soto, the set designer, flitted madly about, instructing his staff on last minute touches. Jackson John carried coffee to Norm Rector who sat in his Director Chair nervously glaring at his watch every thirty seconds.

"Must be something I don't know about," hissed Norm.

"Fucking queen star bitch," hissed Jackson.

"What? Am I crazy? How long does it take the bitch?"

"You'd think we're filming <u>War and Peace</u>."

"Well, <u>I do</u> like the script."

Sylvia entered the set and examined the décor.

"Babe, you look fabulous," cooed Norm.

"Fabulous," echoed Jackson.

"Fucking paint is still wet on this set," Sylvia said, sweetly.

"Goddamn. GEORGIO!" yelled Norm.

"Georgio looked over the top of the set, paint brush in hand, perched uneasily on a fourteen-foot ladder.

"Hello, hello," he waved.

"Fucking paint is still WET."

Georgio rushed down the ladder. On the third from bottom rung his foot slipped and he crash-stretched, his one leg still reaching the clouds, spun on one heel and pitched backwards onto the cold cement. He rose immediately, embarrassed, and took charge of the drying process. Hair dryers whirred, burly grips fanned. Georgio ignored his pulled groin, his banged vertebra which now sent spasms of pain down the front of both legs, and the nausea which accompanied his head slamming into the hard concrete.

"I haven't even met this guy," Sylvia mumbled to Norm.

Her teeth capped with yellow vinyl, her cheeks layered with plastine wrinkles, her breasts bound tight.

"Welcome to the club."

"No."

"I ask and it's always 'No can do'."

"Producers like him?"

"Producers love him."

Sylvia walked back to the set nestled inside the huge Hollywood hangar moving slowly and carefully, slipping comfortable into old age. She brought a rasp up to her voice and quietly spoke the monologue she would use today, occasionally turning to the script, sketching, playing the words. The set was cluttered with all the memories Georgio imagined an elderly woman of the early Nineteenth Century would surround herself with. Faded tapestries and oils, pewter lamps, thread-bare velvet covered chaises. Curtains heavy, dust dancing in the sunlight. She picked at the objects and began sorting out her own soulful musings on immortality.

"Thought we could run it a few," said Norm, "before we give it to camera and lights."

"Hard to start with this," rasped Sylvia.

"With any other actress, I agree. Piece of cake for you."

"Fuck-off."

"Start in the chair – take your time – "

"It's sad."

"What?"

"Old age."

"Tell me about it."

"Norman you are not old."

"I take issue with that. C'mon, in the chair."

Norm moved his chair forward a bit.

"Stop the work," he ordered. Hammers stopped, fans unplugged. "It's all about acting everyone. It's all about the acting after all, Darling. No camera. Nothing. Don't push. If you get stuck go back. I'm a mouse. Not a peep from me."

Sylvia sat in the chair and closed her now ancient eyes. Norm Rector shuddered a bit, so good, so Goddamn good to be back, to have nothing in the world under the sun littering the landscape of the moment. Him facing her as a camera, waiting for her prayer. Wonderful silence. She raised her head and spoke with closed eyes.

"Yes, I . . . yes . . . remember."

"Yes," Norm murmered, "comfortably remember a young man . . ."

As she spoke, the extraordinary compartments of the Director's brain instantly connected in electronic signals of story and line. Characters danced madly as he visualized an overlay of youth darting in and out of her delicate memoir. She rose, gesturing to her room, her life. Inside Norm's wonderful head, lines were deleted, action defined. She moved to the large window and peered out thinking cobblestone roads and vendors, and carts and history and . . . On the other side of the long curtained window, by the black backdrop and backlights, under the hanging flats and trees of past epics . . . someone. She paused. Norm thought camera angle, thought color, composition, not seeing what she saw.

Her pause enveloped the set. Norm marked how long the pause lingered but played the mouse and did not interrupt, again not seeing what she saw.

Jackie beheld her at the window. He moved closer in his almost slow motion toeless step. His uncombed hair dripped wild yellow about his head. His clean white linen suit. His faded red shirt. His eyes.

"It's alright, you know," he said. "It's good, it's so good to remember."

"What?"

"It's alright."

"What?"

"Becoming old. Remembering. Even dying. It's just a . . . transfer . . . to the light you see."

Andy buzzed around behind him.

"There you are. C'mon. They're rehearsing."

"It's good to be old. To be comfortable no matter what. It's hard, that's all."

"Jackie. C'mon."

"Jackie?" Sylvia asked. "Jackie Nef?"

"Sure."

"C'mon, you've got a costume fitting," whispered Andy.

"I'm going to be fitted with a costume now."

Sylvia turned back to Norm and away from her interminable pause.

"I've got to pee."

Monsignor O'Brien was bingoed out. He'd pulled numbers long into the night and announced them loudly to the table filled gymnasium of St. Peter Claver High. By nine-thirty his rich baritone had become a gasping falsetto. Bev Della-Fuentes played to her remarkable average of three victories a bingo night.

"Betty Grable's number, Legs eleven," Monsignor would shout.

"BINGO!" she'd scream.

An average. Three victories.

"What do you think Monsignor? Vegas next time?" she asked as she folded chairs and stacked them with the other members of the Catholic Women's Guild.

"You're remarkable, Bev," he replied, counting the bingo booty.

"I think she cheats," said Cyndy Padilla.

"How? Think you're so smart?" laughed Bev.

"I'm gonna figure it out," Cyndy laughed.

Monsignor O'Brien was sure she cheated too but figured 'what the hell'. He flicked off the lights, waved goodbye to the last of the guild, then crossed the lower school playground to the Rectory. He paused in the kitchen, picked up the pot roast sandwich Mrs. Bocca had left for his snack, carried it and the receipts of Bingo Night to his office, tossed the cash into the wall safe behind the painting of John the Baptist, and headed to the piano room and the comforting Johnny Carson. He bit heartily into the sandwich. Plenty of mustard. Good food and Johnny. All this and heaven too. Monsignor laughed out loud.

It wasn't until the commercial break that he noticed Fr. Nicky sitting in the brown leather chair by the window.

"Nick? Is that you Nick?" asked Monsignor pushing the volume down on his remote.

"It's me," answered Fr. Nicky, illuminated by the glow of the television.

Monsignor contemplated Johnny's schedule of guests which included Don Rickles and an eight foot woman.

"Would you . . . ahh . . . like to be alone?"

"Not really."

"Ahhhh," said Monsignor one eye on Nicky Lombardi, one on Johnny and Ed and Don.

"Actually I was hoping you'd come in. I've been doing a lot of soul searching regarding that little conversation we had last week. I don't know. It's a tough call. I talked to a man about it. It's tough. It's on my mind."

"Ahh."

"I was hoping to get your input."

Johnny looked away laughing. Don leered at another guest's enormous breasts.

"My input?"

"It's tough that's all."

"Well ..."

"I mean it would be wonderful if things could be simple. You know . . . one dimensional. Singular in truth. Not even open to discussion but it's not like that is it?"

Monsignor looked at his sandwich. A slice of pot roast broke perfectly against the mustardly yellow white bread.

"I . . . suppose."

"I feel neutral. I'm not sure God would be . . . disappointed in me if I . . . I had considered a leave of absence . . . I'd be remiss if I didn't tell you I had considered a leave."

Go, go, get your ass out. Just let me listen to what the hell they're talking about. Don's in a whirlpool with two girls for God's sake. What did he say to Carson?

"Oh," he said.

"You see Monsignor I . . ."

Suddenly sickening fluorescent ceiling lights blinked on accompanied by the jerking sobs of Fr. Ralph Amarado standing next to the switch.

"Oh dear God My Savior," he gasped weakly falling into a lean against the door frame. "Sweet, Sweet, Jesus."

"What is it Ralph? Are you okay?" Monsignor asked rising, turning painfully from Don and Johnny and Ed.

"Oh, no, no, no," Ralph moaned.

Nicky walked over to the priest as a sickening lump grew in his stomach. He had denied Ralph the needless visit to pursue his own selfish needs and now (What else?), Ralph's mother had died.

"It's your Mother, isn't it Ralph?" he asked gently placing a comforting hand on the shaking priest's shoulder. Monsignor stole a glance at the set where Doc Severson modeled a hat made of coconuts and played his horn.

"C'mon. Sit down."

Fr. Nicky led Fr. Ralph to the large sofa and sat him down.

"It's alright to let it out," Fr. Nicky said as Fr. Ralph collapsed in spasmodic sobs. Monsignor was not sure of this and never felt comfortable around tears. The O'Briens never cried. That was all there was to it. The old man couldn't tolerate it. But whatever .....

"Yes, of course, let it out," Monsignor mumbled.

Fr. Nicky gently rubbed Fr. Ralph's shoulders and spoke quietly.

"It's okay Ralph. It's fine. Let's pray for her together. She's with God now."

Fr. Ralph looked up at him.

"What?"

"She's with God now."

"Who?"

"Your mother."

"My mother?" he screamed. "She's dead? Mother's dead? Oh God. Oh no, no, no."

"She's not dead? I thought . . ."

"My mother's dead?"

"I . . ."

"When did you find out?"

"I didn't. I mean I assumed . . ."

"Well it could kill her. This whole thing could kill her."

"She's not dead?" asked Monsignor.

"I guess not," said Fr. Nicky.

Fr. Ralph stood and gained control, closed his eyes, took a breath.

"This is not easy," he said to no one in particular.

He walked unsteadily to the T.V. and pushed the off button. Don Rickles was standing next to the eight foot woman, his head waist high, now they were . . . gone. Fr. Ralph took yet another deep breath and faced the two other priests.

"A . . . woman is pregnant," collapsing into sobs on the final syllable.

"Ahh," said Monsignor following the T.V.'s final blip.

"Pregnant," he restated tearfully, "pregnant, pregnant."

"Why don't you sit down Ralph," Fr. Nicky said.

"Yes, yes, sit down," added Monsignor, "it's not as though we haven't dealt with this thing before. The Lopez girl last year? Remember her? Now that was very tough. Fourteen. Thank God they come to us."

"But . . . I'm . . . what I'm saying is a woman is . . . pregnant and . . ."

"Thank God they come to us."

"No . . . I . . ."

"Monsignor," said Fr. Nicky, "I think what Ralph is trying to say is that some woman that he personally knows is pregnant."

"And she's not married, eh? Well Ralph that is why God gives us the tools of compassion to deal with . . ."

"Knows Monsignor," helped Nicky, "as in . . . KNOWS."

Monsignor looked at Fr. Nicky, then Fr. Ralph. A slight quiver of his left eye was the only indication that the revelation had indeed entered him.

"Ahh," he said.

"What can I do?" whined Fr. Ralph. "What? Oh God help me. I mean . . . we're all priests aren't we?"

Chuckie Dumas shooed everyone out of the costume room.

"You have got to gain some weight. Not to worry. Chuckie fixie. You're not sick are you? Not that I mind. None of my beeswax. Say no more. Put some pads everywhere but let me tell you they won't know you're wearing pads and really, after all, you won't know. . . . Amazing stuff. Chuckie fixie."

Jackie observed his deft fingers whirling pins and scissors, chalk and thread.

"Now as I read Karl. . . . Mind if I chat? Can't stop. As I read Karl, I see him boldly reticent. Is that possible? I see him like a good white wine --- dry yet wet."

"Ahh," said Jackie, the pins flying, the scissors flashing.

Andy followed 'The Smiler' into Hangar 12. Rebecca, Gene and Eddie also. They marched in single file. They marched past the tower set, the war room set, the interior of Napoleon's farmhouse headquarters and the make-shift field hospital until they arrived at the magnificent ballroom.

"Fucking Magnificent," smiled 'The Smiler'.

"Fucking 'A'," agreed 'The Scuz' standing by the yet-to-be positioned chandelier, speaking with Norm Rector.

"It's grand Jack."

"This guy," said 'The Scuz', draping his arm around Norm, "this guy got mule balls. Where's he start? Scene right after the Waterloo thing. Dancing. Swordfight."

"Where Karl kills the prince?" Jack asked.

"Exact fucking spot."

"It'll be tough," said Norm.

"Not for you," chimed Jackson.

The two producers turned their heads slightly in Jackson's direction. Norm's friend took a giant step backwards.

"But that's why you get the big bucks. Right?"

"Got to keep the modest lifestyle going."

"Modest lifestyle," chuckled 'The Scuz'. "That's good. What the fuck. C'mon. What's happening?"

"Well essentially the dance will be choreographed in this area . . ."

"Tight waltzes," added 'The Smiler' offhandedly, "there was nothing bouncy about these fucks."

"True. Yes . . . uhh . . . then the fight . . . here and over by the fireplace . . . very forties Flynn."

"No shit," said 'The Scuz'.

"I loved that fucker," added 'The Smiler' nostalgically.

"Where's the guy? Where?"

Andy broke from the pack of retainers, from the retaining wall of assistants that kept 'Scuz & Smiler' from spilling over.

"We . . . we got him fitted up . . . he's fitted pretty well up and he should be out . . . soon."

"He's got at least fifteen," said Norm.

Sylvia glided onto set from her trailer. She had on a blue

terrycloth robe and stocking slippers. Her hair was in curlers and her cream face wore no makeup.

"I see the scary boys are here."

"Only a star," proclaimed Jack 'The Smiler' Runyon, "only a hundred percent star, Lombard, Monroe, West could waltz her ass into a room no makeup, no-do, and still be big. Luscious."

"Luscious," agrees 'The Scuz'.

"Where's the guy?"

"He's not here yet," smiled Norm.

"He's here, I mean in the building. In wardrobe," chimed Andy.

"I'm here."

They turned to the far side of the ballroom where he stood resplendent. Blue and gold, cinched and tight. His plumed hat danced in his fingers.

"There's something here alright. There's all sorts of things here."

He rolled toeless to the group and held Sylvia by the hand.

"First you're an old woman and now you're a young woman."

"I . . . I don't . . . I'm not made up or anything. . . . I thought we were just going to rehearse and maybe . . ."

"Aren't you beautiful. So beautiful. Isn't it all odd?"

Sylvia looked at the hand that held her.

"I'm ... I'm not wearing panties," she said sincerely.

Leonie could not enter the grounds of the studio.

"I'm ... actually I'm an actress with the production."

"Just give me a name miss," the gate-security man said.

"It's Prussian."

"A person's name."

"Jackie Nef."

He gave his list a quick glance.

"Nope."

"No?"

"Nope."

"Wait, he's the star of the movie."

"Well they never list stars. Stars go crazy if they get their name on a list."

"Okay … uh … Andy Nef."

"Nope."

"Jack Runyon."

"C'mon, everybody knows 'The Smiler'."

"So can I get in?"

"Look miss, what I mean is anybody could just walk up here and say Jack Runyon."

"But I know him."

"What's your part?"

"I'm not sure . . . yet."

"You're in the movie but you don't have any idea what the part is?"

"I have an idea . . . sure I have an idea."

"What?"

"It has to do with swimming."

"Is this a put on?"

They swirled blithely in circles of eight, lightning and armament flashing, rumbling around them, shaking the glass of the high windows. The men tall and hard, the women lithe. They danced.

Stars turn left and right. Extras and principles bound tightly in Nineteenth Century heel-step and swirl.

Andy saw him rise on the one foot bearing toes and fall backwards as though away but always gently pulling Sylvia with him, arm full of star, and off to the next smooth circle of dancers. He moved alone and still with her. He smiled and closed his sorrowful eyes.

"The last fucking Prussian," 'The Smiler' whispered.

'The Scuz' squeezed his arm, "The last . . . the last fucking . . . Prussian. Yeah."

★ ★ ★ ★

Koro was now head for there remained only five healthy men (if healthy is measured in slow step to a well) and he wore the mantel of authority uneasily. He was not a chief or headman or even advisor to chiefs or headmen. His lineage embracing a tale of survival. A man of obedience and service. He missed Aina in the mornings profoundly. He reached for her upon waking, then sat and stared at her rolled mat for several moments before water. She always seemed alive then, and he would sit half up and consider the truth with a nod.

"Ahh," he would sigh and go to the water.

One morning, beginning his comforting routine, he saw that Mada had not left the window slit from the night before.

"Ho," he beckoned from the well. "Ho, ho."

She said nothing, remaining still, her head resting on the warm flat rock.

"You are in the sun now," he said gently.

Koro took his cup and swished it lightly through the water so as not to dredge up the filthy underlying coating of mud and stick. He crossed the yard and offered her the water but she did not reach for it.

"Dead?" he uttered aloud, suddenly frightened.

"No," she said. Her eyes closed.

"You are in the sun. Drink."

She put her fingers into the cup and then licked them.

"He does not touch me," she said miserably.

"He does not touch you?"

"I am afraid."

Koro stood from his squat and glanced around the grey-white huts and to the Big Boy rise.

"Yes," Koro agreed.

"Yes, what?"

"I am afraid, too."

After a moment, Koro reached down and with great difficulty (for he had difficulty with most things, this good man) pulled her to her feet.

"You are in the sun," he repeated patiently.

They walked to her hut and he held the tin door ajar for her.

"Sleep," he ordered gently.

He turned for his hut but stopped and looked up to the rise. He could not see the Big Boy or the wild dogs. The burial rock piles shimmered.

"He slapped that big nose," he said proudly.

"Yes he did."

"He walked up to it and he slapped it. He was a great warrior. Did I say how when I found him he …."

"Yes."

". . . not eaten at all. Even the beast respects him."

"Yes."

Big Boy suddenly walked up to the largest of the mounds and discharged his low deep moan six times, each one ending in a strangled sigh. Koro noted how he seemed much larger this morning.

"Killed him quickly."

"Yes."

"Did not eat him."

"Yes."

"Yes."

"Yes."

★ ★ ★ ★

"I despair sometimes, you know, I just despair for the world. Look. There's this woman putting her groceries into her car when some guy comes up behind her ...."

"What?"

Susan looked over towards the kitchen where Andy stood staring at the twinkling hills.

"Are you drinking something?"

"Screwdriver."

"You're drinking too much you know."

"What about the groceries?"

"It was just on television. Some woman got grabbed in a parking lot."

Andy watched the hills, shimmering at the sky. He sighed.

"What?"

"Jesus."

"So what do you think they're doing," Susan asked not pointedly but being pointed.

"I don't know."

"It's twelve, you wrapped at six, she took him home."

"She didn't 'take' him home. She asked him if he'd like to see her beach house."

"It's supposed to be unbelievable. Have you seen it."

"Have I seen it? How the hell would I see it?"

"So what do you think they're doing?"

Andy noticed, how the smog-moon was stationed just beyond the low cloud cover.

"She's very beautiful."

Andy nodded. The bosom of L.A. pressed against the tight wet sky.

The doorbell rang and a door opened to Leonie.

"Hi. C'mon in," said Susan.

"Hi. I was wondering . . . hello."

"Hello," said Andy.

"I was wondering if Jackie was home. I . . . the funniest thing happened today, you won't believe it, but I was supposed . . . I've got this little part in <u>Prussian</u> and I had a costume fitting and, it's really too much, this security guard wouldn't let me in . . . is he home?"

"No, no he's not," answered Susan, "I don't imagine he'll be very late, do you dear?"

"I really don't know how long he'll be. But ... well no actually I don't think he'll be very late."

"Where is he? Oh gee, I'm sorry I asked that. That is absolutely none of my business . . . absolutely none . . . of my business."

"No, no. That's alright. Want some coffee?"

"I'd love some thank you."

Andy thought he heard his name called from the street. He listened but he heard nothing.

"They gave me the part because of Jackie. I know that."

"I'm sure that . . ." started Susan.

"No really, they did, and I don't mind a bit. I've only gotten five or six other paychecks from acting jobs out here in ten years. I know five for sure but I recall a sixth ... funny. Anyway this will be the most money I've ever earned and I don't talk, at least I don't think so because nobody has given me the script and I do need the money and I'm thirty nine years old now. I tell . . . I tell everyone I'm thirty eight but it's a goddamn lie. I'm getting there. Beats the rat race I guess, but I've got friends that have been in the rat race and they think I'm in the rat race. My father told me not to end up waiting tables. Said it was alright to start waiting tables, but to end up there . . . well . . . but he had a small town type of sensibility and really had no idea of the type of business, I suppose, the type I was getting into. He always said life was a crapshoot but acting was ridiculous. You think he'll be home then? Soon?"

They walked down the narrow path to cool sand. She reached out and took his hand, swinging arms like pendulums and thinking how young and girlish and prom-like. He held his head back in his odd head cock.

"You hear the ocean but you cannot see it."

She listened as though she had never walked on sand. She listened thinking how amazing his dance and now walk upon the sand was. They walked closer to the fall of evening waves until their feet sloshed and the sand beneath them roiled.

"I am feeling," he said, his fingers tightening comfortable around her delicate hand, "I am feeling . . . young with you . . . I am feeling alive."

She summoned her cultivated disinterestedness but it could not calm her beating heart.

"I walk here a lot. I feel …. away from all the Hollywood stuff when I'm on the beach."

They stood at sea.

"How about those guys huh?" she laughed. "'Smiler' and 'Scuz'?"

He smiled.

"How about those two? Talk about Hollywood."

"I like them very much."

"Talk about Hollywood," she agreed.

She looked up at him, still gazing into the empty sea-night. She pulled her beach smock over her head and stood beside him naked. He turned and looked at her. He took her breasts, each in a delicate hand and held them lightly. She pressed forward and kissed him gently then leaned away and smiled.

"Let's fuck our brains out."

And they tried to.

Chaca introduced the intense young woman to the pediatrician on the second floor of the community center.

"Dr. Elsworth, I'd like to introduce you to Sheila Montez from Social Services."

"Hello," smiled the young man in jeans and white shirt.

"Miss Montez is doing the first inspection of our center."

"I hope you find everything tip-top. I'm sure you will. The drug awareness program is something special. Got to run – sorry."

He popped back into his bright office.

"Dr. Elsworth treats the parents, too, you know. One of the . . ."

"How many hours a week does he come in?"

"Eight. They all come in eight."

"How many doctors?"

"Sixteen. General family practice is on the first floor. Pediatrics are . . ."

"Why doesn't general do all of it."

"It's a big community, Senorita."

She looked hard at him.

"It's Miss Montez. You're the head here?"

"There's a community board."

"But you're in charge."

"I do what they ask me to do."

"Sixteen doctors seems excessive."

"They all volunteer. Some even bring their own supplies. All of them are affiliated with Bridge Memorial."

"Many home-boys around?"

"Home-boys use the Center."

"Many?"

"We got a Rec room. We got a gym."

"Where do you get financing?"

"What I need? A lawyer to talk to you?"

"A good home-boy knows lots of lawyers."

"Where I get my money is none of your business."

"It is if you want city money, or state money or federal money, hombre."

"Mister."

"Okay, mister. You got one deposit of three hundred thousand dollars and another one, recently, of almost one million."

"My business."

"Know what it looks like to my supervisor? And to his supervisor? Three hundred thousand? One million? Come off it home-boy."

"I don't do no drugs. I don't sell . . . nothing. You see the signs? I swear on my mother's soul it isn't drug money."

"Then where does it come from?"

Below them the laughter of running children. Old men and women chortled.

"A man. You don't know him."

"Look, I want to believe you. I do. But they are all going to want the facts. These are hard people. What's his name?"

Some things are diminished by discussing them. Chaca plunged his hands into his pockets and hung his head.

"God," he said.

★ ★ ★ ★

It had gone into him after a sigh. Jackie felt heavy. Felt this then was death. It had cowered away in corners. Death he thought. He turned to where Harlan had crawled to the throw of light and for some reason wanted a vision of the thin black man firm in his eyes at the last breath. But, of course, he did not die. He expanded and thin veins opened, blood rushing into another, as though another cold heart beat anxiously within him. He rose a little off the ground then settled again in dust. He rose again, this time spinning slowly.

★ ★ ★ ★

She slept curled on her side, right knee pushed almost to her breasts. Silk sheets covered only her creamy thighs. A breeze blew through the bedroom windows. He lay on his back, his forearms over his eyes, listening to ocean. The breeze blew warm yet chilled him. He rose, draped a blanket over his shoulders and walked out of the room. In the living room he slid the glass partition to dew and fog. He shivered but let the blanket flutter about his shoulders cape-like.

A man leashed to a crimson Irish setter jogged by, undisturbed by the blanket nakedness.

The flowers on the Altar were in memory of Robert and Margaret Foley who perished in a Florida car crash almost seven years ago. Their adult children, none of whom is presently a member of St. Peter Claver (part of a vigorous white flight) still remember their parents on Mother's Day. She lay in the brown shining coffin packed like a rare lacquered box to be mailed, not really fitting its container. Flowers pushed up at her feet and down on her hair. Three older women sat in the first stall of this gigantic Spanish Church, pulling at their shawls, badges of grief and woe and misery.

Fr. Nicky Lombardi's Solemn Benedictus echoed through the empty hall, words falling back on one another,

> "I am the resurrection and
> the life: he who believes in Me,
> though he were dead, shall live;
> and everyone who liveth and
> believeth in me shall not die
> forever."

Fr. Nicky looked down at the Monday morning dead and stood quietly. Outside the sounds of children, marching under the watchful Benedictines, stomped through the adjoining playground.

"And . . . hutt! One! Two!" Brother Emilio actually screamed.

The three old women did not seem to hear them, or even understand Fr. Nicky's service, lost as they were inside themselves and their own language.

Outside the heavy feet of children marked time. Fr. Nicky walked close to the coffin and looked down at the face of this thirty eight year old transsexual.

"Josie Gaspar Rodriguez de Francia is resting now."

He saw how thin her lips were, remembering them lipsticked in heavy red, the corners always given a light line up so that she looked nearly clownish. Of course, not many people could bring themselves to look closely at this tiny prancing alcoholic. The neighborhood children accepted her, however, and on several occasions when she had wavered, fallen from her huge platform pumps and could not right herself unaided, they helped.

"Thanky," she would say with the slightest breath of embarrassment. "Thanky, thanky, thanky."

Nicky looked at the three women. One was the mother. Which

one? And the wife? Which one? Her shaved chest. Her bound crotch. Her long hair under the tight net. Red, red wig.

"Josie can . . . be sure of God," Fr. Nicky said, although he was not sure of this. But he would have liked to know the wife. Curious. In life he always kept distance from Josie, watching from behind the flat vocation of his calling.

"Why?" she would sob. "Why if God loves all babies, why doesn't he love this baby? The world is disgusted at me. I have a college diploma. I am descended from Kings. God doesn't love me. Oh, Oh, Oh."

Fr. Nicky would watch her throw hands high in dramatic despair, but never see how her fingers were fleshy and without calluses, smooth and almost new. Hands then for simple display. Fingers not meant to grab the world or break a violent fall. Fr. Nicky imagined Josie Gaspar Rodriguez de Francia in a slow side-walk tumble, tucking those elegant appendages behind her and out of harms way. Taking supreme satisfaction in something beautiful. One thing saved. When they mocked and laughed, when they pushed and hurt, she would hold her rapturous hand up to them and for a moment they would all be lost in the line of thumb and the blushing lacquered nails.

"So then . . ." Fr. Nicky sighed in the direction of the mourning women, ". . . as I . . . have said . . . Josie . . . Jesus. Can you ladies understand me at all?"

They moaned slightly and looked tearfully at the coffin.

"Old Josie has bit it this time. She's a goner alright."

Fr. Nicky walked around Josie stopping between the body and the mourners.

"Look, this ought to be easy for you. You don't understand me and I don't make any sense so, what the hell. The thing is here I am, a Priest, sending poor old Josie on her way and all I can think about is myself. Hey ladies, it's the Twentieth Century out there.

We are not living in the days of heroes, of pioneers. We're smack up to our asses in everything awful and I don't want to man the gates anymore."

Andy sat at the kitchen table sipping coffee.

"Do you think we ought to take it as bonus, all at once or what?"

"Whatever," said Susan, cutting a bagel.

"Actually I was thinking of incorporating. I don't know. I want to set up Trusts for the kids, that's a for sure thing."

"Sounds good."

"Lots of money."

"Sure is."

"Lots and lots of it."

"You think she fucked him last night?" Susan asked matter of factly.

"Susan!"

"No?"

"I don't . . . fucked him? Jesus."

"I'm curious. Aren't you curious?"

"No."

"No?"

Andy looked over the canyon in usual morning fog. Susan called to the boys.

"C'mon guys. Jackie, C'mon . . . Elliot . . . Elliot C'mon . . . Tom . . . let's move it."

They growled in their cells. Susan entered into the smelly caves of hibernating and woke them.

"Mom," moaned Jackie, "Elliot's farting. Oh God make him stop."

"Stop farting. What do you want for breakfast?"

"I'm not farting."

"Shut up," screamed Tom.

"They're silent-but-deadly! Mom, oh God, make him stop!"

"Hee, hee, hee."

Andy stood up and drained the coffee passing Susan as he moved to the door.

"Got to be at the set by eight."

"Have a nice day."

"Jesus."

"What?"

"Have a nice day!"

Susan kissed his nose.

"Have a shitty day."

"Jesus. Hey, eight million one hundred and twenty five hundred thousand. That's not bad huh?"

Down the hall Elliot farted emphatically.

Andy edged out into highway for the one hour, twelve mile drive to the studio. Funny how the most common of torturous drives can offer quiet reflection. Then the studio loomed dangerously. Inside the hangar several hundred extras swirled through their paces with assistant directors and choreographers. The ballroom sequence would require five filming days, possibly more, and the set exploded with energy of star-suns although no star was present. Andy walked over to the ballroom set where Smiling Jack and 'The Scuz' were standing with the hysterical Larry Deeds.

". . . so he thinks," laughed 'The Scuz', "he can say whatever the fuck he wants. He figures I'm a kid and if he wants to tell me to shut up, I shut up. He tells me so I stand there thinking for a minute, then I take out my cock and hit it on the fucking dining room table. I didn't say a thing. I didn't have to. He got the point."

'The Smiler' joined him in a soft, easy chuckle. Deeds shook ever so slightly.

"Yea, well, we all have problems with our fathers growing up. I wish we <u>had</u> a dining room table to slap my cock on."

Norm swirled out of his trailer, like a wind-burst, Jackson close behind.

"Ladies and gentlemen," he said as he walked to the set, "this is for everyone, dancers, actors, technicians alike, I wanted to share with you my delight at the rushes I just viewed. They were spectacular. We are going to have one <u>hell</u> of a feature."

The hangar echoed with applause.

"Now let's keep this level of intensity. Energy is the key. The Key is energy."

"I'll fucking say," chimed 'The Smiler'.

Norm smiled in morning control.

"There they are Jackson. There are the big boys."

"We are going to have one hell of a feature," he repeated.

"Fucking great, great," said 'The Scuz'.

"I love to hear shit like that," said 'The Smiler'.

"They here yet?"

"They've got ten o'clocks. I want to work with Ty Miller on his suicide. Tough scene for him to start with."

"What's tough?" asked 'The Scuz', muffin crumbs shooting from his mouth. "Action shit. Miller's done that shit before. He giving trouble? He gives trouble fuck him."

"Fuck him where he lives," added 'The Smiler'.

"Fuck him where he breathes," added 'The Scuz'.

"No, no, no. He's fine. He's really fine. He's been a gem."

"A gem," chimed Jackson.

Ty Miller, four weeks out of San Martens Alcohol and Drug Rehabilitation clinic walked wearily from his dressing room. His first job in almost three years, playing the small but important role of Thomas Bryant, English arms dealer to Europe. He arrived at the set three hours early, carrying his script like a life preserver, chatting easily with costumers and lighting designers and makeup artists and property people and most everyone else he had, as a young movie star, fired or abused. He couldn't remember all the tantrums. They ran together. He decided to live the rest of his life in general apology. He walked over to Norm.

"Morning all," he mustered.

"Bloody, bloody stuff today," said Norm pleasantly.

"Good stuff. This is terrific stuff," Ty overstated.

Still young and hard only his eyes gave away years of self-abuse.

"C'mere," kidded 'The Scuz', "let me smell that breath."

Ty laughed when before he would have quit. He saw them clear now. He saw their teeth glitter sharp and perfect. It was, after all, just a joke.

"That's cold Sid," he laughed.

"Let's do it," ordered Norm.

Norm led the actors onto the ballroom floor.

"Cutting his own throat on a ballroom floor. I don't get that," sighed 'The Scuz', watching the creative folks walk away.

"Symbolism," said 'The Smiler'.

"Shit. Remember what 'The Elder' said?"

They looked at each other like children then chanted.

"Symbolism? FUCK SYMBOLISM."

Andy noticed Leonie in a serving girl costume standing by a long banquet table, milling with other women dressed in the same blue or brown drab clothes.

"You got in this time?"

"Yea, thanks. Then the costumers didn't want to fit me and the second A.D. didn't want to give me a script .... show business huh? I got it all ironed out now."

"What's the part?"

"Yes m'lady, No, m'lady."

She laughed quietly. Seemed younger than the night before.

"Well, I'm glad you've worked it all out. I hope you enjoy being with us."

"Is he here? Oh gee there I go again. Hey sorry. None of my business."

"He's got a ten o'clock."

"It's really none of my business."

Across the banquet set, in the far corner, the farthest from Prussian headquarters, Norm clapped a waltz beat out for Ty, for the elegant arms dealer, Thomas Bryant. Norm talked as he clapped, dropping ideas and specific placements but never crossing into the realm of actor and never, ever interpreting so much as a moment. His brilliance was the broad hint. The din of idea.

"Da, da da . . . da da. . . . Waltz time, of course. Everyone is dancing and dancing. Eyes closed to any impending whatever . . . And Bryant whirls perhaps . . . I don't know, you could try it, I just want you from here to here . . .and the razor out and . . . slice, slice . . . however . . . now I'm going overhead in one shot . . . you'll love this dear boy . . . what I'm . . ."

As Norm explained the shot, Jackson slipped out of the hangar and back to room 3C where the rushes were being transferred.

"So?" he said entering the room.

Joe Pound whose singular domain was this editing room, looked up from his splice block.

"It's got to be the camera. Something's got to be wrong with the camera. I ran it frame at a time, magnified. There."

Joe flicked on the large monitor to the rough cut ballroom waltz of yesterday.

"Here it comes . . ."

Jackson leaned into the frame.

"Here . . ."

They looked together at what Jackson had seen earlier in rushes amid the swirl of color and blur. Karl's feet. The Prussian's feet. They were not touching the floor.

"Hey, where are you baby?"

Jackie turned. Sylvia sat beside him in the back of the stretch limousine while she glanced through the shooting schedule.

"I've got a week in here somewhere. My contract always calls for a week in the middle." She slid snuggling close to him, "Now if you could swing the same week, or even a few days in there, we could take off. Maybe go to the desert."

Jackie looked at her a moment.

"If . . ." he said finally, turning away. Then back again. "If a man loved you . . . touched and loved you . . . could you accept that man as . . . a part . . . a part of say . . . another man?"

"Part of another man?"

"A joining . . . but that's not it . . ."

Jackie took a deep breath and stared ahead.

"Like two men in one?" she asked.

"Yes ... but more complicated."

"You're bi-sexual?"

"I'm . . ."

"Hey, lots of guys are bi-sexual," she said with bravado, hearing herself speaking with alarm.

"No, no, I'm not . . . we're like . . ."

"We?"

"It's complicated."

"And it's early in the morning."

Ventura Boulevard flashed outside, vegetable stands and T-shirts. They stopped at an intersection where the electric stop light had broken down. A policeman directed the flow of traffic. He signaled a curb full of pedestrians across the street. A tall beautifully angular black girl, hair cropped hard and dry walked in long easy strides throwing out hips with each step, her hands evenly at her side. She stopped at the curb and turned purposely looking directly into Jackie's window. He opened the door and stood looking back.

"Why don't you take a picture," she finally said and turned away.

"C'mon, c'mon," the policeman gestured.

Sylvia pulled him back into the limo.

"So," she said after awhile, "tell me one thing."

"Alright."

"Which one fucked me last night?"

"The other one," he said.

Henderson Anderson dropped off the roll of film at Speedy Development in Santa Monica. He'd have to make the return drive for the pictures by five and of course the Photofast near his apartment building would have been much more convenient but he felt he could take no chances. At Denny's on Sunset he ordered the Big Breakfast, then washed and shaved off the evening in the men's room. A teenage assistant cook entered the facility in mid-shave.

"You know, you're not supposed to shave in here."

Henderson Anderson quickly reached into his back pocket

and flashed his private detective license and badge. The badge was the family crest of the woman who owned the agency. It was a Cocker Spaniel on a leash.

"On a case, son."

The boy nodded and backed out.

Henderson slipped the spotty credentials back into his pocket and completed his toilet. Afterwards he would drive over to the studio parking lot and lock a tail on his pigeon. He could catch a cat nap in his car.

"They'll sweep into the area here. Julio? Enough light?"

"I can give light," answered cinematographer Julio D'Jordevich.

"So they'll sweep into here," Norm improvised to the still and attentive ballroom crowd, "and . . . and . . . if Ty . . . if you're here with a drink and of course you're sick of . . . of everything . . . the war ... the .. uh ... Karl with the woman you love etc, etc. you cross . . . you dangerously cross and . . . by the way just a thought, what if suicide is not spelled out . . . maybe it could seem as though a fight was . . . maybe, I don't know some challenge. . . .What was before this? What happens directly before this?"

"Ty sees the stacks and stacks of bodies from the battle on the carriage ride over to the ball," Jackson answered, script in hand. "Yes, yes. Remember piles of bodies and, of course, by this time Napoleon was throwing kids, for Christ sake, at them. So stacks of dead kids . . . Christ what an image . . . so you're sick, dear boy, I mean Gawd!"

"So he is resolved to kill himself?"

"Oh yes, I'd say."

"Want to try?"

Norm smiled and squeezed Ty's bicep.

"I'm very, very proud of you," he said sincerely.

Ty Miller, who a year ago would have punched anyone touching him, felt invigorated. He moved to his position by the far tapestry of the grazing black lion and slipped nervously into the skin of Thomas Bryant.

"Are they here?" Norm asked.

"Sylvia's in her chair, all made up," answered Jackson.

"My Karl?"

Jackson shrugged.

"Now Jesus," moaned Norm.

"He's got to be here somewhere. He came with Sylvia."

"I mean all we need is his body for Christ sake. He doesn't say a word in the scene."

Jackie quietly walked over to the ballroom from a water cooler where he had stood dabbing fingertips of water into his aching eyes. He moved past Andy and 'The Smiler' and 'The Scuz' past Norm and Jackson and stood oddly balanced in the center of the parquet floor. His uniform perfect, his gold braids shimmering. Leonie turned with the rest toward the glo-worm, the human flare and for a moment she was afraid, for a moment she was afraid for him, that he would somehow consume himself in hot blue flame. She took a step to him but Sylvia swirled laughing around him and squeezed the familiar hand, the delicate known fingers.

"Hi Ty," she waved across the room.

"Hi Syl," he smiled. The last time they had worked together he had uttered some remark about her mother and she slapped him. He countered with a sweeping left hook that laid her down for the count. Sylvia, he silently thanked the patron Saint of all comeback attempts, holds no grudges.

"Now darlings," Norm began, "music plays, da-da, waltz, dance etc. . . . say start over here and end . . . Jackie Love, look at you . . . end smack where you are . . . you must have a sixth sense. Swirl, swirl . . . Swirl and . . . end dance, polite applause

. . . remain in position . . . people in the back, dancers, remember when these dances ended yesterday how we stayed in position – STAY – IN – POSITION . . . very important . . . remembering these were very, very formalized people – and the polite clap – applause – and Ty – slash."

Norm jogged over to Ty and whispered, "Shall we shoot it?"

Ty took a deep breath and smiled.

"It's only film."

"How are we for camera?" Norm bellowed.

"Could I see one rehearsal?" asked the cinematographer.

"See it when we shoot it!"

"No guarantees."

"Hey," Norm shouted dramatically, "life has no guarantees. Let's do it."

"Positions," yelled the first A.D.

The dancers positioned themselves with their partners. Fabulous ladies. Warrior gentlemen.

Leonie and the corps of serving girls lined up precisely behind the buffet in pressed drab outfits and flat hair-dos.

The orchestra pantomimed playing as the music would be added to a rough cut. Norm stood on his raised director's platform and nodded to the first assistant.

"Camera one," shouted the first assistant.

The operator nodded.

"Camera two."

"Why not?"

"Three?"

"One sec .... okay."

"Prussian, scene one-o-two, 3C sequence take one."

Snap.

The dance-master clapped out a quick, waltz rhythm, a German round and the guests twirled and smiled easily,

professionally toward the measured conclusion. Jackson uneasily stared at certain feet, hoping tiny slides but not risings. The
dance-master's voice rose in concluding da-da phrasing, rotating
his charges into a final position.

Sylvia looked up adoringly at her Karl, her Jackie who stiffly
applauded in the bewilderment of war and the dance while Ty
looked up from his goblet of caramel colored water brandy sub-
stitute amidst the ball streamers and four wall tapestry. Looked
up with uncommon dismay over world lust and his particular
inclusion in it and let the goblet slip through his trembling fingers to the floor. Thomas Bryant again for the first time in a last
moment. Sweat poured from Ty/Thomas. The stretch of ballroom
floor seemed unimaginably long, viewed almost as limitless as the
end of the world.

Sylvia/Miranda continued to gaze up to Jackie/Karl. He
looked oddly to the sky in camera nakedness. Ty/Thomas walked
to them as if in a trance. When he was ten or twelve feet from them
he stopped and screamed.

"Prussian!"

Jackie beheld Ty standing drunk in the early Nineteenth
Century, a tear in his eye, a dagger in his hand.

"So it is then for the young warrior, the young hero, that all
honor falls?"

Ty cast a disdainful eye to Sylvia.

"And all riches flow. It was been my tragedy to live in a world
of liars."

With that Ty slid the golden blade across his neck, looked at
them both dumbly, perfectly as the blood pack flowed red and
heavy and sank to his knees.

Jackie staggered forward, mouth open. Thunderstruck.
He knelt and swept the actor, the dying Thomas Bryant into

his spindle arms. Ty looked wildly up at him in death throe or career woe. Blood dripped onto Jackie's fingers and he started to cry. Huge tears barreled down his powdered face digging cinema canals. Ty looked up startled. Sylvia could not move. Norm attempted brilliant calm. Slowly Jackie raised a long slender finger to Ty's temple.

Sheila Montez was troubled to the point of sleeplessness. She sat in the kitchen of the small stucco house she shared with her mother and brother, sipping ice water at three a.m.

"You will see everything," they had told her. "You will see things you cannot believe and cannot forget and sooner or later you'll end up sitting at a table shaking your head."

Sheila shook her head. She'd seen it all. The point was simply, no one could spend an unlimited amount of time in the field, analyzing, weighing, transcribing, deciphering and categorizing all the suffering and unrelenting madness of an undulating population. So ultimately they were right. Finally, at twenty nine she had indeed seen too much, too many. A flood of life, narrow and bitter, washed affliction over her. She sat at her three a.m. table and smoked and sipped ice water and felt old, driven haggard by the title of Social Service Field Representative. Yet it was not so much the horror that jammed her report portfolio, the burned babies, the fourteen year old pregnant mothers, the deathly chill of indifference, it was that she was no longer moved by it and this is why she sat, again, as the night before and the night before that, in smoke.

And now, of course, drug money. What other explanation? Under their noses. Maybe this guy Chaca has got a Robin Hood complex. Sell crack to the rich, give to the Community Center.

Who knows? One thing Sheila took for a fact. One and a half million dollars couldn't have simply fallen out of the sky. And he actually said God had given it to him.

"Sheila?" her mother called from her bedroom.

"Yes Mother."

"Are you gonna sit up all night?"

"Maybe."

"It's not good."

"Good night Mother."

Ty Miller showered off the blood of his eighth and final close-up, slipped on shorts and T-shirt and walked out of his trailer. Surely, he thought, surely there's a lot worth going on for. For the first time he could remember, cocaine was not on his mind. He thought possibility. He thought rain and birds. Strange. But he had his umbrella, and behind the overcast, the drizzle, ... was the flicker of light.

He stood naked facing the wind. A blanket, flew capelike behind. Beside him, the beautiful woman also naked pushed herself against him looking up, her round buttocks reflecting the sea. Several lights dotted the back dropped beach and a wave in decline washed over his ankles.

Leonie closed the paper, put it into her large canvas bag and instantly took it out again. She unfolded it and stared. This time it looked as if the woman had one hand on his shoulder and the other on his . . . no. She closed the paper again, put it back into the bag and fled toward home. On her landing she stopped to calm her palpitating heart. She climbed the remaining stairs and sank weeping at her kitchen table. Hard tears.

She wept for several minutes until no more tears came and her head throbbed and her eyes scraped painfully in their holders. Then Leonie climbed into her bed, fully dressed and pulled the covers up to her chin.

Pedro sat in the corner office eating a burrito.

"Don't drop that on my new carpet," Chaca ordered, pacing back and forth behind his large desk.

"You know I got that carpet for nothing. Next to nothing. I want it to last. Hey, when I was a crazy guy I had less stuff filling up my mind than now. You know what? What are we doing? I'm doing nothing and I'm in trouble. Look what the little bitch sends me."

Chaca handed Pedro an official looking envelope, the seal of the City of Los Angeles leapt out at him. Pedro pretended to read it.

"Ooohhh," he said shaking his head.

"You know what this means? She wants to see our books. She wants all our records. That's pretty terrific. That's some little bitch. I don't got records. I don't got books."

Chaca put the letter back onto his desk and ran his fingers through thick black hair. He flopped into his chair, looked up to the ceiling.

"I don't know," he said and paused.

"You work to get something going. To do the good things and it's all so . . . I mean, it should be so simple. He gives us. We fix this. We make a good connection. Church. Doctors. I mean it should all be so simple. Now they want books and shit. They want records like you can't do good without a whole shit load of numbers. She knows as much as I do. Ain't it like before? I mean we got it WORKING. And ain't this the life?"

"This is the life," Pedro agreed stoically. Listening and understanding as best he could.

Chaca popped up from his chair.

"It's like people can't open up their eyes anymore. That's it, you know. They all looking at the ground."

Wild little Mookie burst in at this latest pronouncement. Breathing hard.

"You supposed to be at school man," stormed Chaca. "Brother Michael gonna kick some ass."

"Recess, Man," he cried. "Look," Mookie held a copy of 'Night Post', the California weekly. 'FAT MOM SELLS KIDS FOR COOKIES.'

"That's shit, man. Fat moms don't sell kids for cookies."

Pedro, not so positive, nodded in agreement.

"Not 'fat moms' man, look."

Mookie pointed to the photograph directly below the glaring headline. Chaca moved slowly forward and took it in both hands. Pedro leaned close over his shoulder. For a moment silence is King.

"That's him," said Mookie, not sure of the goodness or badness of it.

"Who's the Guapa?" asked Pedro.

Chaca looked at him angrily for a concentrated thump of a second. Pedro tried to smile. What a world then. What a funny little place.

He had not gone home with Sylvia that evening. After the day's filming he had become tired and lay for awhile in his trailer. When he finally rose to a sitting position he noticed that he was in darkness except for the tiniest glare of work light illuminating a distant bathroom at the far end of the stage floor.

"Tired," he said out loud.

He walked to the tiny sink of his bathroom and as was his habit and need, dabbed cool water into the corner of his eyes.

"The baby blues," he uttered again.

He stepped down from his trailer and walked across cold concrete towards the work light under which, hours earlier, had swirled the officers of the Fifth Prussian Regimental Configuration and their guests. It was a good silence, not a stony one. This was tranquility without reticence.

Standing directly under the lights he realized for the first time he still wore the Prussian Warrior's dress black uniform and unconsciously straightened himself. He stood facing the three-lion tapestry where earlier Ty Miller moped in suicidal proclivity, justice swelling his head. Yet it was silk lions woven fluffed and sighing on the far wall that pierced him and not unlike Ty Miller's Englishman Bryant, a pretend death washed through him.

Words.

Wondrous how they came in floods and images. The memory of somewhere death and somewhere life. Into his mind came, God is in you now. Take him to the light. But do not stay in the light. Take him as a guide. Be his landmark, yet not as companion. Not for a moment remain in the light. The Light.

Andy walked up to 'The Smiler', a copy of 'Night Post' rolled tightly in his fist.

"Mr. Runyon . . . ?"

"What the fuck's up? You look like a piece of dog shit. What the fuck? You sleep anymore or what?"

Andy raised the paper.

"It's this. It's this. Look."

"Seen it."

"I mean, Jesus."

"So?"

"He's naked for God's . . ."

"So?"

"And she, she's naked."

'The Smiler' considered his right hand for a moment, then looked over to Andy.

"I just noticed, my hand don't shake anymore. So what? C'mon, big deal. Nobody reads 'Night Post'. Old women. Morons. Press conference tonight on set. They'll be here. Reporter. Variety. Times. Television. Feed those animals. Buffet. Something. Give it to Rebecca and tell her champagne. And listen. What the fuck does that Mick do?"

"Eddie?" replied Andy dumbly.

"We got another Mick?"

"Eddie Burke's one of your attorneys."

"He's a lawyer?"

"Well, he's . . ."

"He's a lawyer or he says he's a lawyer. I don't know. I just don't know. Gene's not a lawyer."

"No sir. Gene's an accountant."

"I lose track. I'm so fucking excited about Prussian."

"Yes sir."

"He's great you know. What is it? It's more than Sid and me expected. It's more."

"Yes sir."

"Gene's a good accountant."

"Very good."

"Eddie Burke."

"He's a lawyer."

'The Smiler' smiled.

"Rebecca's a little piece of candy huh? Jesus would I like a little of that. Not in the cards though. We're friends. Sometimes she tells me who she's fucking. I like that. Hey, c'mon. Nobody, NOBODY reads 'Night Post' Won't affect the picture at all."

Andy staggered from the monster's lair, down the studio corridor and out into bright western sky. They would be filming all night long and he knew he should sleep. The 'Scuz' and 'Smiler' loved the night stuff. They were night guys. They cooled off and grew young at night. He should get some sleep now but instead walked, slowly, a slope shoulder head down walk, with his naked brother rolling toeless in his head.

She was called on Thursday and Friday for background but she did not go and they did not miss her. There were seventy serving girls, one more or less was hardly noticeable. She stayed indoors and made quiche with eggs whipped high and lots of onions and cheese and garlic. Sorrow is in the corner. Sometimes it cannot be explained. She made tea. She toasted english muffins.

Henderson flashed his bogus credentials at the flustered gate attendant, asked where <u>Prussian</u> was being filmed and rolled his car into lot 16. No joke now. No idiot telling him which way to go. He patted his wallet, then removed it from his pocket to check and double check its contents. Neatly folded between his Ralph's Check Cashing Card and his license lay the 'Night Post' check for $3500.00.

"That's cash," he muttered out loud, "that's the whole fucking potato."

He slipped the billfold back into his pocket and swung the car into a position facing the ten acre knoll which was being transformed into a battlefield. The attendant had told him it would be an all nighter, not even starting till dark, but he had position and he knew it.

"I've got the position," he muttered again, nodding behind the wheel.

He squiggled his ample ass against the back of his seat, scratching, an under-the-wallet-itch. It felt good. A good scratch for a good itch. $3500.00 felt good too and <u>that</u> is only the beginning. Henderson Anderson planned to make a career out of the geek.

It had been cloudy with a spittle of dirty rain but now the high afternoon sun had blasted apart the sky and it was summer again. He walked the residential street surrounding the studio complex and stopped to remove his shirt and shoes. The sun felt good on his bony square shoulders.

Jackie walked on. A beautiful Black child, perhaps three, shot out of his drive on a three wheel plastic motorcycle.

"I'm riding," he screamed.

He crossed the street and watched some older boys playing basketball.

One of the kids held the ball.

"What man?"

Jackie stared silently ahead.

"He crazy man."

Jackie walked away from the game to the street corner. The studio loomed bright and white and strangely puffed up from every sidewalk.

He ducked behind a low hedge and squatted on the grass. Hidden from the street, car rush, facing an ordinary ranch house he stared into the grass.

Jackie stared quietly at a birdbath, distorted as it was, from his angle. He could not see any birds, only an occasional throw of water over the sides from a pricky little Jay. The tiny blue head, angry eyes, shook itself and peered over the edge of the birdbath at the man. He disappeared throwing more water over the side. Jackie slept under the sun.

They piled into the station wagon. Jackie, Jr. had Fain and Goodson with him. Elliot brought Josh Stoops and Tom pulled in Manny Fortez. The war scene as promised.

Al Merrill pulled into his garage across the street, got out carrying what looked like another rifle box and waved.

"Hi Suzie." She hated being called 'Suzie'.

"Hi Al."

"Where are you going?"

"We're spending the evening at Andy's shoot … if these guys will settle down."

Al chuckled tenderly and pulled a rifle out of his bag.

"Want to take this? This'll maintain order. This beauty was patented in 1900 in Switzerland. It's the Schmidt-Rubin short rifle. It's got a box magazine, six cartridges per magazine, weighs eight and a half pounds. Got a nickel plated envelope and a muzzle velocity of 1920. Not bad for a 30.7 N.C. propellant."

"I just want them to shut up, not kill them," she shouted pleasantly as she backed out of the drive.

"Maybe next time," he said happily waving the assault rifle.

"He's cool," Tom said to Manny.

"Awesome," Elliot said.

A city bus squeezed Susan over. She hit her brakes and raised her middle finger in salute.

"Oooooooooooo," they all commented.

"Sorry," she said looking at them through the rear view.

Elliot happily gave the finger to the world.

"Stop that," she said.

"You don't even know what it means, dork head," said Jackie, Jr.

"It means FUCK YOU. Tee hee hee."

Chaca walked warily into City Services and asked for Sheila Montez. She came from a maze of cubicles to the reception area.

"Mr. . . . ?" she said businesslike extending her hand.

"Chaca."

"I remember."

"Look. I don't know. This is tough because see, I thought about it and I admit it looks like drugs."

"What looks like drugs."

"The whole thing lady. All of it. But as God looks down on my Mother it's not. Things are working out. Also we got a lot more money now. New money. He sent it over."

"Who."

"You know. I told you."

Sheila Montez took a deep breath and felt uneasy in the role of inquisitor.

"I don't know. You told me God gave you the money. Chaca, I'm not trying to ruin your Center. Quite frankly it seems too good to be true. It's an oasis."

"Thank you."

"But the question of financing has to come up. God may love people but I doubt very much if he hands them dollar bills."

Chaca looked at her for a long thoughtful moment. Then he smiled.

"I know a girl, who knows a guy and the guy can fly. Come with me and we'll find him."

"I . . . I don't get off 'til 5."

He stood straight and tall as though he suddenly had a stash of secret evidence.

"Five?"

She nodded.

"I'll be outside, Senorita."

★ ★ ★ ★

Big Boy heard it first from his grave perch overlooking the village. No one had appeared all day save a child who walked to the well, looked into it then walked back to his hut unmoistened.

He shook his huge head a crazy shake for at first he felt the broken flap of a desert fly entering his ear. He shook again. A twitch. Still the fly buzzed, growing larger and larger until it was no longer a fly but a distant bird, two birds, running madly to the rise out of the sun. Suddenly the birds seemed to stop in the air and slice sideways to a point some five hundred yards from his tree. Big Boy rose, his eyes narrowed and cold. Big Boy skipped instinctively to his tree, his dry and lifeless tree. He moaned low, then sighed and faced fully the eyes of the now sloping bird. The tall woman staggered from the largest hut holding several children by hands and shirts, pulling them close. She looked past Big Boy, past the tree to the slow rush of birds. The small man stood next to her, then another came and other women holding tight the clothes of children. Over the rise Big Boy saw a flash of light break from one bird's mouth and one hut, next to Lumpapa's hole, exploded in dust and flame. Its rusted tin sheet roof rose into the air reflecting chunks of the sun. Below him, Big Boy saw the people running madly toward the rise. His rise. The woman turned from her flight, pulling away from the others, and ran toward Lumpapa's hole. She was at the well when that hut exploded and she fell back toward the others. Big Boy moved closer to his tree. He had seen this in other ways. So when he watched, pressed as he was against the ancient tree, he was not unmoved. They scrambled up the side of the rise to the graves and the horrible birds continued after them. Big Boy watched. He would remember this, these birds, as somehow he remembered that long, low, line of lion killers. The people stopped and the tall woman raised a hard and bloody fist, screaming to the birds as she did. They moved toward her, flashed hot and angry and the people were gone among the graves. One of the hovering birds saw him and turned. Big Boy moved away from the trees and the bird flashed hot. The forever tree split and tumbled. Big Boy ran to the desert. From a corner of his dry and smoky eyes Big Boy saw him by the well. His matted hair, his dirt, his shape. Big Boy saw him hold the bloody goat high over his head but desert stones pushed between his tender paws and he turned away, into the dusk.

★ ★ ★ ★

"You guys can't do that," sneered Sid 'The Scuz' Morris.

"Oh no, you guys can't do that," echoed Jack 'The Smiler' Runyon.

"Im – fucking – possible."

"Abso- fucking – lutely."

They nudged each other playfully. Norm Rector looked on.

It was six-fifteen in the evening and they stood inside a crater on the field of Waterloo.

"We say we want to get back. We say it's gonna be the way <u>we</u> remember it and fuck all this location shit."

"Fuck Europe."

"Fuck those guys."

"Fucking Frogs. Fucking Limeys."

"Fucking Polacks."

The dinosaurs laughed again. From inside the crater the laugh echoed into a roar as if the meat-eaters had cornered a Brontosaurus.

"It's unbelievable," chimed Norm. Jackson stood beside him holding the director's script, a frightened smile pasted on his pale face. All around people wore frightened smiles. These are dinosaurs soon to be extinct but decidedly still alive. Still among us.

"Fucking-A," the terrible lizards laughed.

"'Don't you guys know anything?' 'You guys can't film the whole thing right here in L.A.'"

"You gotta go to Europe. You gotta get help."

"Help this," laughed 'The Smiler' grabbing his crotch. "Help this, right here."

"This fucking set is dressed beautifully."

"You didn't go after the best for nothing," said Norm.

"It's beautiful. Beautiful. Where's Sylvia? Where's the kid? Where's the army?"

"We got a while yet. I've given the set over to the effects master."

"O-fucking-kay. Can't wait," said 'The Scuz'.

"Rebecca?" yelled 'The Smiler'.

"Sir?," she shouted, standing in a safari outfit.

"What the fuck you supposed to be? Great white hunter?"

"I thought it might get dusty."

"Great fucking white hunter."

Everyone laughed. Andy looked up over the rim of the crater as Susan pulled through Security and parked next to Henderson Anderson who still slept behind his wheel waiting for nightfall. The barbarians, led by Elliott leaped from the station wagon and ran screaming toward the acres of pre-carnage.

Tom turned toward the field. His eyes somehow caught the sleeping driver. The man sitting unconscious, head tilted back, mouth open. Tom stared for a long moment, turned away, looked back, then trotted over to his savage herd.

Fr. Nicky Lombardi was at the foot of the long back steps to Leonie's apartment when Chaca rolled into the parking lot in his gleaming low rider. Pedro and Mookie sat in the back, deep and cool. Sheila Montez sat in the front passenger side, straight and tall.

"Yo," Chaca yelled at the Priest.

Fr. Nicky waved slightly.

"He there?"

"I . . . I don't know. I was out for a walk."

"This is Sheila Montez," said Chaca, gesturing to his passenger.

"Hello Sheila."

"Hello."

"Miss Montez is with L.A. Social Services. She says I'm dealing drugs."

"That's not tr . . ."

"I'm killing people with drugs or something so I can get money for the center."

"Bullshit lies," shouted the excited Mookie.

"Hey. This is a Priest, man. Watch your mouth."

"No, that's alright. Why do you think that?"

"She thinks we're 'crazy guys'," muttered Pedro.

"Hey," yelled Chaca again.

"I asked him where the money came from for the land, the building restoration. Lot of money. You think Social Services, City Services doesn't want to know that? We've seen it before. The Marabellas had an all-night grocery. It was legitimate but we know how they got the money. I'm not accusing anybody, but if you ask a straight question you ought to at least get a straight answer and not that God threw the money at you."

"God?" Mookie asked Chaca.

"Not God. I didn't mean to say God."

"God wouldn't have that picture," said Pedro.

"Which picture," asked Mookie.

"The beach, no clothes, that woman with the big . . ."

"I just meant that it's not so good to say God. You know what I mean Father?"

"I . . ."

"Anyway I figure the MAN will explain it to her, she'll see that it don't have nothing to do with drugs and that's it. He home?"

"Father?" Leonie called from the top of the stairs.

"Hello."

"Hey girl," waved Chaca. "He here?"

"No."

"I got to see him. It's important."

"I guess he's working."

"That movie, I heard."

"I don't know where he is."

"Like you say . . . the MAN is working. I need him. I got some shit needs straightening."

Leonie looked down at Chaca, at Sheila Montez and Pedro and Mookie and Fr. Nicky Lombardi. Behind them the red low rider coughed and heaved. "Just a second." She got her employment card, issued to <u>Prussian</u> cast members, and locked the door. Her eyes gleamed wet.

Jackie remained on his side when the water from the sprinkling system pelted him. He opened his eyes and looked out at the steady spray.

"Water," he mumbled.

He pushed himself into a sit.

"Not rain though." His tongue out to catch some drops.

He sat for several minutes. The water soaked his red shirt, his pants, his hair.

He sighed, and walked out from behind the hedge and began to retrace his steps back to the studio.

"No!" snapped the soaking Jackie, a slight bark coming from the back of his throat. The basketball players backed to the far court.

"He crazy man."

"Crazy."

Jackie threw his red shirt down into the gutter and walked on.

"They'll be worried about me," said Jackie out loud.

A young black woman pushing a double stroller with infant twins approached them. Jackie stopped and gazed expressionless at the children. The woman looked ahead, increased her speed and rolled them rapidly past.

"You see?" Jackie shouted. "I don't want to KNOW that shit. I don't know it. I don't want to know it."

The woman began to trot away.

Jackie put his hands against his ears and pressed.

Suddenly his feet hurt so he sat on the curb, took off the shoes, left them and walked on.

Dark and getting darker. He circled homes and cars toward the Security entrance. Birds watched him.

"Birds," Jackie said.

A boy, perhaps ten, stood watching from a driveway.

"You're talking mister. Who are you talking to?"

"Nobody, I think."

He looked at the brightening moon over the child's house, then back to the boy. He smiled. Once. Perfect but not pure. A kind of smile the six year old could easily see as a lie.

"You a nut?" he asked softly.

"I'm not sure. I think so."

Jackie felt a stabbing, ripping pain in his intestines. It moved to the very front of his eyes and nose. He fell forward with an awful thud and rolled bunched onto his side. The child took two steps back.

"You fell down."

"No, oh no," cried Jackie holding himself.

Jackie rolled to his hands and knees. He stared at the red wagon.

"That's my wagon," the child said. "It's a wagon."

"It's a god-man." said Jackie.

The child watched the man speaking to his wagon and did not think odd or strange. He looked at his wagon proudly.

Jackie knelt on both knees, then lay slowly on his side.

A small fire truck was in the wagon too.

Plastic soldiers. Baseball cards.

". . . I think you . . . are you afraid?"

"Don't be afraid," the little boy said, now closer to his wagon.

It also had a cowboy lunch box. It had a plastic cash register.

Jackie looked at his finger, holding it up. The long one on his right hand.

"I'm Jackie Nef. I'm all Jackie. My fingers don't burn. I'm just Jackie and I'm thanking you now for my life."

He reached out to the fading dream.

Then Jackie pulled his hand back and looked at the innermost part of his soul for ten years. Alone. Suddenly Jackie turned and moved toward the light.

He moved into the light, fully, joyously, unafraid. He sighed once, smiled and left.

"Where'd you go?" the child asked.

"Can you see me?"

"You were gone."

"Can you . . . ?"

"Sure. That was neat."

"Neat," yelled Jackie. He trotted down the lawn to the side-walk and headed in a run to the studio entrance.

"Neat," yelled the boy.

"Neat," yelled Jackie.

★ ★ ★ ★

Big Boy roused himself. The morning sun was concealed behind white and grey billowing clouds, and spray of rain patted the dusty covering of ground. He stood and shook himself into day, still exhausted from the pursuit of the birds. The spray of rain became heavy pellets. He licked at his damp skin. Behind him lay the flat hot expanse to the mountains. He turned once in the wet direction of the peaks then began to trot toward his rise. His tree.

Hours later birds loomed. Smaller, less deadly but a promise of something horrible. They circled the rise of the hill.

Big Boy saw all this from the far side of the village. He did not have to slow his trot and consider the strange quietness. A silence of the plain. A good silence. He raised his face under a downpour now, and looked at the rise, where bird and dog ripped and tore. He turned to the half destroyed hole of Lumpapa. Sniffing, he stood at the center of his universe. He pawed at the damp and odorous earth for several moments. The rubber soul and partial canvass of sneaker emerged from under years of packed waste and dirt. He took it into his mouth and shook it, then released it to the ground. He smelled it. He ran his blubbery tongue across it. It smelled . . . good. Big Boy lay down and lay that unbelievable chin on the sneaker carcass. A whisker touched easy on the name penned on the inside of the heel. Harlan. #1 B.A.D. Big Boy whimpered once, then slept.

★ ★ ★ ★

The cavalry mounted themselves on the side lawn by the executive studio suites formed by the stunt coordinator into ten squadrons of 128 men and horses in each. A lieutenant and two lance officers commanded each unit. The squadrons slowly pulled out, one through ten, in two specific ranks of 64 files. By the time the lead officer arrived at the battlefield the line of horsemen snaked from one end of the studio to the other.

The first assistant director swung over the front of the soldiers in a cherry picker. He gripped the side of the yellow basket for dear life.

"Not so jerky, Goddamn it," he shouted down to the operator.

"Okay people," he said into the speaker system, "thanks for being so patient, we've got thousands here, not the easiest thing. You've heard of a cast of thousands? Here it is. Cast of thousands. Okay. Cavalry first. Where are the Prussians? Raise your hands. Cavalry please raise your hands. No, not all of you. Prussians. Okay. Stop. Pinch yourself people. The cavalry in light blue. Raise hands. Good. You guys are the Prussians. See the light blue flag at the western part of the field? Go there. Now please ONLY the Prussians. Beautiful. Stay in formation. Let's try for the French. Dark blue. C'mon now get with it people . . ."

The positioning of 1280 horsemen, 3500 foot soldiers, six

batteries of cannon, assorted dead peasants and even a pond of ducks (wings clipped) was an event in itself. The studio had not seen this kind of activity since 1939's <u>Someone's Got To Do It</u>, a failed romp about Rome's conquest of Gaul.

"What is this costing?" asked a startled Susan.

"So much I feel stupid telling you. Where are the boys? Are they with anybody?"

"They're here, Andy, don't worry about them. Are you okay?"

"Where is he?"

"He's not here."

Leonie walked over to them. She was dressed as a peasant.

"Hi."

Andy and Susan looked embarrassed and returned the greeting.

Susan imagined how Leonie felt holding that picture. Him naked. Her naked. A world watching. Maybe she never saw it. No. She saw it. Susan knew she saw it.

"You're all in your costume, aren't you?"

"Why yes."

"It looks nice."

"Listen, I'm really sorry to bother you, but if . . . I know you're really busy and all . . . but if there was any way I could maybe bring a few people onto the set . . . and if it's a problem I under-stand . . . I . . ."

"No problem, sure," said Andy feeling let off the emotional hook. "Where are they?"

"At the gate."

"I'll go over there right now."

He jogged away.

"Quite a project," Susan said after a moment.

"It's not a very good script. I mean . . . what do I know from good."

"Oh, I'm sure you have a good idea," Susan said dumbly. "I mean . . . sorry."

"The people I brought have to talk to him. He'll be glad I brought them. I'm not going to bother him. I don't want anybody to think I'm going to bother him …. wherever he is."

"I'm sure you won't bother him."

"I only came over and got in costume because these . . . friends of his wanted me to take them. Otherwise I would never bother him. Never. I'm not even going to speak to him because I don't . . ."

"Hi," he said from behind them. Henderson Anderson squiggled up, eyes steering wheel level.

Leonie and Susan turned around and looked at him standing shoeless and shirtless, standing green stained and toeless.

"I'm Jackie Nef," he announced.

Susan moved to him.

"You must be freezing."

"Freezing? Shit. I'm warmer than toast. Where's my trailer? There it is. It's got a star."

Jackie walked between them and headed across the battlefield. He turned and looked at Leonie.

"C'mon."

She ran to him tripping in a crater, rose wet and dirty, and wrapped herself around him.

Susan stared. Henderson Anderson clicked away madly, then reached for his video camera.

Sylvia was leaving her trailer.

"There you are," she said, draping her arms around him. "You'll never guess what these assholes did. They called me for six-thirty and when I get here I find out I'm not even working tonight."

She was small and tight and astonishingly lovely. She wasn't wearing perfume and even though the evening chilled the air, she smelled wonderful. She looked at Leonie, mud caking on the side of her face and hair.

"You got shit all over you honey. You believe these assholes? I'm a movie star. Am I interrupting something?"

Jackie held his hand out and helped Leonie into his trailer.

"Yeah," he said.

"I'm interrupting?"

"I'm Jackie Nef. You remember I told you about two guys in one and how . . ."

"This is a brush off? This a let down?"

"No."

"Good, because I think I love you."

Across the field Susan watched, saw Jackie put his hands on his hips then reach out and take Sylvia into his arms. She fell against him.

"Listen Sylvia, listen."

Sylvia listened but Jackie did not speak for a while.

Across the field Leonie's friends also saw him and stared. Sheila and Chaca and Mookie and Pedro and Fr. Nick. He seemed to look over her head to them.

"I'm trying to be alone now. I'm really not sure how Jackie Nef works. I want him to be kind and considerate. I want him to have the compassion of his friend but I know . . . I can't be my friend. He had a three thousand year head start."

She pushed away from his embrace very slowly and looked at him. She smiled, also slowly. His face smiled back, a corner of his mouth rising into an innocent half sneer.

"You don't . . . love me?"

"Yeah."

"You don't?"

"NO . . . I mean, yeah, I do."

"Only not like the other guy."

"Yeah."

"He loved me?"

"He loved me, too."

She put her head on his chest again, then pushed back off and stared.

"Well . . . see . . . he's in the light Sylvia. He truly is."

She leaned in and up and kissed him on the chin.

"They made a mistake. I'm not working tonight."

He nodded.

She turned and walked toward her limousine.

"We got a great scene on Tuesday," she choked out over her shoulder.

"Yes," he remembered, "you're old."

"Yes," she said turning, "and you're a memory."

She waved and got in the car.

Leonie helped him pull into the black battle uniform. Plumes and belts, stirrups, the rest. They did not speak. She felt comfortable and herself. There was a loud bang on the door and Jackie opened it.

"I got to pee," said Tom.

"Sure. C'mon. I didn't even know you guys were here."

"We're here. Elliot's here. Jackie's here. Mom brought us."

Tom peed and emerged from the camper toilet zipping his fly. Leonie pulled tight gloves over the bony fingers of his Uncle.

"Fly," said Tom softly.

Leonie stopped and turned toward the fantastic critter.

"Fly, Uncle Jackie, I won't tell."

Leonie looked back to Jackie, then to Tom. Jackie smiled.

"I can't Tom. That was before. It's just me now pal."

Tom thought for a moment, the corner of his lips flipped half up, then mooned into his own smile. "Okay."

He buckled his belt and looked back at the two.

"The flying was awesome."

"I love you, Tom."

"I love you too Uncle Jackie," he snickered and closed the bathroom door with a Karate kick.

Jackie straightened himself and seemed much taller than before. In the tight britches the slightest touch of a belly rounded out. His face seemed less hollow. He kissed her lightly on the lips and walked to the door.

"I brought your friends. I brought Chaca. I brought the Priest."

"I'll tell them I love them."

"That's all?"

"I'll tell them I'm Jackie Nef."

"That's all."

"That's all there is."

He walked from her bedroom to the kitchen and smelled the oddly crisp air of a cool Los Angeles night. Funny how the wind tumbles, beginning over the hills and dropping to the sea, finding him at this open kitchen window. A dog barked somewhere. He listened to rivers. Somewhere rivers. Leonie curled tight into the comforter in another room.

As he closed his eyes he remembered that rivers die and fold into themselves. That dry winds move terrible fine sand over the earth. And that her beloved bones burned blue lying on the rise over the schoolhouse.

CPSIA information can be obtained
at www.ICGtesting.com
Printed in the USA
JSHW022028310523
42513JS00001B/37